REDS
ON THE
RUN

John Sandham

Grosvenor House
Publishing Limited

This book is published by
Grosvenor House Publishing Ltd
Link House
140 The Broadway, Tolworth, Surrey, KT6 7HT.
www.grosvenorhousepublishing.co.uk

This book is a work of fiction. Any resemblance to
people or events, past or present, is purely coincidental.

A CIP record for this book
is available from the British Library

ISBN 978-1-83975-793-8

CONTENTS

About the Author

Dr John Sandham was born in Cardiff, Wales, in 1962. He trained to be an engineer in the Royal Air Force (RAF), and during his 12 years in the RAF, he served in the United Kingdom; Central America during the height of the 'Cold War'; Ascension Island; and Bahrain during the first Gulf War – 'Operation Desert Storm'.

He has been involved in building several businesses; and also achieved the award of 'Doctor in Professional Studies' at Middlesex University, England, in 2014. John lives in Bedfordshire, England, with his wife, Ruth, and enjoys writing, travelling, snowboarding, and walking.

Author's note

This is a work of fiction based partly on my own experiences as an engineer in the Royal Air Force when stationed in Belize, Central America, during the early 1980s. It is not meant to be an accurate depiction of any specific events that happened during the Guatemalan civil war, but I would encourage readers to find out more because the facts are now available, and the reality is far more shocking than anything I have written within these pages. I have created a story and characters that give a fictional 'snapshot of that time'. Unless otherwise indicated, all the names, characters, businesses, places, events and incidents in this book are either the product of the author's imagination or used in a fictitious manner. Any resemblance to actual persons, living or dead, or actual events is purely coincidental.

GLOSSARY

RAF	Royal Air Force
BFBS	British Forces Broadcasting Services
NAAFI	Navy, Army and Air Force Institutes
SMG	Submachine Gun
SLR	Self-Loading Rifle
SAC	Senior Aircraftman
JSP	Joint Service Publication
Flight	A flight is a military unit in an air force, naval air service, or army air corps. It is usually composed of three to six aircraft, with their aircrews and ground staff
BDF	Belize Defence Force
NCO	Non-Commissioned Officer

Map of Belize, showing borders with Guatemala and Mexico

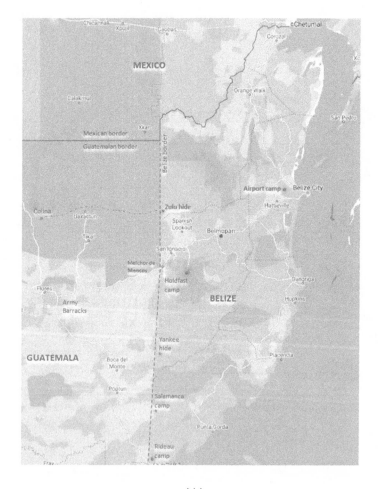

PROLOGUE – THE SETTING

In 1977, the US State Department published a human rights report that ended military aid to Guatemala. The document detailed abuses and acts of violence that forced President Carter's US administration to cut direct security assistance. Central America was in turmoil; General Efrain Ríos Montt became President of Guatemala in 1982, after coming to power in a military coup where he promised Guatemalans, "I will not steal, I will not lie, I will not abuse." At that time, President Reagan's US administration had prioritised the fight against communist rebels, and their civilian supporters, over respect for human rights. The US administration manipulated its own policies '*to not supply arms to General Montt*', by supplying arms to Israel, in the knowledge that Israel would then deliver them to General Montt.

Given Ríos Montt's staunch anti-communism policies and his ties to the United States, the Reagan administration supported the general and his regime, with the US president paying a visit to Guatemala City in December 1982. During a meeting with Ríos Montt on 4 December 1982, President Reagan said:

> "*President Ríos Montt is a man of great personal integrity and commitment... I know he wants to improve the quality of life for all Guatemalans and to promote social justice.*"

In reality, the indigenous Maya people of Guatemala were being brutally attacked as part of the 'scorched earth' policy that intended to root out and obliterate left-wing communist rebels, commonly referred to as 'the reds'. This was during the period when the 'Cold War' between the USSR (Eastern Block) and the USA and its allies (Western Block) was at an elevated level.

Thousands of indigenous Mayas were being brutally killed between March 1982 and August 1983 to stem the rise of communism in Central America. The Guatemalan army sought to wipe out rural support for the communist rebels. This was the most violent counterinsurgency period in what was already an extraordinarily long and brutal civil war. During this time, thousands of Maya people were shot, raped, tortured and 'disappeared' in one of the most violent episodes of the Guatemalan nation's history.

It was problematic for the Guatemalan army to identify who were the reds and who were innocent Maya people. Sadly, tens of thousands of innocent

Maya people were killed indiscriminately. This 'scorched earth' military strategy had been agreed at the highest political levels, going right to the president himself. Orders were given to the army, who then went on a campaign of death and destruction, destroying anything that, in their opinion, might be useful to 'the reds'. Their intention was to drive them out of their hiding places, usually villages and farms in the jungle, and thereby extinguish all resistance against the right-wing military government that was in power.

Any property that was considered useful to the reds was destroyed as part of the army's campaign. This included anything that could be considered a weapon but also included vehicles, animals, homes, and any other buildings that might be used for sheltering 'the reds'. Whole villages were burnt to the ground. The army took anything they wanted for themselves, including food stores, crops, water sources, and even some of the people, although this had already been banned under the 1977 Geneva Conventions.

One piece of intelligence that came via the CIA stated:

'The commanding officers of the units involved have been instructed to destroy all towns and villages which are cooperating with the 'Guerrilla army of the Poor' (EGP) and eliminate all sources of resistance.' It went on, *'Since the operation*

began, several villages have been burned to the ground, and a large number of rebels and collaborators have been killed. When an army patrol meets resistance and takes fire from a town or village, it is assumed that the entire town is hostile and it is subsequently destroyed.' When the army encountered an empty village, it was assumed to have been supporting the EGP, and it was destroyed. There are hundreds, possibly thousands, of refugees in the hills with no homes to return to.'

There were accounts of people being buried alive, burnt alive, women being captured and raped repeatedly, and the killing of infants. It was understood that hundreds of innocent men, women and children, with no political understanding or views, were being killed on a daily basis.

A 1982 confidential 'CIA cable' noted a rise in *'suspect right-wing violence'* in the capital, with an increasing number of kidnappings (particularly of educators and students) and an associated increase in the number of corpses recovered from ditches and gullies. The cable traced the wave of death squad repression to the 'Archivos intelligence unit', whose agents were given full authorisation to *'apprehend, hold, interrogate and dispose of suspected rebels as they saw fit'*.

This virtually indiscriminate killing of men, women and children, of anyone regarded by the army as possibly supportive of the rebels, was not simply the result of a twisted anti-communist ideology that dominated the Guatemalan military and political elites, but was also endorsed and militarily supported by the Reagan US administration.

The Guatemalan army was being secretly funded and armed by the USA. The communist rebels were being funded and armed by Cuba. The east-west support for this civil war kept the guns firing, and the fires burning, and tens of thousands fleeing and dying.

Ríos Montt died in April 2018 aged 91, and is widely held responsible for unleashing a scorched earth campaign on the nation's Maya population, particularly in the departments of Quiché and Huehuetenango, that, according to the 1999 United Nations truth commission, resulted in the annihilation of nearly 600 villages, and the deaths of up to 70,000 mostly indigenous Mayas. According to the UN-sponsored report, 'Guatemala, Memory of Silence': *The massacres that eliminated entire Maya villages are neither perfidious allegations nor figments of the imagination, but an authentic chapter in Guatemala's history.'*

The report documented that in the 1980s, the army committed 626 massacres against Maya villages. It has been documented that as many as one and a half million Maya peasants were uprooted from their homes and that many were forced to live in re-education concentration camps and to work in the fields of Guatemalan land barons. It is estimated that more than 200,000 people died or disappeared during the civil war.

CHAPTER 1. GOING TO BELIZE

It was 2 April 1982; Britain was about to go to war with Argentina over the sovereignty of the Falkland Islands.

Reagan answered the phone; it was the UK Prime Minister, Margaret Thatcher, "Hello, Ron, Margaret here."

"Yes, Margaret, what can I do for you?"

"We might need some help with our Falklands deployment in the South Atlantic. Could you possibly provide us with any support?"

"What type of support?" Reagan asked.

"We could do with having one of your aircraft carriers on standby; some re-armament support, and also, additional refuelling capability from Ascension Island."

Reagan replied, "Well, Margaret, as you probably already know, I've already made a statement saying we will remain impartial with regard to the Falklands, but I'll see what we can do. Leave it with me for now, and I'll get back to you."

"Thanks, Ron," she replied. "How is Nancy?"

"Just fine," Reagan replied.

"That's great. Give her my love," Margaret said.

"I shall. Goodbye, Margaret," he replied and hung up.

She remembered meeting Reagan in 1975, when he had been visiting Europe, in advance of his first run for president. He wasn't nominated at that time but was selected in 1980, beating President Jimmy Carter to take his place in the White House. She recalled them starting out with a more cordial relationship. Their joint belief in capitalism and democracy had eventually made them political soulmates; both committed to freedom and resolved to end communism. The prime minister smiled as she realised how they had warmed to each other.

Later that day, Reagan called back, "Hello, Margaret, you'll be pleased to hear that we've decided to assist you in the South Atlantic, but it must be with the utmost secrecy."

"Of course, Ron," she said sincerely.

He went on, "We'll keep an aircraft carrier on standby for you. We can also send additional armaments, including Sidewinder air-to-air missiles and Stinger hand-held missiles, and we'll share any useful satellite and signals intelligence. With regard to the fuel, we have instructed our tankers to fill up all our underground fuel facilities on Ascension Island."

She felt very relieved. "Thanks, Ron."

"You're welcome, Margaret; that's what friends are for. Is there anything else we can do?"

Margaret smiled. "That's very good of you, Ron. Nothing else I need right now, but I won't forget this. Thanks again."

Reagan interjected, "Before you go, Margaret, I do have a small request. As you know, there's a growing problem in Central America with Cuban-trained communist rebels. The Guatemalan president has asked for our help, which officially we have declined, but secretly, like you, we are helping out where we can. What I would like your guys on the ground to do, is to stop these commies from crossing the border into Belize. It makes it too easy for them to escape, and I'm sure you don't want the commies building an infrastructure in Belize. Can you beef up the border patrols to stop Belize becoming a safe zone for the rebels?"

"That sounds like a very reasonable request, Ron. I'll speak to the chief of the defence staff and sort it out."

"Thanks, Margaret, goodbye for now."

"Goodbye, Ron," she replied.

* * *

As a boy, Danny Sinclaire had lived in a small town at the heart of South Wales coal mining industry in the sixties and in the early seventies. He had moved with his family to South Africa for four years before eventually returning to Wales at the age of 16. He had always been the type of working-class boy that would take on the bullies at school, and occasionally came home from school with a black eye, so it came as no surprise to his parents when he announced he was going to apply to join the Royal Air Force.

At the age of 17, after going through the selection processes, he entered the RAF as an aircraftman to train as an engineer. Danny spent his first few years improving his engineering and combat skills, and by the age of 22, he was working on ground equipment in the General Engineering Flight at RAF Brawdy in West Wales.

The work could be monotonous, and Danny particularly disliked early mornings, especially after having had too many beers in the local town of Haverfordwest the night  before. He was on the early shift, his alarm went off at five in the morning, it was dark and cold, he groaned and rolled out of bed, had a quick shower and shave, then headed over to the hangar where he met his colleague sharing the early shift duties with him. They unlocked the hangar, winding the handles that operated the large hangar door, which gradually slid open. They both had a moan about the icy weather; Danny said, "It's fucking freezing out here.

Let's get the airfield done, and then we can get back for a mug of tea." His colleague agreed. They went into the hangar to get the tractor and refuelling bowser and then drove it out onto the aircraft pan. They used the diesel in the bowser to refuel the Houchin electrical aircraft generators that were plugged into the Hawker Hunter fighter jets sitting on the concrete pan.

When they had finished refuelling and testing the generators on the aircraft pan, they drove back to the general engineering hangar, reopened the hangar doors, and parked the tractor and refuelling bowser back in the hangar. Danny then picked up the keys for the Land Rover, which they  needed to use to carry out height and operational checks on the aircraft arrestor gear at the ends of each runway. This all had to be completed by 7am before the first Hunter took off to check the local flying conditions. After finishing all his duties, Danny thought to himself, *It's freezing cold, dark, wet and windy, and I can't feel my fingers. I bloody hate doing earlies.*

Danny had already been at RAF Brawdy for over two years. He had settled in nicely and enjoyed playing rugby, surfing on the local beaches, and going out on the town with his mates. The surrounding area was very lively in the summer due to the base being so near to some of the best beaches in Wales. It would swell with tourists during the summer, and Haverfordwest, where he often went socialising with his mates, was always busy. All of this socialising was a lot of fun, but he was now becoming bored with working on the same equipment in the hangar, day after day. It was time for a change.

When Danny got back from the icy, snow-covered airfield that morning, he went straight into the crew room, still shivering from the cold, and put the kettle on to make himself a hot mug of tea with two sugars. He tried to remove his green woolly hat, but it had frozen to his hair, so he left it in place and decided to wait until the ice had melted.

Every month, he and everyone else in the flight had to read station standing orders and then sign against the list of names attached to the back of the orders.

He picked up this month's issue and sat down, flicking through the pages. In the final section of the March 1982

station standing orders, it was asking for electrical and mechanical engineers from the General Engineering Flight to volunteer for an overseas posting to Belize, Central America. It explained that the work entailed maintaining ground support equipment in jungle hides as part of the General Engineering Flight.

Danny chatted with a colleague who had already done a tour in Central America, who described the

'hides' as landing sites where British Harrier GR3 jump jets, and helicopters, could be quickly refuelled and re-armed whenever necessary. Some of the hides were at Belize Airport Camp, and the rest of the hides were at secret locations near the border. Harrier GR3 jump jets were in Belize as a deterrent and would be used to protect Belize if the country came under attack from neighbouring Guatemala. These landing sites were also being used by Gazelle and Puma helicopters, dropping off British soldiers and supplies for the border protection forces patrolling the Belizean border with Guatemala. There were a few aircraft hides and army outposts based strategically along the border to monitor and prevent any Guatemalan army or rebel incursions.

Danny read the orders with interest. *Well, one of the reasons I joined the forces was to leave Wales and see the world, and it's got to be warmer there than it is here.* He assumed that going to Belize would be something completely different. He had never been to Central America or anywhere in the 'Americas'. It was only going to be a six-month posting. *It's not that long; what the hell?* he thought. In his head, Danny imagined Belize to be a sunny, exotic, and exciting place to be. All his friends told him he was absolutely mad. Why would he want to volunteer to go to such a hot, humid, dangerous jungle? There was a civil war ongoing in neighbouring Guatemala that could easily spill over into Belize.

Danny's boss, who didn't want him to go, said, "There are poisonous snakes, spiders, and mosquitoes that will eat you alive, according to one of my mates that did a stretch there."

"Mosquitoes have never liked the taste of my blood, Sarge, and anyway, I joined up to see the world and got bloody posted back home to Wales!" Danny retorted.

Everyone he spoke to told him this was a bad idea and that he should stay at Brawdy with his mates, but Danny was a risk-taker and was looking for adventure, so eventually, and unsurprisingly, he ignored their advice and decided to apply for the posting anyway.

Danny completed his application and was selected to go to RAF Sealand, alongside many other serving airmen and soldiers, for personal weapons training and selection processing. When Danny arrived there, it was a warm, still, and sunny day in the May of 1982, and 'Only You' by Yazoo was playing on the radio.

Danny pulled up outside the guardroom in his brown Ford Cortina and switched off the ignition. He took out his wallet, removing his identification card so it was ready for inspection, then reached over to the passenger seat and picked up his beret, put it on his head, adjusted it slightly; folding down the right side over the top of his ear, and then got out of the car.

As he walked towards the guardroom, he stopped briefly, looking at the Spitfire 'Gate Guardian' with admiration and pride, before heading towards  the reception hatch at the guardroom. The Spitfire made Danny think about the long history of the base. His warrant officer back at RAF Brawdy had told him that it was originally a civilian airfield and was taken over by the military in 1916 for training by the Royal Flying Corps.

Looking around the entrance to the RAF base, he thought, *This place looks very quiet; I wonder what the next few weeks hold in store for me?*

There was a senior aircraftman desk clerk sitting at the counter. He looked up at Danny through the hatch and said, "Hello, Corporal, what can I do for you?"

Danny was feeling tired and just wanted to get to his accommodation. He replied, "I'm here for a jungle combat training and selection course," and handed over his ID and induction paperwork to the desk clerk.

The clerk ran his finger down the list stopping at Danny's name, and said, "Okay, Corporal, just a moment please." He then walked over to a pile of brown envelopes and started thumbing through them until he found the one with Danny's name on it. He walked back over to the hatch and handed it over to Danny saying, "Everything is inside the envelope, there's a map inside with your car pass. You're in the temporary accommodation, block 16 at the top of the hill. The code for the door lock is in the envelope, your bedding is on the bed, and the mess hall and the NAAFI shop and bar is across the road. You must meet up with Sergeant Blake in the weapons training school tomorrow morning at eight, it's on the map, just a five-minute walk from your accommodation. Anything else I can do for you, Corporal?"

Danny picked up the envelope and said, "No, that's fine, thanks," and walked back to his car.

Danny drove up to the entrance barrier and showed his ID card. The gate guard opened the barrier, and he drove slowly up the hill to the temporary accommodation. Block 16 was easy to spot, with its large sign displaying 'Block 16' in thirty-inch-high letters. He pulled into the car park, put the car pass on the dashboard, got out of the car and took his dark blue RAF holdall out of the boot. He walked up to the entrance and punched the four-digit code into the code lock on the front entrance door, and turned the latch to let himself in.

Once inside the temporary accommodation block, Danny surveyed his surroundings – it looked clean and tidy. *Better than I expected*, he thought. He took the stairs to the first floor and pushed back the double fire doors. Looking at the numbers on the doors, he could see that his room must be about halfway down the corridor, on the left-hand side. He turned the key in the lock and let himself in. The room was small and quite basic, with a metal frame single bed, a wardrobe, a sink with a square mirror on the wall above it, and a chocolate brown carpet covering the floor.

Bedding, plus a couple of pillows, had been thrown haphazardly on the centre of the mattress. *This'll do for six weeks, if I get to stay that long,* he contemplated as he looked out of the window. He noticed the mess hall was opposite the accommodation block. *Not far to go for food,* he thought, then unpacked his holdall and made the bed.

Danny kicked off his shoes and relaxed on the bed, falling asleep for a couple of hours. When he awoke, he looked out of the window and he could see the sun was setting. It was Sunday evening. *Tomorrow morning is when the fun really begins*, he thought. He got up and walked across the road to get something to eat in the mess canteen. It was quiet in the mess, not many people around. *Not surprising for a Sunday,* he thought. He went up to the servery, picked up a plate with cutlery, and moved along the servery, helping himself to roast beef, Yorkshire puddings, vegetables and gravy. After he had eaten his meal, Danny then walked across to the NAAFI bar and had a couple of beers. Again, it was very quiet, so he spent some time chatting to the barmaid before heading back to his room.

Over the next few weeks, Danny did a lot of training – including physical and written tests, firing a variety of weapons on the range, learning jungle driving techniques, camouflage, first aid, and working in small units. Throughout the training, any applicant could choose to leave, but Danny was enjoying the challenge and was getting to know some of the other volunteers from both the RAF and the army.

Gradually the applicants were whittled down until by week four, there were only six left, two teams of three. The next two weeks were spent doing more weapons training, especially on the six-hundred-yard range. It was Danny's first time on a long-distance range; up until this point, he had only used weapons on a twenty-five-yard range. Over the next two weeks, Danny was trained on how to improve his accuracy and use of multiple small arms, including a standard self-loading rifle (*SLR*) and a Sterling submachine gun (*SMG*). During the period on the weapons range, RAF regiment weapons specialists assisted with fine-tuning and personalising each of the weapons to the individual's own line of sight. This was especially important for Danny because he was left-handed.

In the final week, the two teams were competing against one another. This involved being operational for 16 hours each day; being trained in a variety of rebel tactics, simulating being attacked, carrying out attacks, rescuing wounded colleagues, unarmed combat, knife fighting, how to respond to aggression, preserving ammunition, and how to survive in the jungle with limited rations. Danny was made team leader, with Kevin, the mechanic, and Mark, the signals radio operator, being the final two members of his team.

Danny and his team were issued with new rules of engagement – Sergeant Blake referred to it as their 'Pink Card'. The normal 'Green Card' rules of engagement in the UK stated that individuals must use minimum force to achieve their aims and always issue loud warnings, "AIR FORCE, STOP OR I FIRE!" up to three times. The big surprise was that the new 'Pink Card' rules of engagement for operating in Belize did not require the issuing of a warning before opening fire. It suggested that a warning should be issued but gave the caveat, *'unless to do so would endanger you or some other person.'* The 'Pink Card' stated, *'You may use deadly force in defence of: You, fellow soldiers, or innocent people.'* Danny tucked the card into the back of his wallet.

Sergeant Blake explained that owing to the nature of the insurgent hostilities in Belize, it might be the case that an armed combatant, whether they were rebels or Guatemalan soldiers, may not identify themselves by wearing a uniform and may conceal their weapons. Under these circumstances, special rules applied, and Danny and his team could make their own judgement of who was, or wasn't, an enemy combatant, even though in the first instance, they might appear to be civilians. If they came across anybody carrying their weapons openly, they could be challenged or engaged. The sergeant went on to explain: "Members of rebel forces are legitimate objects of attack when taking a direct part in hostilities on the Belizean side of the border. Guatemalan army soldiers are also legitimate objects of attack, but only if they threaten Belizean sovereignty. The Belizean civilian population as such, as well as individual civilians, shall not be the object of attack."

By mid-July, they were at the end of their six weeks, and the two teams were trained and ready for their posting to Central America. Danny was the highest rank in his team, a corporal, so was in charge. Mark was an army private, and Kevin was a senior aircraftman (SAC) in the RAF.

Danny travelled to RAF Brize Norton in Oxfordshire a week before Mark and Kevin. He was flying to Belize a week earlier than them to do the handover with the current team leader. Danny felt excited and a bit nervous but was looking forward to getting on the flight. He boarded the Vickers VC10 with 140 other passengers and flew to Dulles International Airport, Washington, where everyone got off for a couple of hours while the aircraft refuelled. Then on to Belize International Airport, a patch of hot concrete in the jungle shared by the RAF and the Belize Civil Aviation Authority. It was early August 1982, and it was nearing the end of the rainy season. The journey had been long but uneventful. Unfortunately, alcohol was not allowed on RAF passenger planes, so Danny was already thinking about having a nice cold beer once he got to the Airport Camp.

As the seatbelt lights went out in the cabin of the VC10, some people started standing up and opening the overhead lockers, taking their things out and generally milling about. A set of steps was rolled up to the VC10. Danny could see the air traffic control tower and terminal building close by. There was a slight thud as the rubber bumper of the steps touched the side of the aircraft. When the front passenger door of the VC10 opened, the cool air inside the aircraft was hit by the hot humid air from outside, creating an immediate haze around the exit. Danny was six rows back from the exit, and he took a moment to adjust to the heat before unclipping his seatbelt. *It's going to take quite a few days to acclimatise,* he thought as he got off the plane to collect his kit bag. Everyone got off the aircraft and walked across the concrete to the terminal building, which was not more than 50 yards away, but by the time Danny walked in, he was already soaked through with sweat. There was no air conditioning in the terminal building, just large fans circulating the hot air.

He eventually picked up his holdall from the baggage carousel and headed out to the transport, a Bedford four-ton flatbed lorry that was to take them to the

Airport Camp. The main camp was three miles away, where he remembered being told the headquarters for No. 1417 (Tactical Ground Attack) Flight was situated. The flight had four aircraft, with their aircrews and ground staff, and was in Belize as part of the British protection force, flying Harrier GR3 vertical take-off fast jets.

CHAPTER 2. AIRPORT CAMP

At the time, the country of Belize was a very poor and unpredictable country. The Falklands War was not long over, and there were many  *Guatemalan exiles living and working in Belize who sympathised with Argentina, and similarly believed that Belize should be part of Guatemala. They mistrusted both the current Guatemalan government and the British forces protecting the newly independent country of Belize.*

Danny climbed into the back of the Bedford four tonner with his blue kit bag. Wooden bench seats were bolted in along either side of the lorry. He sat down, resting his kit bag on his knees.

The four-wheel-drive lorry kicked up clouds of dust for about 10 minutes as it bumped along the dirt road between the terminal building and the British forces Airport Camp until finally, they all arrived, dusty, sweaty, hungry and thirsty.

Danny had been travelling for 16 hours. He was hot, tired, and thirsty. *I could down an ice-cold beer right now,* he thought to himself. A small group of people were waiting for them outside the station headquarters – a corrugated Nissen hut opposite the flagpole on the main road through Airport Camp. When he arrived there, with many other soldiers, airmen, and some civilian workers, they were all greeted by a welcoming committee and taken into the admin offices to get all their paperwork sorted out. They were briefed on the Airport Camp station standing orders and the 'Off-base Rules' around socialising and curfews. They were taken through all the usual arrival and familiarisation processes, such as the obligatory tour around the camp, picking up their bedding, and being escorted to their accommodation. When they visited the store, they were all handed bivouac storm capes by the duty storeman.

Danny looked at the long, green, wax cotton cape and said, "This looks like it should cope with the worst of the rains," and the storeman agreed.

"You're right. When it rains here, it comes down like a flood, and if you haven't got that with you, then expect to get soaked through."

"Okay, understood." Danny smiled.

The corporal who had been waiting for Danny, and was now escorting him around the base, was called Bill, and he was the person that Danny was replacing. Bill was sounding upbeat and obviously happy to be handing over his duties. Six months of living in a tin hut in the jungle had been tough, and he was now looking forward to getting back home. He pointed across the playing field to a row of Nissen huts, which was where everyone at Airport Camp was accommodated, and said, "That's where you will be living for the next six months."

Danny smiled and raised his eyebrows, "Not quite the Ritz, is it?"

"No," Bill laughed. "Do you fancy dumping your holdall and then popping over to the NAAFI bar for a couple of pints of the local brew, Belikin lager?"

"Sound like an excellent plan, Bill!" Danny responded with a big smile on his face and gave him a 'thumbs up'.

Danny was shown into what would be his living accommodation for the next six months. It was quiet, no one was there except for them. The building was an eighteen-man corrugated tin Nissen hut, which was 16 feet wide by 72 feet long. Each bed space had a metal frame bed with a foam mattress, a double door

wardrobe with a padlock, and a small side table. There were square tables running down the centre of the hut, and washing lines hung between the wardrobes, with various garments draped over them. Large white fans were bolted along the top of the semi-circular tin roof, they were buzzing as they turned slowly, wafting the scorching tropical air around. Danny threw his kit bag into his wardrobe and said to Bill, "I'll sort that out later; it's like a bloody oven in here, way too hot to unpack right now." He clicked the padlock on the wardrobe, put the key in his pocket, and then they headed over for a beer.

It was sweltering inside the bar, and Danny quickly realised that it was much hotter than he expected. Bill looked at Danny and could see the sweat rolling off his forehead into his eyes; he said, "Don't worry, mate, you'll get used to the heat, but it'll take you a few days to acclimatise."

"The sooner the better, Bill!" Danny replied while wiping the sweat off his brow.

They ordered a couple of beers. The barman took a couple of glasses out of the freezer under the bar and then poured them two pints of Belikin beer. They were ice cold, and Danny relished that first pint; it went down very easily and very quickly.

He and Bill had found a table under a fan, which gave them a little relief from the heat.

Bill asked, "So where do you come from, Danny? I can't quite pinpoint your accent."

"I know, most people can't figure out my accent. I am originally from South Wales, but my father is a builder, and we moved around a lot with his work, including four years in South Africa, and eventually living in England, so I suppose that's why my accent is difficult to pinpoint," Danny replied.

"Ah, I see." Bill nodded. "So it's not the first time you been somewhere this hot them?"

"That's true," Danny replied.

They chatted about the job, how often they went out, what the dangers were, what to look out for. Bill cautioned, "Whatever you do, don't forget to go to the armoury in the morning and check all your weapons are there. It's compulsory to carry weapons when you are heading down to the hides on the border. There are a minority of local people who don't want us here. As you get closer to the border, there are more Guatemalan refugees living and working with the locals, who view us Brits with suspicion. Just stick to the rules and you'll be alright."

They carried on drinking and were joined by a few more soldiers and airmen, who then started regaling Danny with stories about where to go and what to do. No doubt, looking forward to taking Danny out for a tour of the local bars and the local women. After chatting to Bill and the others over a few beers, Danny had a better understanding about the local area, the no-go areas in Belize City, and the work he was expected to undertake over the next six months.

It was usual for the team leader to arrive early and carry out some reconnaissance. Danny had arrived a week earlier than his two colleagues, Kevin and Mark, who he had been teamed up with at RAF Sealand. Danny's role was to do some preparation and handover work with Bill and his team, get to know his way around, and meet the key individuals he needed to work with and report to. One of the first people he needed to see was his boss, Warrant Officer Briggs, who was in charge of the General Engineering Flight. He would meet him the following morning.

By the time they had finished drinking in the bar, it was dark and much cooler. Danny went back to his Nissen hut, where a few of the airmen were playing cards, others already asleep, and some were still out in the local bars. He introduced himself and was warmly welcomed by the other guys sharing his accommodation. After having a quick chat, Danny unpacked his holdall and set his clock radio for seven the next morning.

Danny awoke to the sound of his alarm. Some of the airmen were already up and heading to the shower block. Danny could hear the DJ talking on the radio. It was the local British Forces Broadcasting Services station, BFBS Belize, who coincidentally started their breakfast show at seven. He listened to the first song played, Dire Straits

'Private Investigations', then got out of his bed and went to the shower block. The outdoor set of concrete cubicles was shared with the local insects and lizards, and covered in patches of slimy black mould. Danny avoided touching the walls, had a quick shower, shave, and got dressed, putting on his lightweight jungle fatigues, with 'Chant No.1 (I Don't Need This Pressure On)' by Spandau Ballet playing in the background. The transport was the same vehicle that he had arrived in; the Bedford four tonner open flatbed with bench seats. Danny jumped aboard, and it left for the airport at 7.45am sharp, as it did every morning.

He would discover over the next few days that there was no need for an alarm clock, the BFBS breakfast DJ came on automatically over the loudspeaker every morning at 7am, with the same track Dire Straits, 'Private Investigations'.

Danny arrived outside the airport's RAF engineering compound, where the Harriers, Pumas, and Gazelles were hangared. There was a guard on the gate checking IDs; he knew most of the people already and just waved them through, but could see Danny was new.

The guard asked, "Just arrived, Corporal?"

Danny replied, "I arrived yesterday afternoon. I have to report to Warrant Officer Briggs," handing over his ID card.

The guard looked at his ID and pointed towards a portacabin about 50 yards from the gate.

"That's where you'll find Warrant Officer Briggs," the guard responded.

Danny walked across the concrete towards the portacabin, knocked on the door, and a voice inside said, "Come in."

Danny opened the door and went inside, it was one of the few buildings with an air conditioner. *Nice...* he thought, as the cool air enveloped him. He closed the door behind him and went over to the warrant officer sitting at the desk in his khaki shorts and jacket and introduced himself, "Danny Sinclaire, sir."

Warrant Officer Briggs looked him up and down and said, "Hello, Corporal Sinclaire, I was expecting you," and motioned to Danny to sit down in front of his desk. "Please, have a seat."

Danny sat down and handed over his joining papers. Warrant Officer Briggs glanced at them and said, "Thanks, we'll sort out the paperwork later." He went on to explain that Danny's primary role would be ensuring the hides were operationally maintained and ready for use whenever necessary. There were two teams maintaining the Harrier landing sites along the border, and Danny would be starting work in a week once the rest of his team had arrived. In the meantime, he needed to get familiar with the role, and the best way to do this was by having a detailed handover from Bill.

Warrant Officer Briggs had asked Bill to organise a tour of the operational hides to get an understanding of these remote landing sites and what the job entailed. The warrant officer made a call to the hangar and asked Bill to come over to his office. He knocked on the door, walked in, and said, "Sir?"

Briggs looked over the top of his glasses and said, "Bill, take Corporal Sinclaire to get his papers signed off. Make sure you take him to the armoury to check his weapons have arrived."

Bill knew what was needed, he had gone through the same procedure six months earlier with his predecessor. He walked Danny around the site introducing him to the key people and eventually going to the armoury. The armourer had received Danny's weapons the day before. Danny filled out the forms and checked his weapons as the armourer passed them to him one by one, saying, "A standard SLR with two 20-round magazines, and a Sterling SMG with two 34-round magazines."

Danny inspected the weapons, and after a few minutes, said, "They're all fine, thanks."

The armourer replied, "You'll need to speak to the regiment guys next door and get a slot on the range before you can take these out on operational duties." Danny went there next with Bill and booked his slot as instructed.

Danny spent the next few days getting to know his way around, testing his weapons on the range, and getting everything signed off by the various sections on Airport Camp. He had been allocated his own long wheelbase Land Rover and trailer, currently being used by Bill and his team. It was just the right type of vehicle for the potholed highways and dirt roads that would get him around the different outposts. Many of the roads in Belize could become virtually impassable in a normal car during the rainy season, but the Land Rover would usually get through.

Bill explained, "You've arrived at a good time, Danny, it is coming towards the end of the rainy season now, so there are fewer storms, but you can still expect a few very heavy downpours and some spectacular thunder and lightning, nothing like you see in the UK, a lot bigger and louder!"

Danny smiled and said, "Well, it's only rain, Bill, and at least it's warm rain."

Bill smiled and raised his eyebrows as if to say *You'll soon see!*

The very next day, Danny discovered that the lightning displays were particularly impressive, arcing across the sky like long crooked fingers, followed by loud claps of thunder and rumbling that reverberated through his whole body. The rain fell in waves; Danny had never seen such heavy rainfall. It was as if the Gods had opened a dam in the sky, it just kept coming down, flooding the playing field outside his Nissen hut. The noise of the rain falling on the corrugated tin roof was so loud, the airmen inside had to shout to be heard. Danny stood in the doorway with a couple of the other airmen, watching the forked lightning as the storm passed over Airport Camp.

Bill walked over to the doorway and tapped Danny on the shoulder. "I told you it was nothing like you'll see in the UK."

"Never seen rain like it!" Danny replied.

"If I can change the subject, we're jumping on a Puma tomorrow morning to do a whistle-stop tour of all the hides and outpost camps. I can brief you on our ground equipment and the sodium lighting at each of the sites. Shall we grab a seat and I'll show you where we're going?"

"Sounds like a good idea, Bill," Danny replied.

They walked over to one of the tables and sat down. Bill took out a map of Belize and pointed at various positions on the map, saying, "The pilot normally does a round trip and will not want to hang around too long at each site. We'll be flying to Zulu hide first, then Holdfast Camp, Yankee hide, Salamanca Camp, and lastly, Rideau Camp. Rideau, Salamanca and Holdfast are all used as company level patrol bases. The Yankee and Zulu hides are normally unmanned unless there is an exercise going on. All the sites are used for landing our helicopters and Harriers. We keep aviation fuel there, and some diesel for the standby generators."

"That all makes sense, Bill. What's the plan for the morning?" Danny asked.

"Probably best if we go for breakfast around 7.30am," Bill said.

"Sounds good. Breakfast at 7.30am, I'll be there," Danny replied.

The next day, Danny met Bill for breakfast and then went to the armoury to get his SMG and two magazines. The shoulder butt was folded in, which made it easier to carry. Danny preferred this weapon; it was light and reliable, easy to strip down and clean. This was his personal SMG, he had used it during his weapons training at RAF Sealand, where the sights had been adjusted for him by the RAF regiment to give him the best accuracy. It was compulsory to carry weapons when going to the outposts and hides. It was an area where rebels operated, and there was also a concern that the Guatemalan army might decide to invade like Argentina did in the Falklands. The Guatemalan government had always held a claim to Belize, saying it was previously taken from them by the British, so there was always a slim possibility of them deciding to take it back.

Danny walked over to the Puma waiting on the playing fields. The RAF pilot was stood in the doorway, and Bill was outside sitting on the steps. Some provisions and mail were loaded onto the Puma, and then they boarded, following the crew instructions to their seats. They both put their headsets on, strapped themselves in, and the Puma roared into the sky and headed towards Zulu hide.

As they approached the hide, Danny could see a cleared patch of jungle, a couple of generators, and  two air portable

 Avtar fuel pods in the far corner, each capable of holding two tonnes of aviation fuel.

They landed, and Bill gave Danny a quick tour of the site before they re-boarded the Puma and spent the rest of the day visiting the remaining sites, enabling Danny to familiarise himself with them and their set-up.

Salamanca Camp was the fourth site and was different from the other's because its position was so remote. It was located in the southern part of Belize jungle – beside the Columbia River at the foot of the Maya mountains. Salamanca Camp was surrounded by dense rainforest, where the noise of the jungle was constant, whether it was the buzzing of the insects or the shrieking of the monkeys hundreds of feet into the canopy. It was like a cacophony of nature, where birds sang in the treetops, snakes rustled through the undergrowth, and soldier ants walked along in their regiments carrying leaf litter to their colonies.

The next location, Rideau Camp, was 25 miles away. There was a British army contingency there, carrying out patrols along the border with Guatemala. They patrolled in the villages, hills, and the jungle of the

Maya Indian reservation, spending between five to seven days on patrol. One of these patrols came aboard the Puma and got dropped off on a hilltop close to the border. *Rather them than me!* Danny thought, now feeling happy that he was able to get back to his tin Nissen hut at Airport Camp, which suddenly felt much more appealing and civilised.

As they returned to Airport Camp, touching down again on the playing field, Danny thought about Kevin and Mark, the other two members of his team who would be joining him shortly. *Good thing I got out here early for the handover, I've got a lot to go over with them,* he pondered.

The Puma took off again, heading back to the hangar, where they dropped their weapons off at the armoury and headed over to the NAAFI bar to mull over the day with a few beers and have something to eat.

A week later, Danny went to the airport terminal and greeted Kevin and Mark as they came through customs with their kit bags, saying, "Hello, guys, nice to see you again. I've got a Land Rover outside; I'll give you a lift around to the Airport Camp. Once you've got your bedding and filled out all your paperwork, I'll take you both over to the NAAFI bar for a few cold beers and brief you on our duties." They both thanked Danny, threw their kit bags in the back of the Land Rover, and drove to Airport Camp.

CHAPTER 3. THE ONLY GOOD RED IS A DEAD RED

Carlos Cruz was a belligerent, self-important young man from a wealthy land-owning family, who owned a large farming estate on the outskirts of Guatemala City. Carlos had grown up being doted on by his father, and like his father, he had become a racist, bigoted, and aggressive tyrant. He often watched his father as he strutted around his estate like a peacock, shouting his orders at his staff. Carlos wanted to be just like his father – imposing, powerful, tyrannical, and rich. His father had very close links to both the political elite and the army. His wealth and connections made him a very influential man. He employed hundreds of peasant workers, kept under tight control by his 'private army' of ex-soldiers patrolling and managing his vast estate.

By the time Carlos was 21 years old, he had developed a distorted understanding of what 'normal' life was like, especially for the poor people of his country. He only saw them as servants to do everything for him. He enjoyed giving them orders. They would pick up and wash his discarded clothes, cook his meals, fetch him drinks, and keep the mansion and its grounds looking immaculate. It was also an expectation of his that the prettiest young women they employed were not just there to cook and clean but were also there for his personal pleasure. From a teenager, Carlos would often tease them, trying to take advantage of them, and encouraged them to provide 'additional services' for 'additional rewards'. His father had done the same thing for years, and his mother didn't seem to notice. *Just men being men*, he thought.

In 1979, following in his father's footsteps, he became a commissioned officer in the Guatemalan army. By 1982, He was a lieutenant, commanding his own platoon of 40 soldiers, proudly assisted by Sergeant Garcia, a very experienced senior non-commissioned officer. The platoon was split into four squads, with Sergeant Garcia supporting Lieutenant Cruz by ensuring each of the corporals in charge of the squads understood their orders.

At the age of 24, Carlos did not feel out of place giving orders, it was something he had got used to growing up. He enjoyed being in charge of his own platoon, the camaraderie, and the excitement he felt when his platoon obliterated a communist rebel enclave. Carlos had been raised by his parents to hate communism. In his mind it was like a disease slowly spreading through the land that needed eradicating, and his platoon was the weapon to do just that. They went out on regular patrols, searching for rebel hideouts. His job was to ensure that the reds had nowhere to hide. Carlos and Sergeant Garcia had a phrase that they often repeated to the platoon, 'The only good red is a dead red!'

Today, Carlos listened to the radio with interest; there was a coup being reported. General Efrain Ríos Montt has just become President of Guatemala after coming to power in a military coup. It was the 23rd of March 1982, Montt was speaking to the nation and promised Guatemalans, "I will not steal, I will not lie, I will not abuse." Carlos wondered how this would affect him and his family – and decided it was probably nothing to worry about, after all, his father had always been very close to the military, and was also a very wealthy, respected man in the city. He poured a large glass of aged rum, sipping it slowly and enjoying the warmth and flavour. *There's nothing I can do; I'll just keep killing the reds, and then wait and see what happens,* he pondered to himself.

* * *

Sisasi was a twenty-three-year-old schoolteacher. She smiled to herself as she walked through the village towards the schoolhouse wearing her favourite pastel blue floral dress. It was made of cotton and had a large bow tied at the waist. As she walked, it flowed backwards and forwards just below her knees. She felt happy wearing it; the dress suited her bubbly personality.

Her straight, shiny black hair fell halfway down her back in a loose tangle, and every now and again she would unconsciously reach back with her hand and pull her hair forward, draping it over her shoulder. At five feet six inches tall, she was the tallest woman in her village, and still unattached, much to her mother's disappointment. Many of the single men in her village had tried and failed to woo her.

She sat down on the wooden bench outside the schoolhouse, listening to their new president on her small transistor radio, feeling sceptical about his promises. It was a scorching hot day, beads of perspiration glistened on her shoulders. As she continued to listen to the broadcast, Sisasi wondered what this meant for the people living in Colina. She thought, *Our politicians never seem to deliver on their words*. She moved the radio around to try to get a better signal, and as she moved, her silky, mahogany coloured skin shimmered in the heat.

Polo, one of her teenage pupils, had been watching her from the schoolhouse. He was always delighted to see her and felt completely besotted. His heart ached for her, but he knew she was out of his reach. He daydreamed that one day when he was older, he might have the slightest of chances to hold her in his arms.

The coup had come as no surprise to Sisasi; after all, she, her family and friends had been living through many years of civil war. This was just something else that may, or may not, make a difference to the world they lived in. She was working in the local school alongside Father Michael, the local priest, teaching Spanish and English.

She could hear Father Michael arriving on his motorbike. He was a rotund, balding American priest in his fifties. He always wore a long black robe tied at the waist, accentuating his rather large pot-belly, and a wide-brimmed straw hat to keep the sun off his bald patch. He had been living near the village of Colina for the past 20 years, and had been Sisasi's mentor, teaching her to speak, read, and write in both Spanish and English, and along the way, Sisasi had picked up some of his cheeky wit. Sisasi loved reading, and languages, which was unusual because most of the adults she knew, including her parents, did not speak any other languages and could not read or write. Some of the parents looked at Father Michael with suspicion, and thought schooling was a complete waste of time, "It's better to teach them how to grow maize and live off the land," they would say to each other.

He had found an ally in Sisasi, she was very intelligent and articulate. She helped him with encouraging the parents in Colina to send their children to school, and she was a natural in the classroom. The pupils in her class always enjoyed joking with her, albeit she would sometimes cut them down mid-speech with her sharp one-liners when they were being too boisterous; or if an individual pupil misbehaved, her large brown eyes would emit a laser-like glare with such intensity, she could gain their attention and obedience in an instant. Sisasi had the utmost respect of her pupils; they looked up to her and enjoyed their time with her.

When Sisasi was a young girl, like all the other Maya children in the village at that time, she had also been taught how to live off the land by her parents. Subsistence farming in the jungle provided their main sources of food. After Father Michael arrived and had set up classes in the village, Sisasi had wanted to learn to read and write, even though her parents tried to discourage her, but she was persistent, and cajoled her parents into letting her go to the missionary school. Her father had eventually conditionally conceded saying, "So long as it does not interfere with your chores."

All her life, she had grown up learning that the jungle was an environment full of dangers, and that due to the ongoing civil war, it was much more dangerous, even in their remote northerly location. The small village where she lived and worked was east of the sacred Uaxactun Ruins. Maya people had lived in this part of the jungle for millennia, and there were many old paths and temples known only to them, which had been used by their forefathers for thousands of years.

The village was at the end of a long and bumpy road which connected to the local farm. This was where her mother and father, and many of the other adults in the village, were currently working during the week to earn hard cash. It meant they could buy tools and seeds, enabling them to maintain their own smallholdings in Colina. Sisasi had three older siblings, who had all left the village, two of whom had gone across the border into Mexico. Like many of the people in their district, they had left Guatemala, hoping for a better life.

Two years previously, Fabio, her twenty-five-year-old brother, had just vanished without a word. After leaving to go to work at the local farm, he had never returned home again. She worried about him and wondered, was he still alive? She often thought about him, remembering how funny and how strong he was. He had fierce deep-set eyes and jet-black hair. He had always been a spirited and outspoken young man. Nobody knew what had actually happened to him, but there were rumours that he had joined the rebel army with some of the other young men that had been working on the farm. Like many people in their district, he had disappeared unexpectedly, and was just another missing person. She missed him, the whole family did, and she thought about him almost every day, hoping that one day there would be a miracle, and he would suddenly turn up on the doorstep.

The people who lived in the villages to the south were gradually moving further and further north towards Mexico and away from the troubles of the ongoing civil war. Many thousands had also moved west, closer to the Belizean border, or even gone across the border into Belize, where they felt safer. They had carved out new clearings in the jungle, where they could live and subsistence farm. This was true of some of her own family and friends too; many of them had been leaving the area over the past few years because they no longer felt safe.

Father Michael paid Sisasi a small amount of money each week for her support, teaching reading, writing and arithmetic to the young children in the village. He had watched her growing up. She had a natural way with children, and when she smiled, her round cheeks would reveal dimples and her pearly white teeth. Father Michael had instilled in her that education was a good thing and could bring her people out of poverty. Her parents still believed that the most important things to learn were tending to the crops and the pigs, but the small income Sisasi brought into their home helped, so they reluctantly agreed that she should continue working in the school.

Sisasi had spent many hours talking to Father Michael about his life in the United States, and found it hard to understand how different it was there. It seemed to her that everyone was rich, so very different from the world that she and her family lived in. Their village was very remote and difficult to reach in the hills of the north-eastern district of Guatemala, near the Mopan River. All the Maya people in her village lived in poverty. Life was very primitive compared to western standards. Their houses were made of wood with thatched roofs, with openings for windows that allowed a variety of insects and small animals to come and go. Mosquitoes and other bugs were particularly active and irritating at dusk, but it was just the way they were used to living.

The Mopan River wound its way through Petén, the northernmost area of Guatemala, and across the border into the Cayo district of Belize. There were no tarmac roads and no electricity or running water. The roads didn't even make it as far as their village. The dirt road that vehicles could use ended about a mile south of their village, so the rest of the journey had to be walked, or for larger loads, a donkey would be used. Father Michael had a small motorbike, which he used to get around the local community. He was adept at getting his motorbike up the narrow paths, although occasionally, even a motorbike could be challenging to get up the steeper paths in the rainy season when the paths became muddy and extremely slippery.

Sisasi and the other adults in Colina knew that the civil war was still going on in other villages and towns; many people were just disappearing or being found dead in a ditch. Colina was still unaffected, being so far north, but many people had been leaving their villages further south and would pass through, following the old, well-trodden roads and footpaths towards Mexico.

Some would stop and ask for food and water, and some would tell terrible stories of their villages and crops being burnt to the ground. Many of the people passing through spoke of army soldiers not only burning down their houses and stealing all their food, but also raping their women and killing anyone who tried to stop them. Some told stories of men that stayed to fight to protect their homes and their families. They were all eventually killed by the army, but not just the men; even the women, children, and the elderly were annihilated.

The violence was escalating to unprecedented levels, and Sisasi, alongside many others, worried that the troubles would, sooner or later, reach their village. She had also heard stories that it was not unusual for drunk soldiers to start gun and machete battles between themselves, seriously injuring or even killing each other. So many people were just disappearing, life was so precarious, and for some soldiers, their lives seemed to carry no value at all. Sisasi thought about her absent brother, *I hope you are alive and well, Fabio*, and felt worried for her family and friends in Colina.

Sisasi knew that the northern area of Guatemala was also very active with armed communist rebels fighting with the Guatemalan army. She had been told that many of the rebels had been trained in Cuba, and were ambushing the army soldiers, killing as many of them as they could, then retreating quickly back into the jungle. It was a very worrying time for her village.

She could often hear distant gunfire and explosions; in fact, most evenings, she and other villagers would sit quietly and spend time carefully listening to the menacing noises, trying to decide whether it was any louder than the day before; to determine whether the soldiers were getting closer to their village. Some villagers in Colina had already packed up and left to follow the old northern footpaths. They knew that following these old routes would eventually lead them across the Mexican border, where they could then clear a new area in the Mexican jungle and start again – a place where they hoped to be able to live and farm in safety, although they didn't know for certain whether this would be allowed.

Sisasi and other villagers in Colina often talked to each other about leaving and going across the border to Mexico or Belize. They knew that there was so much danger around them, it felt pervasive. Other villages had taken to defending themselves, and the elders in Colina decided that they, too, must do something to try to protect themselves, their crops, and their village. After many discussions, they formulated a plan to build mantraps and hideouts, just in case any soldiers attacked their village. After everything that had happened to people in other villages, it seemed like the only sensible thing to do. They needed to think up ways of protecting themselves.

The villagers had different paths they would take to get from the village to the crops, the pig pens, and back to their homes. These were the standard ways in and out of the village. Sisasi's father, who was a respected elder of the village, discussed options with the other elders as to how to protect themselves, and they decided that they needed escape routes which should be off the normal paths and kept secret, so that only people in their village knew of them. Over the next few weeks, in between tending to the fields, they cleared some of the undergrowth to allow access to the new pathways, which would allow them to get to higher ground. The new paths and hideouts dug into the hillside were well camouflaged, with the entrances well hidden by branches and palm leaves.

They dug deep holes as 'mantraps' in which they secured strong pointy stakes. The mantraps were approximately six feet deep, and the pointy stakes were about two feet high. These dark, damp holes attracted snakes, scorpions and spiders, and the villagers also caught and dropped extra snakes into the traps. They kept the traps covered with small twigs and branches, strong enough for a small animal to cross, but a man would fall through and be injured or killed. Similar traps were also dug in people's houses, but they were covered with stronger pieces of wood during the day and then removed at night when they went to bed. In that way, if anyone sneaked into their houses during the night, they would fall down a hole and be impaled on the pointy bamboo stakes, and the alarm would be raised.

They also made very clear and straight 'decoy' pathways, which could be easily seen and followed by the soldiers. A series of booby traps were laid along these paths, designed to impact any 'would-be' pursuers, the most dreaded of these were the ranks of spears attached to arched lengths of tensioned bamboo, or large logs held high in the canopy to fall on their heads. They were just waiting for the soldiers to step on the discreet trip wires, positioned just beneath the leaves and soil, that would trigger the release of their deadly weapons. The bamboo spears were set around waist height for an average man, and designed to smash into the soldier's abdomen at high speed, killing or seriously injuring them.

It was every villager's responsibility to learn the correct and safe paths and understand where all these dangerous traps were set. Even the children, as part of their school lessons, were taken on walks by Sisasi to the school hideout, so if they needed to evacuate, they would know where to escape to, even if they were alone.

CHAPTER 4. DISTANT GUNFIRE

It was coming to the end of the rainy season. During this period, the tropical thunderstorms delivered wave after drenching wave of torrential rain that would turn paths into torrents, followed by baking hot sunshine, which quickly evaporated the water on the ground and in the tree canopy, leaving the jungle enveloped in an ethereal haze. On the ground, wet leaf litter and puddles formed plumes of vapour rising up to the foggy haze that filled the spaces between the trees and branches. The heat from the sun kept it rising higher and higher past the tree canopy and towards the waiting sky to join the next storm cloud that was starting to form. The continuous haze disrupted the sunlight, making the jungle canopy look like a shimmering mirage, warping the view of the canopy under the blazing heat of the sun.

It was early September 1982, Sisasi was in the schoolhouse teaching Spanish to 10 of the village children, who were aged between six and thirteen. The oldest boy, Polo, was 13 years old, he liked being at school, particularly because he was so infatuated with his teacher, who would often catch him gazing at her with a fixated look of desire. She knew what that look on his face meant, and would give him jobs to do to stop him from daydreaming, sometimes acting as her teaching assistant to help her with the younger children and stop them from being disruptive. He felt very proud and grown up when she asked for his help, thinking, *One day...* In his parents' eyes, it was time for him to stop going to school and start helping them out more with tending to their crops. In their eyes, he was becoming a young man, and it was time for him to take more of the workload. He was skinny but strong, and currently sprouting up like a beanstalk. *Not long and I'll soon be grown up,* he thought, but growing up just seemed to be taking too long. He gazed over, daydreaming again, as he watched Sisasi.

Father Michael would also assist at the school with giving lessons, including bible studies. Sisasi looked up to him, he was very clever, he could teach so many subjects; languages, arithmetic, and the scriptures. He was the most educated person she knew, and he had taught Sisasi to become a teacher. He helped her with putting together her lessons, which was challenging considering the varying ages and abilities. He had explained to the villagers over the past 20 years that a western style education could complement their local knowledge; most of Sisasi's family, and the older villagers, thought this type of western education was unimportant.

Sisasi would often hear the sound of distant gunfire, but today it seemed closer. The chatter in the classroom stopped abruptly, and everyone paused to listen. They could hear rapid gunfire, seemingly getting louder and closer to the village.

Father Michael said to Sisasi, "Ring the school bell, Sisasi. I think it is time to be cautious."

Sisasi replied, "Yes, Father, I'll do it now." She picked up the school bell and swung it backwards and forwards for about 30 seconds. The bell could be heard from all around the village, and the villagers in Colina knew that a constant ringing of the bell meant it was time to go to their secret hiding places.

Sisasi grabbed her rucksack and gathered up the children. They all knew the drill as it had been practised many times before, but this time it seemed more earnest. Their teacher looked concerned, and it no longer felt like they were practising, it was definitely more serious. The group of pupils left by the rear of the schoolhouse, Sisasi leading the children up the hill to their designated hiding place. Along the way she set the man traps with Polo's assistance. A few other elderly villagers joined them, but many of the schoolchildren's parents were still working a day's travel away at the farm. They could sometimes be away for weeks during harvest time, but the villagers worked together as a community, and the children were well looked after. When Father Michael could see the evacuation was in progress, he got onto his motorbike and headed out of the village. *Hopefully, they will all be okay*, he thought, but he knew it wasn't a certainty.

After two hours of waiting in their hideout, as Sisasi listened carefully, the sound of gunfire faded into the distance and then stopped. Then everything sounded normal again. She slowly opened the camouflaged door, covered in grasses and palm leaves, and tentatively peeped outside. She could see there was nothing unusual happening, the danger had passed for now.

Sisasi then opened the door wide, walked out, and asked all the children to follow her. She led the children back down the winding path to the schoolhouse, but sensed that the mood of the group was sombre. They had practised using this escape route before, but, somehow, it had felt like a game to the children then; but this time it felt real, and they were all scared. Sisasi could see the fear in their eyes and reassured them all that they would be safe with her. That seemed to help them, for now.

Later that day, Sisasi heard that a neighbouring village had been surrounded by the army. Many people in the village had managed to escape into the jungle, but the soldiers had taken that as a sign of guilt; that because they had run away, they must be communist rebels, enemies of the state, or they were helping the rebels. Running away was enough justification for the lieutenant to give the order, "Kill all the reds you can find, take what you want, and then burn the rest to the ground."

All the villagers that had remained in their houses were shot dead, and their houses were burnt to the ground. Carlos told his platoon of soldiers, "Men, we are doing our duty as ordered by our president. We must leave nowhere for these reds to hide; they must be wiped out! This is our signal to all the other villages in the area that helping these communist rebel scum will not be tolerated!" Carlos actually didn't care that much about killing the villagers, they were unimportant to him, less important than his pet dogs. As part of his training, he had cut the throat of one of his dogs to prove to himself that he could kill anything, even his own dog that he had raised from a small puppy.

These villagers were not like him, not educated or even civilised. He considered them of no real importance to him, his president, or his country, albeit they were cheap, almost free, labour for his father's farms. He had been raised by his parents believing that not all, but most of them were troublemakers, whingers, communist sympathisers, always complaining about their lack of pay and the injustices they suffered. It was all very troublesome to him and his family. His father had always said, "You need to show these people who's the boss!" Carlos had always taken this to mean, *You need to show these people who is in charge through a show of force.*

He had grown up within a wealthy community of family and friends, who often spent their time joking about the indigenous workers, and congratulating themselves on how they had brought these natives out of the dark ages and trained them to do their bidding. His father often compared training a new servant to training a new dog, saying, "If they don't do what they're told, give them a slap or a kick up the arse. If that doesn't work, use a big stick, and if that doesn't work, get rid of them, but annoyingly that means starting from scratch again."

Carlos was very proud of himself and his platoon. *We are doing the president and our country a great service*, he thought, *we are clearing the jungle of these red commie traitors*, and although he didn't really know, or have any evidence whether or not they were traitors, he decided that the best strategy was to kill all the people that lived in the areas where the rebels operated, just to be sure. In this way, he could be certain that all the reds in the zones he was patrolling were cleared out. He had discussed this with his commanders, and no one disagreed with his strategy. When Carlos talked to his fellow officers about their patrols, he justified his tactics, saying, "It's better if you just kill them all, and their little chocolates," meaning the Maya children, "you definitely won't have a 'red' problem if they're all dead!"

After a couple of days of rest, Carlos led his platoon through the jungle, north towards Colina village. There had been a lot of rain, it was slippery, muddy, the going was arduous, and he decided it was time to stop. They set up camp in a clearing just over a mile from the next village. Carlos and his platoon had taken food from the previous village, including killing a pig they found. They lit a fire and set up a makeshift spit roast. The soldiers sat and watched as the fat dripped into the fire sending up plumes of flames and smoke. They drank cheap rum and took turns raping two pretty young women they had kidnapped. They were like cats playing with two mice. They knew that when they had finished with them, they could not leave any witnesses, so it would then be time to finish them off, but for now, they would have their fun.

In Colina, the villagers listened; the jungle was very quiet. They could see a plume of smoke in the distance, rising into the evening sky, so the elders sent a couple of older boys to run down the path to investigate. They headed towards the location of the smoke, and as they got closer to the army platoon, they started hearing the soldiers in the distance. They seemed in high spirits, laughing and joking. Every now and again they could hear the young women screaming, then it would abruptly stop. The smell of pig cooking on the spit filtered through the trees. It seemed to them that the army soldiers were probably there for the night. The two boys had seen and heard enough; they turned around and headed back to their village.

They reported what they had found out to the elders; an army platoon of about 40 soldiers. The Colina elders discussed what to do. They had heard many reports of soldiers wiping out other nearby villages, which is why they had prepared for this possibility. They decided that the soldiers were just too close and that they must ask all the villagers to spend the night in their hideouts and stay safe. The villagers went out into the night to their designated hiding places. As they went into the jungle, they set their booby traps and hoped that the soldiers would not come to Colina.

Some of the families decided it was too dangerous for them to stay near Colina, even in their hideouts; it was time to leave. They packed up some essential items and headed north towards the Mexican border. Many of the parents from Colina were still away on the farm and were relying on Sisasi and their extended families to watch over their children. She was like an aunty as well as a teacher, and she took them with her to the school's hideout that the villagers had built for their safety.

Some of the man traps they had dug deep into the jungle paths had partially filled with rainwater, but the sharp bamboo stakes, tipped with poison, could be seen pointing up. They were like outstretched fingers, waiting to catch some unsuspecting soldier, able to seriously injure or kill anyone that slipped into the hole.

Tensioned bamboo branches, with short bamboo spears attached, and ankle level triggers, waited patiently for their unsuspecting prey to come along, ready to send their poisonous spears plunging into the abdomen of any soldier that stepped on the trigger mechanism. As they climbed the hill, everything behind them was set, the route was now deadly to anyone following. They were all worried and scared, but hoped and prayed that the soldiers would not come.

At dawn, Carlos gave his orders for the platoon to pack up so they could head further north, following the road up the hill, and then take the path to Colina. The bodies of the two young girls, with their throats slit, had been thrown in a ditch close to their previous night's camp. They had walked for about half an hour when Carlos put his hand up in the air, and the platoon stopped. Carlos listened. "Tell them to be quiet!" he whispered to his sergeant. The message was passed along the line and they all fell silent. Carlos then pointed up the hill towards Colina, and beckoned for his platoon to carry on walking. The message to keep quiet was again sent down the line, as they moved slowly and quietly up the path in single file, all keeping a watchful eye out for any enemy rebels and traps. It was dangerous walking in single file, but the jungle was so dense here it would expend too much energy to try to cut an alternative route through.

They arrived in the village without any resistance, the only noise was a dog barking, but no one came out of their houses. The soldiers surrounded the small village and went from house to house, but no one was home. Carlos barked orders at his sergeant to search the surrounding area. Twenty of the platoon soldiers helped themselves to any food and water they could find, and then Carlos ordered them to burn the houses to the ground. Carlos had already given orders that an empty village must always be presumed to be a 'red' village, therefore everything must be burnt and destroyed, except any items that were useful and they were able to carry with them. Their patrols would normally last two weeks, and they had enough rations to see them through, but if there was fresh food or liquor, that would be worth carrying.

The villagers knew the soldiers were nearby, they could smell the smoke from their burning houses. Their hideouts were well camouflaged, but they had no guns, so their only tactic to avoid being caught was to keep quiet.

One of the younger children with Sisasi started to cry. Sisasi pulled her up onto her lap and cradled her, putting two fingers on the girl's lips and shaking her head, No. The young girl settled down. Out in the jungle, the soldiers searched carefully, looking for escape routes, such as tracks, flattened plants, broken branches, while also being wary of booby traps.

Two of the soldiers found the tracks that headed up the hill towards the place where Sisasi was hiding with the children. They moved slowly and identified the first trap, a hole in the ground. This had been deliberately left open as a warning. They knew they must keep looking, and skirted the trap, looking down and seeing the bamboo spears. What they didn't know was that next to the open trap was another hole that was so well camouflaged, it was almost invisible. The lead soldier, who had tentatively skirted the first trap, felt the ground giving way beneath him and started falling into the second trap. He knew what was happening but could do nothing to stop his descent. It was as if time had slowed down, every thought was heightened. He realised immediately that he was in mortal danger; he thrashed his arms and legs around in a vain hope that it may alleviate his fall, but nothing would stop him now. He felt his boot hit something on the way down, the points of the bamboo spears ripping through his jungle fatigues into his flesh. He screamed out in pain, but there was nothing that his colleagues could do. It had all happened so quickly! His screams could be heard in the village. Carlos immediately sent four more soldiers to find out what had happened.

The soldiers looked into the hole and could see their friend was badly hurt. "Don't worry, we'll get you out," one soldier said; another cursed, "Bastards!" They worked together and eventually pulled him out of the hole. He screamed out in agony as they pulled him up against the barbs of the bamboo, but it was the only way to get him out. Eventually, they came back into the burning village carrying their colleague, who was badly injured.

Carlos swore at the soldier, "You fucking idiot! What do you expect us to do with you now?"

The injury was bad, and there was no way of extracting him from here. Carlos ordered eight of his men to carry the injured man back to the clearing, where they could call in a helicopter to evacuate him.

Carlos shouted across the village, "Sergeant!"

Garcia stopped what he was doing and jogged over to where Carlos was standing and said, "Sir?"

Carlos ordered, "Get the rest of the platoon together. We need a search party to find and eliminate these reds! They must still be out there somewhere!" He huffed angrily, "Sergeant, go and find these reds, find them now. We'll make them suffer for what they have done!"

Sisasi was scared, still sitting silently in their hideout, with all the children looking nervously at her. They had all heard the soldier fall into one of the traps; it was awful, they could clearly hear him screaming in pain through the trees. Sisasi felt sorry for him. *This will only make them angrier*, she thought.

She agonised with herself about whether or not she should move the children out of their hideout and venture deeper into the jungle. She thought she could raise the alarm with neighbouring villages and maybe get some help? She could still smell the smoke from their burning houses and realised the surrounding villages would already know that Colina was burning. She decided that she, and the children, must try to escape. It was just too dangerous to stay around here any longer.

CHAPTER 5. SEND A CLEAR MESSAGE, NO REDS!

It was mid-September 1982, torrential storms had been passing over Colina every afternoon for the past few weeks, making the ground very soft, slippery, and muddy. The going would be tough, but she knew this area well. She had grown up learning about these roads and paths and also knew very well how to wield a machete. All the village children started using machetes from as young as four years old; they were an essential tool if you lived in the jungle. Like many people in this northern district, Sisasi had thought about leaving, as all her siblings had done, but felt a responsibility towards her parents and the school children.

It was mid-afternoon and all the booby traps were set. Sisasi was trying to decide whether she should try to escape with the children. She could take the children deeper into the hills, further away from the soldiers, but they would have to stay off the beaten track or it may be too easy for the soldiers to follow them. They would have to carry machetes to cut a new path through the dense vegetation. The noise of the machetes would echo in the canopy, and the sound may alert the soldiers of their whereabouts.

She considered all her options. If she was going to move the children, it would have to be mid to late afternoon. At this time of the year, the rains were very predictable, with storm clouds forming around three thirty in the afternoon, followed by rumbles of thunder and warm heavy downpours of rain that clattered through the tree canopy creating a constant white noise around the jungle. The occasional bolt of forked lightning would light up the dark clouds, followed by loud claps and then distant rumbles of thunder.

Sisasi was thinking through a plan to get the children to safety. She initially considered heading north towards Mexico, which would be the easiest and more obvious route, so she decided against that idea. If she went east instead, it would initially involve taking the children up the well-trodden path through the jungle for about a mile, and then cutting east on the old rarely used path towards Uaxactun in the east, a sacred place for the Maya peoples. She realised that if she led the children down this ancient, ancestral path, they could hopefully stay safe. These paths were only known to the local Maya people, and she felt that the spirits of her ancestors would be there, watching over them and keeping them safe along this rarely used and overgrown route. Taking this route would avoid the most commonly used paths and keep the children safer.

The best time to move from our hideout is when the rain is heavy; the constant noise in the tree canopy is so loud when it rains that it will hopefully drown out any noises we make, she thought.

She whispered to the 10 children, "Children, listen carefully. I'm going to take you all up the path into the hills, it's not safe to hide here for much longer. It will be difficult for the soldiers to follow us, but if they do, they will have to move very slowly because they will be worried about our booby traps. If we all leave when the afternoon rain starts falling, it will be noisy, and the steam will rise from the jungle, making it difficult for us to be heard or seen."

She looked at the oldest child and said, "Polo, I need you to be brave and help me. Can you do that?"

Polo replied proudly, "Yes, Miss Sasi, I can help you." He imagined himself as her 'second in charge', like a soldier.

Eventually, the sky darkened and the rain started falling, gently at first, a quiet pitter-patter, growing louder and more menacing minute by minute. Sisasi waited until the rain was getting heavy and the steam rose from the wet jungle floor. She spoke gently so as not to alarm the children, and said: "Children, it is time to leave." Sisasi took the children out of their hideout and up the hill, under the cover of the thunderstorm, moving them away from their hideout as quickly as she could. They were half a mile north of Colina before Sisasi slowed the pace; the warm rain was still falling hard, they were all drenched, but they were all alive too, and she felt relief that she could see no one following them.

Her second in charge, Polo, asked, "Miss Sasi, where are we going now?"

Sisasi replied, "To safety, Polo, to safety. We'll take the paths of our forefathers, which are quite well hidden, to the Uaxactun temple. The spirits will guide and protect us on these paths."

Polo felt relieved that his teacher knew the old paths and the old spirits. In his mind, this included Jesus, but all of their ancestors too. Their priest, Father Michael, had told them about the spirit of Jesus. His people had already believed in the spirit world long before Christian missionaries arrived, so it was not a huge leap of faith to believe there was a top spirit called God. His family had always told him that the ground they stood on, the earth itself, was God. Everything came from it, and everything went back to it. Polo stopped briefly and crouched down to touch the muddy ground with his outstretched fingertips and said faithfully, "Thank you, God."

Sisasi looked at Polo and smiled at him. *He is turning into such a lovely young man*, she thought.

Sisasi had decided to use the hill paths first because they could move quickly, and the rain would wash away their tracks, so it would be difficult for the soldiers to follow them, and see where they had broken away from the main path onto the more ancient and secret paths. If the soldiers did follow them, she thought they would be likely to stay on the main northerly path towards Mexico. Eventually, she hoped, they would all get to a safer place. After about one hour of walking in the rain they came to a long arc in the path which had been described to her by her father as the 'giant bow' in the forest. He had told her to imagine an arrow shooting from the centre of the bow. It would follow the path east towards the rising sun and eventually arrive at the Uaxactun temple. The path was only occasionally used and slightly overgrown. Therefore, they would need to use their machetes to cut through some of the light undergrowth. Sisasi was aware of a Maya settlement near Uaxactun, she felt sure that she could get help there.

* * *

Carlos was still in Colina, feeling angry that one of his soldiers had fallen into a trap. His platoon was trained to spot rebel traps; they worked in teams to find these traps and make them safe. *This should not have happened!* he thought. He felt agitated, and said to his sergeant, "Garcia, this is obviously a 'red' village, or they would not have set traps and run," Carlos justified in his own mind why he was giving his next order. "We must find these commie bastards and kill every single red that we lay our hands on!"

"Yes, sir," said Garcia, and he continued sending out the patrols to make safe any traps and search for anyone hiding out there. Carlos considered that most of the Maya people living in the jungle were uneducated heathens, more like wild animals. He had no compassion or empathy for their cause, he agreed with his president's policy of 'beans or bullets'. They could support the president and get fed, or die; he didn't care one way or the other. Carlos kept his decisions very binary; if they hadn't decided to take the presidents beans, then they definitely got the bullets! He thought, *Better to be safe than sorry. This red village is now part of the problem, and therefore needs to be completely eliminated.*

Carlos had no time for the reds, and the best thing he could do for his president was to wipe them from the face of the earth. In his mind, the reds were like a cancerous tumour, and his platoon was the scalpel that was needed to cut out this cancer in their beautiful country. His platoon had been briefed that Guatemala was a battleground between communism and freedom.

Carlos was a right-wing patriotic supporter of the current government, with a goal of completely eradicating communism, using the '*scorched earth*' policy. As he looked at the houses burning, he thought, *These fucking stupid reds are ruining our country.* This sentiment was shared by his friends and family, they agreed that it was better that the *Indios**[*] knew their place: as unskilled, low-paid labour, working as cleaners, cooks, gardeners and farm labourers.

Carlos's parents would often rant and rave at their servants. Carlos once watched his father shoot a farm labourer dead because the labourer shouted angrily at his father, claiming his father had raped the man's wife. Carlos felt proud of his father, there was no risk of prosecution, and force was needed to maintain good order. The beating and occasionally killing of peasants had been accepted by his family and peers as a necessary penalty to ensure they knew their place, whether this was on their farm or in their home. It had been happening for decades and wasn't considered illegal or evil, but was sometimes deemed necessary to maintain the status quo. His father had once discussed it with him, comparing it to shooting a lame horse. He remembered his father saying, "Carlos, I don't want to beat my Indios, because it makes it harder to get the crops in when they run away, but if they steal the corn, or don't work hard, then I must make examples, and take the appropriate action. They need to know that I am the boss!"

---

[*] Indio: a derogatory and racist term used when referring to indigenous Maya people

This approach made complete sense to Carlos. He had his place, they had theirs. In his opinion, this was just the way civilised society operated. The *'haves'* and the *'have-nots'*. He had grown up with servants in his house, who were almost invisible to him. They meant nothing to him other than to pick up after him, make his bed, wash his clothes, clean the house, and cook his food. In his mind, this was just the way it had always been, and this was the right way. *I don't hate them; they have their uses. After all, it's not their fault they're so backward; they haven't long come out of the jungle into civilised society.* He mused to himself, *They're really like clever little monkeys, they can be trained to do certain things, but ultimately they have limited intellect and therefore limited capability.* As Carlos was considering his superior intellect, a voice came over the radio informing him that they had found a hideout with an elderly couple and a baby in it. They could be heard pleading for their lives over the two-way radio. Carlos ordered the prisoners to be brought back to the village.

The translator had found out that the couple were the grandparents of the baby, and the parents were a day's travel away, working on a farm.

Carlos asked the questions, "How many people live in the village?"

The interpreter relayed the questions, and the old lady answered, "Ten families, approximately 50 people live here in Colina."

"Why are they hiding?" said the interpreter.

The old lady answered, "Some are not hiding, they're working away. Those of us that have stayed are afraid of you, afraid of the soldiers. We know what has happened to people in other villages."

The baby in the arms of the old lady was hungry and crying. Carlos said, "Shut that chocolate up," referring to the baby.

Garcia quickly snatched the baby from the grandmother, who cried out in horror as he swung the baby boy by his legs; at the same time, the baby's grandfather lunged towards Garcia as the baby was being swung around, trying to stop Garcia from killing his grandson, but then, simultaneously, two loud shots rang out from the rifle of a nearby soldier. The first shot hit the old man in the right shoulder, throwing him backwards, spinning him onto his face, the second shot into the centre of his back killed him instantly. Garcia was not fazed; he continued swinging the baby boy until his skull crashed against a nearby tree and then tossed the lifeless body into the nearby bushes.

Garcia looked down at the old man on the ground with disdain, his dark eyes as emotionless as a shark's, and turned his attention to the old lady, who by now was screaming uncontrollably. He walked over to her and shouted, "Shut up," while thrusting his rifle butt hard into her ribcage. She heard a loud crack as a couple of her ribs broke from the force of the impact. She screamed out in terror and pain, the same soldier that had just shot her husband lifted his rifle and took aim. "Not yet!" ordered Carlos. "We need to know who else is hiding out there, and where the booby traps are!"

Carlos addressed her directly, "You will tell me what I want to know. Now, where are the traps and hideouts?" Initially, the old lady refused to help, but the soldiers held her down and placed her hand on a boulder. Carlos then used his rifle butt to shatter the tips of her fingers, one by one, against the boulder until the pain in her hand and rib cage was too much to take.

He was just about to crush her third finger when, terrified, she called out to them, "Please, no more, stop! I'll show you."

She had agreed to help them, but the rest of the villagers had already heard her screams and guessed what might be happening. The shots and the screams had been enough of a signal for the other villagers to escape further into the jungle. Some of them followed the northerly path towards Mexico, and the rest just headed deeper into the jungle where, although it was very difficult terrain, there were plenty of places to hide. Some of them were hoping to cross over the border into Mexico, and others had scattered both east and west in the hope of finding safety and shelter in other Maya villages.

After clearing the traps on the hill path and finding all the other hideouts empty, Carlos called over to

Garcia, "Tie her to a tree. Don't kill her, leave her to die slowly. It will leave a clear message."

Sergeant Garcia did as he was told, he would rather have killed her, but if some of these red villagers tried to return, hoping to save her, they would now be met by a small contingent of soldiers who would be left behind.

Garcia pointed at four soldiers from his platoon and ordered them to "Strip her naked and tie her to that tree over there," pointing to a nearby tree. He thought, *Most of these reds only carry machetes; four guards will be enough*. He gave them their orders. "She is not to be gagged or killed. Keep her alive. If anyone returns to the village and tries to save her, kill them." Once they had tied her to the tree, Garcia proceeded to gently run his razor-sharp bayonet down her body. She pleaded for mercy, but he had done this many times before, making enough superficial cuts to ensure she would gently bleed, but not enough to kill her immediately. This would attract flies and other insects to come for her blood; laying their eggs in the wounds, in which their maggots would hatch after a couple of days to devour the rotting flesh. It would take a few days for her to die, and it would send a signal to all the reds out there that nobody was safe to live in this area. If they set traps, they were considered as hostiles, as reds, the enemy. They would all die horribly, even this old grandmother.

Carlos looked at the old lady and thought, *Harsh, but we cannot let these reds win, our way of life will be destroyed.* He believed that all these people were reds anyway, and if they weren't, they were feeding them and helping them to try to overthrow his president. Leaving the old lady tied up would send a clear message, 'No reds are safe living in his country, not even if they're deep in the jungle.' He would find them and either drive them out or kill them, he didn't care which. He knew within a couple of days she would die; her flesh would be rotting, and she would look and smell disgusting. It was a tried and effective method of stopping his patrolled zone being re-occupied by the reds and made his regular patrols safer.

Carlos looked at Garcia and his platoon with pride; they were all doing their patriotic duty. In their minds, the reds were the fire, and they were the firemen, ready and willing to put the fire out quickly. They had been ordered to clear any reds from this part of the jungle and make sure they didn't come back. Carlos understood that the only way to really be sure that he had done his job was to accept that everyone living this deep in the jungle must be considered to be reds. He justified the platoon's actions to himself, thinking, *If they don't want to die, then they need to get a proper job and not hide out in the jungle. Everyone needs to know their place, then life can get back to normal, and the wheels will keep turning.*

Chapter 6. The old path
to Uaxactun

Carlos and his platoon had a routine, two weeks patrolling the jungle, followed by one week off for rest and recuperation, which often involved the platoon going into Guatemala City, getting drunk, fighting with the locals, and ending up in one of the many brothels where they could take advantage of the services on offer. This was their reward for two weeks of constant patrols and sentry duties in the jungle, after which they needed to unwind and let off steam. It had brought his platoon closer together; he felt like they were his responsibility, and he needed to ensure they could put the previous gruesome patrols out of their minds. They had all seen and shared so much horror, lost friends, and suffered injuries, but they all had each other's backs. They always made the reds pay when one of their own got injured or killed. Going out on patrol after patrol seemed like a vicious cycle that Carlos was determined to end, and the only way it would end was when the reds were eliminated.

It had been a very wet, rainy September; their clothes were constantly wet or damp. It was impossible to get them dry in the jungle because the humidity was always high. Carlos had severe athlete's foot, the fungus made the skin between his toes peel, which made them itch constantly and made him even more ill-tempered. He yearned to be in his comfortable bed at the army barracks. *Only one more week on patrol, thank fuck for that!* he thought as he picked and scratched at the loose rotting skin on his feet before applying some foot powder. At least it stopped the itching for a few hours.

Suddenly, news about the soldier who had fallen into the trap came over the two-way radio. The poison had got into his body, and he had started convulsing and died before they could get him to the helicopter evacuation point. Carlos thought about the young man's family, *This fucking war! These fucking reds!* He realised that the villagers must have used poison on the stakes in the man trap. He felt rage building inside him, he was going to find these reds and make them suffer for killing one of his men. His platoon was like a family to him, and he was responsible for their safety, so he always felt personally accountable when one of his men was injured or killed. He gave the news to the rest of his men, saying, "Sadly, our platoon has lost another good man. Pray for him, be extra vigilant, and make sure you watch out for traps and tripwires! I don't want any more of you dying on patrol."

It was time to get moving and make these reds pay dearly for killing one of his soldiers. Sergeant Garcia shouted out his order, "Move out in single file!" putting his arm straight up into the air and then forward; they all started heading up the narrow muddy mountain path. The lead soldiers moved slowly and cautiously, checking for tripwires and traps. The old lady had already told them where to find most of the traps, but they still needed to be careful. The lead soldier used a long stick to prod anything he considered suspicious. After 15 minutes of walking, he signalled to the others to halt by raising his arm, then went down on one knee and gently scratched the mud away around a trigger mechanism. The rain had washed some of the mud off around the pressure pad, and he could see it was attached to a tensioned bamboo spear.

Carlos moved up to the front of the column and congratulated him, "Well done, Private."

Above their heads, they could see a tensioned bamboo spear with poisonous barbs attached to it. Carlos motioned to the soldiers to step back, and then he walked to the side of the path before cutting the vine attached to the trigger. The bamboo spear came whipping across the path at tremendous speed, but this time no one was injured and the danger was averted. They used their machetes to cut the bamboo spear into pieces, so it could not be reused, and then carried on heading north.

Patrolling carefully, and looking out for traps, was time-consuming, but they were making it safer for both themselves and the next patrol. Carlos had orders to eradicate all the reds and anyone else helping them. He knew there was no way of actually knowing who the reds were, as they often didn't wear any sort of uniform. They could be men, women, or even children, so the only way to ensure he had 'eradicated the reds' was to kill them all. After all, they had killed one of his men, so he felt justified in his assessment that Colina was a red village.

* * *

While the platoon was dealing with the traps and making slow progress up the northern path, Sisasi was making better progress and putting a lot of distance between them and the soldiers. It was already sunset and very quiet. The children were hungry, worried, and afraid. She could hear nothing behind them and could see a clearing ahead. "Time to have a rest," Sisasi said to the children.

There was an abandoned farm where the trees had been cleared. An old wooden house stood on the corner of the clearing, with part of the thatched roof hanging down inside the house. Sisasi decided that they would stop here for the night and find something to eat. She sent Polo with some of the older children to search for food; they knew what food could be foraged. How to find food in the jungle that was safe to eat was something that all these children were taught from a very early age. It was a welcome distraction and the children turned it into a game. Some of the younger ones followed the older children around, keen to help them find the food and learn what to look for.

There was some maize growing near the edge of a large pond at the side of the clearing. Maize crops had been planted by the people that had lived there originally, close to the river that ran alongside this ancient pathway. Some of the plants had been abandoned and left to go to seed. Sisasi looked down at the river. It had been following this route for many centuries, coming down off the hills, flowing fast and cutting a deep scar into the jungle floor. There was a short drop to the surface of the water, and it was moving fast, grinding and snaking its way through the jungle until it reached the flatter ground a day's walk away, where it flowed into a large marshland and lake. Sisasi warned the children, "Listen now, be careful around that river. If you fall in, it will not release you, this river is famous for taking small children away, and they're never seen again." The children looked nervously at the river and decided to heed her warning. The water was murky with churning silt, twigs, and other jungle litter that flowed past quickly.

The river had been diverted by the previous inhabitants of this clearing for irrigating their crops.

This had created a man-made pond, long since abandoned for farming but now being used as the local watering hole for monkeys and other animals. It was a good hunting spot for the local jaguars and also home to many capybara, large rodents who hid amongst the reeds, always keeping an eye out for their enemy, the big cats. The children searched along the bank of the large pond, occasionally seeing the reddish-brown fur of a capybara, a favourite food of the big cats and eagles, grazing on the bank. If they got too close to the capybara, they would bark a warning and then disappear under the water, where they could stay hidden for many minutes. From time to time, a pair of nostrils could be seen breaking the surface of the water, only to vanish again. The children were enjoying the many distractions, and worked their way around the abandoned farm, collecting maize kernels, bananas, nuts, and fresh water brought from the inlet to the pond. There was enough food to keep them going for at least another day. Sisasi was pleased with the collection of food, she knelt down and touched the ground respectfully, thanking the earth and the spirits of her forefathers for providing the food, water, and a safe place to rest. Some of the children copied her, touching the ground and offering thanks. It was good to respect the ground, which they understood gave them everything they needed.

Sisasi took a box of matches out of her canvas rucksack and lit a small fire. She knew it was a risk, and was concerned that the soldiers might see the smoke, but she also knew that she had a good head start. They were a long way from the commonly used northern path. It was also difficult to see very far through the dense vegetation of the jungle, especially as it was getting dark.

They all settled down around the fire to eat; grilling the maize cobs in their husks on pointy sticks of bamboo, held over the open fire until the yellow seeds were soft, hot and succulent. They all shared and enjoyed the food they had collected. They carried on eating and chatting until their bellies were no longer grumbling, and then sat back to relax against the walls of the derelict farmhouse. It was getting darker and Sisasi decided to let the fire die down to a dull red glow. She put some of the leftover food into her rucksack and settled down with the children to get some sleep.

They lay there listening to the jungle, which sounded alive as the monkeys howled, the parrots screeched, big cats moved around in the undergrowth, and mosquitoes and flies buzzed around them. As the dusk became night, the jungle became a much quieter place. The hummingbirds stopped buzzing, the songbirds stopped singing, the capybara, monkeys, and many of the other 'daytime' animals settled down and became quiet, just as the panthers started to prowl. The cacophony of sound diminished as the light reduced. Day had gradually faded into night, and the different nocturnal noises became noticeable. Bats whizzing by, rodents rustling in the grass, and the wind rustling through the top of the canopy. Sisasi loved the subdued sounds of the night; it was as if the jungle itself was relaxing, it made her feel at one with her surroundings. She loved the jungle, her home, it felt serene.

She went and got some smoking embers from the fire and put them on a flat stone near the front of the hut. The smoke from the burnt embers rose gently upwards, and was enough to shift away the cloud of mosquitoes that had been buzzing around the entrance to the farmhouse. Bats were swooping in, picking off the mosquitoes and then the moths that had been attracted by the glow of the embers, before eventually turning back to continue their feast on the cloud of mosquitoes.

* * *

Father Michael rode his motorbike towards Colina. He had seen the smoke and heard stories of nearby villages being destroyed. He was a man of the cloth, and considered it was his duty to go to Colina and see if there was anything he could do to help. Turning off the main road, he rode his motorbike up the bumpy path, using his legs like outriggers.

It was early in the morning on the day after the village had been attacked by the soldiers, and smoke was still rising gently from the ashes of the collapsed houses. He felt horrified at the scene before him. An old man's body still lay where it had fallen on the outskirts of the village. *I know that poor man,* he thought, and bent down to check for a pulse, but the old man was dead. He looked around, could not see anyone else, and felt confused. *Have the rest of them managed to escape this awful attack?* he wondered. He looked over to the site of the schoolhouse, which by now was now a just pile of ashes. The devastation around him was awful, and he wondered what had happened to the villagers, especially Sisasi and all the children. *Where are they all?*

Father Michael carried on walking into the village. The old lady, naked and tied to a tree, came into view. He could see she was terribly injured, but could not make out her facial features very easily because her face had been beaten. It was swollen and covered in dried blood and bruises. Her wounds were attracting clouds of mosquitoes, flies, and other insects, and he felt physically sick inside. What type of person could do this to an old woman? He was sure she must be dead. As he got closer, he could see her chest slowly rising and falling. Father Michael let out a gasp and whispered, "Oh my God, she's alive!"

He ran towards her to see what he could do to help, but one of the soldiers stepped between him and the old lady, lifting the muzzle of his rifle and pointing it at Father Michael and shouting loudly, "Stop, or I'll fire!"

Father Michael stopped abruptly in his tracks, and three more soldiers stepped into view. One of the soldiers laughed, saying, "The bait worked!"

Another soldier remarked sarcastically, "What a catch!"

The corporal in charge got on to his short-wave radio to Sergeant Garcia, who was now about half a day's walk away from Colina. Garcia spoke to the corporal, who explained that a "commie-loving priest" had turned up. The corporal on the two-way radio explained that the priest was threatening to go to the barracks and tell the major about what he had seen.

"What are your orders, sir?" Sergeant Garcia said to Carlos.

Carlos had always considered himself a Christian, but he couldn't have this priest interfering with his work, and thought, *This nosey priest is probably collaborating with these fucking reds!*

Carlos frowned and said to Garcia in a questioning manner, "Why would any man of God want to help these red heathens? Tell the corporal to question him.

He probably knows something about their plans. Use whatever persuasive methods he sees fit to get the truth. If they find out the priest has been helping these reds, they must execute and bury him somewhere nearby where he won't be found."

Garcia relayed the message, "Corporal, interrogate the priest, check to see what he knows. Find out if he's a commie, like the rest of these traitors. If you find any evidence that he is helping the reds, then you know what to do."

"Yes, Sergeant," the corporal said.

The message was clear to the corporal: 'Interrogate the priest to see what he knows, then kill him.' They tied the priest to a tree facing the old lady and left him there for a couple of hours. "Twice as much bait," the corporal said to his colleagues, and they all sniggered. *No need to interrogate him yet, we have plenty of time before the rest of the platoon returns*. He and his three subordinates discussed how they should deal with the priest.

Father Michael was only a few yards away, close enough to hear the appalling things they said they would do to him if he didn't talk. *Talk about what?* Father Michael thought. He was horrified at what he had already seen; was this now to be his fate?

He prayed quietly, the old lady heard him praying and sighed, her head bowed down. She whispered hoarsely, "Where is your God now? I came from the earth, and I will go back to the earth. I'll go to see my husband, my grandson, my ancestors, they're waiting for me with open arms." She knew she was very weak and would probably die soon. The thought of death comforted her.

CHAPTER 7. GETTING TO THE BORDER

Sisasi woke up and looked around, it was just before dawn, and the sun was still below the horizon. It was light enough to see that an early fog and mist had formed outside, hovering around the abandoned farm and surrounding trees. She imagined that the spirits of her ancestors formed part of that fog, that those spirits were protecting her and telling her to keep moving.

She went around gently waking up the children and told them that it was time to carry on. After walking for many hours the previous afternoon, Sisasi guessed that they must now be approximately 15 miles away from Colina. She had estimated that it was 80 miles to the Belize border, and much of the walk would be across difficult terrain, especially for the younger children. They carried on along the eastern path, leaving the farm far behind. They were all wet due to the early morning mist clinging to their clothes and skin. Much of this ancient path had become disused and overgrown because of the new eastern highway south of Colina. Sisasi wondered whether taking this old path was the right decision, it was slow going, and they were making it easier for anyone following because they were clearing much of the overgrown path. They used their machetes to hack their way through some of the more overgrown areas. As the distance increased between them and the abandoned farm, she started to feel more relaxed, and the children seemed to be feeling calmer too. They all walked and chatted quietly. The younger, slower children meant that the pace was not as quick as she would have liked, but she thought, *We must only be a couple of hours from Uaxactun by now*. This ancient and sacred settlement may be a place where they could rest and find some help.

* * *

Carlos and his platoon were now two hours away from Colina. They had camped overnight because it would have been too dangerous to keep going in the dark. There could be more traps to contend with, and it would be too difficult to follow the tracks of the reds at night.

Garcia woke them all at dawn, it was time to track and pursue the reds again, as ordered by Carlos. There were no tracks that could be seen at the moment, they had all been washed away by the heavy rains the evening before. Carlos discussed the best options with his sergeant. There were only two main escape routes:

North to the Mexican border or east to the Belizean border. They decided that it was possible that the reds could have split up and escaped in both directions. *Wouldn't be the first time these reds have split up to avoid them all being caught,* Carlos thought.

They might still be in the jungle, but in his experience that was unlikely. Carlos and Sergeant Garcia decided to split the platoon. Seventeen soldiers, led by Garcia, would follow the northern path towards Mexico, and 18 soldiers would be led by Carlos and head east towards the Belize border. It would be challenging to find their way through this part of the jungle. He could see from the black and white aerial photos that there was a passable route which would take them due east to Uaxactun. There was a government licensed farm marked on the map; a subsistence farmer, licensed by the government to clear a small area of the jungle for farming and habitation, classified as 'known and friendly'. Here, they could pick up water and probably some food too. Carlos was suspicious of anyone that lived in the jungle. He couldn't see the attraction himself. It was hot, humid, with mosquitoes everywhere, such a very uncomfortable place. He would much rather be in his officer's accommodation, which was cleaned and fumigated twice daily; the only insects he saw there were dead ones.

They needed to be back at the rendezvous point for helicopter extraction in a week. It was four days maximum to get back there, so they could only pursue the reds for a couple of days. Carlos explained the strategy to the platoon, saying, "We'll all meet back at this point at 12 noon in two days. That should give us more than enough time to search the surrounding area for the reds, clear them out, and then get back to the rendezvous point." He spoke directly to Garcia, "You head north, I'll go east, let's stay in touch on the short-wave radio."

Garcia nodded and said, "Yes, sir. Two days." He called his half of the platoon together, and they started moving out on the northern route.

* * *

Sisasi and the children arrived on the northern outskirts of Uaxactun around midday. They had been walking since dawn, and the youngest children were completely exhausted, so she asked them to sit down and rest in the secluded shade of the trees. She could see open farmland in front of her, surrounded on all sides by jungle, with a dirt road heading towards the south. She felt a pang of sadness as it reminded her of Colina, a quiet rural settlement. Sisasi looked around, it seemed like a beautifully tranquil place. There were a few houses dotted around the settlement, some with corrugated tin roofs and others with thatched roofs. Many of them were built along the dirt road that ran up the centre of the clearing, and some of them had wooden fences around them to keep their chickens safe. She noticed a couple of large, brown healthy-looking horses grazing in the open field next to a plough. She wondered how a small village like this could afford to have horses, it made her feel wary. *No one in Colina owns a horse, whoever lives here must be quite wealthy. Is it safe to ask these people for help?* she thought.

She could see a water pumping handle at the end of the dirt road where the local farmer had drilled a well. This was where the villagers collected their water and often congregated to chat, but it was very quiet at the moment. What she didn't know was that most of the adults in the village were picked up in an open truck every morning and taken to the local farm where they tended to the crops. The majority of villagers would not return before sunset, but there were a few of the elders left behind to look after the animals and the younger children. This village was not threatened by the army because the land they lived on was owned and licensed by the local landowner, who owned the farm which provided income and food for the villagers.

Sisasi asked Polo to walk with her to the water hand-pump, where he pumped and she filled up their water bottles before returning to the tree line. They all sat in a circle and shared the water and the leftover food they had collected and cooked the night before. Sisasi had no idea of the best route to take to the Belize border from here, so she decided that she must try to find someone to ask for help with directions. She could hear the sound of children playing from the other side of the village and said to Polo, "Wait here and make sure the others don't wander off." She pointed her finger towards the house from where the noise of children playing was emanating. It had a corrugated tin roof and a wooden fence surrounding the back garden. She said, "I need to go over there, where we can hear the children playing. I must find out which is the best route to get to the border. I need you to look after the other children and keep them quiet."

Polo nodded willingly and said, "Yes, Miss Sasi. I'll look after them and keep them quiet."

Sisasi walked down the empty road towards the noise coming from the garden at the back of the house. The wooden fence was too high to look over, so she walked around to the front of the house, knocked on the open door, and called down the hallway, "Hello, is there anyone in? Hello."

An elderly woman came to the door and looked at Sisasi; not recognising her, she asked, "Hello. Can I help you?"

Sisasi looked at the woman imploringly and explained how she and the 10 children had only just escaped from their village, how it had been burnt to the ground, and that it wasn't safe to go back.

At first, the woman frowned at her and looked angry. "Why have you come here? The soldiers may try to follow you and then burn our village!"

"I know you are worried, but I only want help to find the best route to get to the border," Sisasi pleaded with her.

The elderly woman's expression noticeably relaxed, and she explained, pointing her finger, "That dirt road goes south-east from our village, past the Uaxactun temple, and then towards the town of Melchor de Mencos. That's the main border crossing, but it is often patrolled by the army, especially around the border." She explained, "There's another route, more difficult, but rarely used by the army. That path zig-zags through the densest part of the jungle, but it can be easily followed."

"Where does that path start?" Sisasi asked.

"If you skirt along the top of those crops," she said, pointing at the fields, "you will find a path on the other side. It has been used by the local farmhands for years, so it's well-trodden, you can't miss it, just keep following it. It heads east towards the border with Belize. The villagers near the border plant maize crops along it, so when you get to the maize crops, you just need to cross the fields and you will be in Belize. There's a small village across the border called 'Spanish Lookout', you may be able to get help there."

Sisasi smiled at her. "Thank you for giving me the directions, you are very kind."

She looked at Sisasi and said anxiously, "I wish I could help you more, but it brings its own threats to my village. If the soldiers found out we were helping you, they might kill us."

"I understand, these are such terrible times," Sisasi said quietly and touched her on the shoulder, mindful of her concerns.

"How long do you think it will take us to get to there?" Sisasi asked.

She paused slightly before saying, "You will probably arrive at the border by sunset the day after tomorrow. I have been told by the farmhands that soldiers occasionally patrol the border, so you must be very careful when you cross over."

Sisasi thanked the woman and headed back to the children.

***

Fabio, Sisasi's brother, had a long easy gait, which meant he could cover the ground quickly. He had been walking for hours and was finally near the outskirts of Colina. Since leaving home two years earlier, all his combat training had made him physically strong; his physique sent a clear message that he was a dangerous rebel fighter. There was a pink scar on his right thigh that he had picked up in a knife fight with a soldier; it stood out against his brown skin.

A couple of days earlier, after receiving the Cuban intelligence report that described the burning of villages near Colina, Fabio had been incensed with rage. It detailed the destruction of whole villages alongside the disappearance and killing of many villagers in the Colina district.

He frowned angrily, and deep furrows formed between his eyes. *These are my family and friends. My people!* he thought. The 10 comrades he was fighting alongside had all been affected by this long civil war. They had all lost someone, which is why they had decided to join the revolutionaries in the first place. They had all been trained in rebel warfare by the Cuban armed forces for six months. They were trained to get in quick, kill their enemy, and get out even quicker. Such tactics were designed to demoralise and sap the willingness of their enemy to enter their rebel stronghold in the north.

Fabio was leading the group. It was just before dawn, and they were moving in very low light, heavily camouflaged, and operating in the stealth mode that they knew worked best. Arriving in the early hours, he had followed the path up to the village with his small band of comrades, each carrying machetes, light machine guns, and a small number of grenades clipped to their belts. As they approached, they could smell the charred wood. Where Fabio's parents' house had once been located, there was now just charred ground and grey ashes. It was a scene of devastation, not the beautiful village he had left only two years earlier.

He felt distressed by the sight of it, and whispered, "Bastards, fucking bastards!" He remembered his beautiful village as it used to be, and the hard work that the families there had put in to turn it into a thriving community as he was growing up. It was now a smouldering mess, and his heart sank. He wondered how many had escaped; it all felt so surreal. The anger rose up inside him, but he knew that he needed to be careful.

As they crept around in the pre-dawn light, they could see the embers of a fire outside one of the huts that was still standing. Near to the fire, a soldier was on guard duty, but clearly sleeping, sat huddled with his rifle across his lap. Fabio pointed at one of his comrades and gestured, pointing with two fingers at his eyes and then at the guard. His comrade understood the signal and went to investigate. The others waited as he skirted around the only house not completely destroyed. He was back soon, the report seemed good, he whispered quietly, "There are three soldiers sleeping inside, and the one on guard outside is also asleep. Can't see any others. Looks like they're guarding two tortured prisoners tied to trees behind the house."

They went over to check on the two prisoners. Fabio looked at the naked old lady; her head drooped, she had been badly beaten, was possibly dead. He thought he recognised her, she looked quite familiar. As he got closer, he did recognise her, it was Magda, she had babysat for him as a child and had been like an aunty to him growing up. He felt the anger rising up inside him. *These soldiers have no fucking respect or compassion!* and they would soon feel his vengeance. He also recognised the priest tied to the opposite tree, Father Michael, who looked in much better condition. Not stripped or as badly beaten up. Fabio whispered to his comrades, "Let's take the guards out first, then free the hostages. Don't kill them unless you have too. If possible, I want them captured to see what we can find out."

Three of his revolutionary comrades crept silently inside the house, then passed the soldiers weapons out of the open doorway to their comrades outside. Two of them stood over the armed guard that was sleeping outside, their weapons pointed at him, while another got ready to snatch his weapon lying across his lap.

Fabio gave the signal, with a machete in one hand and machine gun in the other. His comrades pushed the points of their machete blades gently against the throats of the three soldiers sleeping inside the house. The first soldier awoke confused, shocked, and terrified, feeling the cold steel against his throat. He wondered how the rebels had managed to get past the soldier on guard? The two other soldiers were also waking up to the horror and realisation that they had been captured. All three soldiers emerged from the house holding their hands up, with the rebels following closely. Their throats were bleeding from where the points of the sharp machetes had been used to wake them up.

The guard outside was more abruptly woken up. Fabio walked over and kicked him hard in the side of his shoulder, toppling him sideways into a heap on the ground, while in the same moment, his weapon was taken by one of Fabio's comrades. The shocked and bewildered soldier was lying in a heap on the floor.

"Get up!" Fabio said. The soldier stood up with his arms in the air. Fabio signalled to his comrades and said, "Tie him to that post!"

The other soldiers were inwardly cursing the soldier who had been left on guard duty outside. They could do nothing about it now, and they had no hope of any immediate assistance. The rest of their platoon was at least a day away, but they were meant to do a two-hourly 'check in' on the short-wave radio. Maybe, when they didn't call, it would be a signal to the rest of the platoon that they had been ambushed and needed help. The rebels tied up the four soldiers for the time being and left them to consider their fate, watched over by some of the rebels.

Fabio went over to release the prisoners with one of his comrades. They cut the ropes; Magda and Father Michael fell forward into their arms. Fabio remembered

Father Michael, a good man who had come to this village and helped to build their community since Fabio had been a small boy. He had taught Fabio Spanish, English, and arithmetic; and also taught his clever sister, Sisasi, to become his teaching assistant and eventually a teacher herself. He was very surprised that Magda was still alive, her face and torso were very swollen. Fabio took his water bottle out and gently poured a little water over her lips. Her swollen tongue reached out, and he gently poured a little more water onto it. They took her to the only remaining house still standing, where the soldiers had been sleeping, and washed her wounds. Maggots crawled out of her open wounds, with some exiting the many lumps all over her body. He also knew from his combat training that maggots could help to reduce the likelihood of bad infection, so he reluctantly let them have their feast. Once she was washed, they wrapped a bed sheet around her and sat her down on one of the beds that a soldier had recently been occupying. One of Fabio's men stayed with her, gently cradling her on his shoulder and dripping water into her mouth. She tried to say "thank you", but her throat was too dry and her tongue too swollen for any words to come out. She gratefully kept sipping the water, and in her confusion wondered whether these were angels that had come for her to take her to her husband and grandson. Tears rolled down her cheeks as she remembered them.

Father Michael had a swollen and bruised face. He had not been beaten as badly as Magda and was able to speak in a whisper after having some water. He explained what had happened to him, but he couldn't tell them what had happened to the village, because he wasn't there when the soldiers had arrived. Fabio said to Father Michael, "Don't worry, Father, just try to rest now." He went back to his comrades and said, "We'll have to interrogate the soldiers. We need to know what happened here, and where the rest of the soldiers are."

Fabio went up to the soldier that had been on guard outside the hut and said, "Where are the rest of your patrol?" the soldier looked up but said nothing.

"You can speak now or speak later, but you will speak." Fabio whispered a threat into his ear, "Talk, you bastard, or I'll burn you alive! Where's your platoon?" but the soldier just looked at him defiantly and said nothing. Fabio walked over to the well and pulled up a bucket of water. He put the water in front of the soldier and then got a small bottle of lighter fuel and squirted some on the soldier's boots and trousers. The other three soldiers were watching; Fabio asked them, "Is this man important to you? Either speak up or he will burn right here, right now! Where are the rest of your platoon?" All of the soldiers looked at him defiantly, not believing he would carry out his threat. Fabio took out his Zippo lighter and flipped the lid, saying to the soldier, "Do you want me to burn you alive?" The soldier just looked at him defiantly, saying nothing. He was tied to an upright wooden post at one of the burnt-out houses. Fabio crouched down in front of him and rolled his thumb gently across the flint wheel. The sparks slowly flickered over the top of the wick until it ignited the vapour coming from the lighter's fuel. Suddenly, the soldier's boots burst into flames, and the flames quickly worked their way up his trousers. The soldiers could feel the heat of the flames burning away his skin, and his resolve broke.

He called out in terror, pleading with Fabio, "I don't want to burn! Please! Put me out! Please…" Fabio threw the bucket of water over his burning trousers and boots and the flames went out.

"Okay, that's more like it. Let's start again, and don't fuck around because next time, I will not put the flames out. How many in your patrol?" Fabio asked again.

The soldier had a terrified look on his face and immediately replied, "Forty, there are forty of us."

"Where are they?" Fabio asked

"They're hunting down the villagers that fled from here," the soldier responded.

Fabio looked confused and shook his head, "Why are they going after these villagers?"

The soldier replied defiantly, "They killed one of our men in a man trap, so they need to pay, they're all reds, killers, just like you!"

Fabio gently rolled the wheel on the Zippo again; sparks flew off the flint and ignited the wick on the lighter. He held it in front of his own face, looking at the flickering orange flame and then looking into the soldier's eyes. The soldier was terrified and pleaded for mercy again. Fabio blew out the flame and flicked the lid closed. He then turned away and walked towards the other three soldiers.

Fabio looked at the other soldiers with disdain, he had overheard one of them say, "For God's sake!" He and his men had seen many of their own people treated in the same way; tortured, burned, and left to die in pain.

Fabio snapped at the soldier, "For God's sake?! You fuckers tortured a priest and an old woman. God is not interested in you!" Fabio pointed at the other soldier and said, "He only has burnt legs, but I want you to understand that I would have let him burn if he hadn't spoken up. If you lot don't want to burn like him, don't fuck around with me! I am not in the mood to be messed around with!"

Fabio had found the soldiers two-way radio in the house they had been sleeping in. He held up the handset and said to the soldier nearest to him, "I know why you have this short-wave radio. I want you to report in to your commanding officer, report in as you would normally. I need them to confirm their location, direction, and any news of other villagers they may have captured or killed. If you do as I ask, you and your friends here will not be burnt alive!" He leaned forward slightly, looking back and forth at all three, and said menacingly, "Do you all understand me? I'm not fucking around!"

All three soldiers all nodded in agreement and muttered, "Yes, we understand."

CHAPTER 8. STAND TO!

Danny, Kevin the mechanic, and Mark the radio operator, had been operational for five weeks. They had got into their rhythm, getting up at 7am, showering, shaving, breakfast, and then jumping on the 7.45am transport to the General Engineering Flight Compound on the edge of the airfield, where they kept their vehicle and supplies. They had developed a good bond, with plenty of banter going on, and were enjoying their time in the jungle. Their off-duty time was mainly spent in the many bars, clubs, and restaurants of Belize City, where they had been introduced to the sun and rum-fuelled lifestyle that the British forces enjoyed. It helped them to cope with the less pleasant aspects of working in the jungle and living in their corrugated tin Nissen huts at Airport Camp. They often went away on the weekends to the local beaches, where they enjoyed scuba diving, sunbathing, and the hotels, which had much better levels of accommodation and comfort than their Nissen hut.

This particular morning, Danny signed out the keys for the Land Rover from the engineering flight office as usual. They loaded up the trailer with maintenance parts for the hide's electric generators and filled the twenty-five-gallon jerry cans with diesel fuel for the Houchin aircraft generators. Once the trailer was hitched, the final job they had to do was to pick up their weapons and ammunition from the armoury. Two loaded SMGs were placed in the quick-release weapon clips at neck height behind the driver's and passenger's seats. If needed, they could easily reach back and pull their weapons from the quick-release clips. There were two self-loading rifles in a lock-box near the tailgate of the Land Rover. The weapons had never been used in action, only on the firing ranges at RAF Sealand, but Danny and the team were aware of the civil war just over the border, and thought of them as an insurance policy. The hides were in very isolated and difficult to get to locations, even for their Land Rover. Mark and Kevin would often have to get out of the Land Rover when crossing narrow wooden bridges to ensure the trailer didn't slide off the edge, watching the mud-caked wheels crawl precariously across to the other side. The aircraft hides were also an insurance policy; somewhere for both the Harriers and the helicopters to land, where they could be refuelled, re-armed, and turned around within minutes.

The initial run today was easier. They signed out their Land Rover and left early, driving towards Belmopan, the capital city of Belize, on the dusty

pothole-ridden 'Western Highway', with clouds of dust billowing around the trailer and off into the distance behind them. Danny often considered it was a joke calling it a 'Highway'. It felt nothing like any highway he had ever driven on. It was steady going, but not quick, as the trailer bounced around too much at anything over 40 miles an hour, and in some places, it was also difficult to avoid the potholes at even 30 miles an hour. They had left Airport Camp at nine that morning and were making good progress. It usually took them around three hours with a twenty-minute stop along the way for a mid-morning coffee and to stretch their legs. They had some generator and lighting checks to do at Holdfast Camp, near San Ignacio, and would then carry on to Zulu hide via

Spanish Lookout the next day. They eventually arrived into Holdfast Camp around noon. Two-para regiment were currently in residence, and patrolling the border in that area. They went to the Holdfast Camp headquarters and collected the bedding for their temporary accommodation.

The Nissen huts here were worse than the ones at Airport Camp. They had managed to cram more men in by using bunk beds, but the alternative was sleeping under a bivouac, so they just had to accept what they were given. As they carried their bed packs over to their hut, they could hear distant gunfire and explosions. This was quite common at Holdfast Camp, it was very close to the Guatemalan border, and the civil war in Guatemala was still raging.

Danny, Kevin and Mark had been concerned about the gunfire in their first week or two of operational duties, but now the distant sound of guns was becoming a normal occurrence, and had become intermingled with the other noises in the jungle, making it less noticeable. Danny found himself listening to the gunfire and remarked to Kevin and Mark, "I think the sound of the guns is a bit louder today. What a bloody nightmare! I'm glad we're on this side of the border."

They all nodded in agreement.

Mark set up the whip aerial on the Land Rover and reported their safe arrival on the two-way radio to Airport Camp. Danny looked at him and said, "You plonker, Mark, you could have just used the telephone in the camp admin office," raising his eyebrows.

Mark looked irritated and said, "Who's responsible for comms, Danny? Yes, I could have used a phone, but it's important that I get the whip aerial up and test the two-way before we are in the middle of fuck knows where!"

"For fuck's sake, Mark, it was only a joke. Stop getting your knickers in a twist," Danny responded.

"Sorry, Danny," Mark replied. Mark knew they were heading up to Zulu hide tomorrow. *No fucking telephones there*, he thought to himself.

* * *

Sisasi had been making good progress since leaving Uaxactun. They were only a few hours from the border, but they had come to the end of the path. *It's going to get tougher from here*, she thought. They had come east from Uaxactun, following the winding path out of the hills and onto the farmland, which was now cleared and cultivated with maize crops. She could see a settlement on the other side of the farmland, which was on the marshy bank of a small lake. Sisasi motioned to the children to stop and then told them to have a rest. Libi, the youngest child at only four years old, was feeling very homesick. She asked Sisasi, "When are we going home, miss?"

Sisasi looked at the little girl and smiled. "You can go home as soon as it is safe, Libi. We all can. I know this is hard for all of you." She looked around and could see the other children were all listening intently. "Try not to think about it, everything will be fine. Once we are safe, I will send a message to your parents. Okay, Libi?"

Libi nodded in agreement and said, "Yes, miss."

They stayed in the shade of the treeline, staying out of sight for now. Sisasi watched the villagers going about their business for maybe an hour. Women washing clothes on rocks at the lakeside, men fishing with nets, some children running around; everything looked normal, no soldiers.

Sisasi looked at Polo and said, "I want you to look after the younger children while I speak to the people over there," pointing towards the wooden houses with thatched roofs on the lakeside.

Polo smiled and nodded, almost standing to attention, and said in a resolute voice, "Yes, Miss Sasi, I will." The other children looked at him and rolled their eyes at each other.

* * *

Carlos and half his platoon had been following the old Maya path that he had identified on the aerial photos. There was evidence that someone had used this route in the last couple of days. They were moving reasonably unhindered, as the undergrowth on the path had already been cleared. Clean machete marks were apparent on the stalks of the undergrowth. Carlos thought, *The reds are using this route*. His corporal notified Carlos that there was evidence of a recent camp where someone had lit a fire. He could see where leaves had been stripped off the maize cobs and evidence of cooking outside the old, abandoned farmhouse. There were many footprints. He analysed the footprints around the house and at the river's edge and said, "Maybe 10 to 12 people here, sir, some chocolates too," meaning the children.

Carlos looked at the tracks himself and replied, "Okay, thank you, Corporal."

Garcia had continued on the northern path and had also found tracks, a small group of four, possibly five people. These were recent tracks, and this spurred him on.

Within an hour they spotted a small group ahead of them. Garcia could now see that they were within 50 yards of the group, and had still not been spotted by them. He was glad the wind was so noisy. He could now see that there were four adults and a baby. Two of the adults were much older. *Must be the grandparents of the baby*, he thought. Garcia sent two of his soldiers to run ahead and stop them.

The family from Colina suddenly heard the sounds of the soldiers closing in on them, but it was already too late to escape; the villagers had been taken by surprise.

The mother was carrying a baby on her hip in a blue coloured shawl fashioned into a sling. When she turned her head and realised there were soldiers running towards them, she screamed and started to run into the jungle, thinking only about saving her baby, but it was already too late. At such close range, the young woman didn't stand a chance of escaping, the burst of automatic weapon fire ripped through her back and she collapsed onto the ground.

Her husband ran towards his wife and baby lying on the ground, crying out, "No, no!"

Another burst of bullets hit him in the back and he fell forward, landing in a crumpled heap on top of his wife and baby daughter. The baby girl, still securely wrapped in her mother's shawl, was wailing loudly.

Garcia shouted at the nearest soldier, "Shut that chocolate up!"

The soldier walked over and calmly took his rifle off his shoulder, spinning it around. Now holding his weapon by the barrel, he quickly slammed the rifle butt downwards, smashing it into the baby girl's face and crushing her skull instantly. It was all over very quickly. The soldier bent down to check the baby was dead, then wiped the butt of his weapon clean on the mother's shawl.

He looked at the dead baby. *For fuck's sake, what are we doing here...?* he thought, feeling a pang of remorse.

Garcia lifted his machine gun, and with two short bursts, the elderly couple were also lying dead. He ordered his men to move the bodies, saying, "Put them over there, out of sight," pointing into the trees, and then walked over to the radio operator. "Get me the lieutenant on the two-way radio." Garcia hadn't seen any more recent evidence of reds on this path, so he decided that it made sense for them to get back to the rest of the platoon.

* * *

Fabio was still in Colina with his men, tending to Magda and Father Michael, while also interrogating the soldiers, when he heard the message on the enemy's radio. Carlos's radio operator had connected Carlos to Garcia, who had been heading north towards Mexico.

Carlos said, "Sergeant Garcia, Lieutenant Cruz here. What's your position?"

Sergeant Garcia replied, "Sir, we are a few hours north of where we left you at the rendezvous point. We've just dispatched five reds that we had been following. One of them was a chocolate. No other tracks found. I think we'll be wasting our time to continue any further north. What are your orders?"

Carlos replied, "Good job, Sergeant Garcia. We've identified that 10 to 12 reds are heading towards Uaxactun, and we are still in pursuit. Looks like a few of them are chocolates, so they won't be moving very quickly. I want you to turn around now. Head back to the rendezvous location and then follow the path east towards Uaxactun. It will be easy to follow in our tracks, so you should be able to set a good pace. Don't worry about traps, we haven't found any, but we'll let you know if we do spot any."

"Thank you, sir, we'll turn around and catch up with you as soon as possible," Garcia said.

"See you soon, Sergeant Garcia, over and out." Carlos handed back the radio to his corporal.

Fabio had been listening carefully on the two-way radio they had seized. He said to his comrades, "Five villagers killed. The bastards! They're heading down the old path towards the Uaxactun temple."

He remembered his father taking him there as a child, a few hours to get to the eastern turn. Fabio understood there were children in the group, and he suspected that his sister Sisasi may be with the children, leading them towards Uaxactun and away from danger.

Fabio felt alarmed and spoke to his comrades again, "They're tracking some people from this village, they could be my family or my friends. They said on the radio that there are chocolates, which we know means that there are children in the group. We may be able to get ahead of the soldiers coming back from the north if we move quickly. Then, we may have enough time to find and ambush the other half of the platoon currently heading east. We must catch up with them if we are going stop them from killing the group of villagers they're pursuing." The rest of his comrades were ready to follow Fabio anywhere and take up the fight, especially when it meant they may save their own people and kill their enemy.

Carlos knew he had reinforcements coming, and he could see his own half of the platoon were not far behind the reds. He felt like a hunter after its prey, swooping in quietly. He ordered his men to pick up their pace.

Sisasi didn't know, but Carlos and his men were closing the gap between them quickly. The soldiers were fit, and able to move at speed. They were still wary of traps, but Sisasi had not had time to build or set up any more traps. The children could only go as fast and as far as the youngest ones could manage, so they had to rest regularly before they could get going again. Sisasi was completely exhausted herself, but she sensed that she must keep going for the sake of the children. Her instinct was telling her it was still too dangerous to rest.

* * *

Danny and his team got a taxi from Holdfast into the local town, San Ignacio, to go for a few beers. There was a midnight curfew, so they knew that they had to get a taxi back by 11.30pm. The driver took them to the

Blue Lagoon Bar, which was quiet, with plenty of available tables. Large fans turned slowly, with their motors buzzing softly overhead. It didn't really liven up until much later in the evening, but they had all been there before. It was nice to chill out for a change and just relax with a few beers.

They would have an early start in the morning to get to Zulu hide, so none of them wanted a late night; that could wait until the weekend. They drank a few of the local Belikin beers and then a couple of large rum and cokes before jumping into the taxi and heading back to their Nissen hut at Holdfast Camp. After climbing into their bunks, they fell asleep almost instantly. Being tired from the drive and slightly drunk worked well to knock them all out cold. They were all rudely awoken by a lance corporal coming into the accommodation at 3am and shouting, "Stand to positions. Stand to positions!"

Danny was still slightly drunk, tired, and angry at being woken up, and said in a slightly intoxicated voice, "Just fuck off, will you? We don't have *stand to positions*, we're all knackered and trying to sleep."

The lance corporal was completely taken aback by Danny's unwillingness to get out of bed. Mark was getting dressed, and Kevin was sitting up in the top bunk.

"Kevin, Mark, don't get dressed, don't go outside, that's an order, and lance corporal, I thought I told you to fuck off? So, fuck off!"

The lance corporal turned around and marched angrily out of the accommodation, but within minutes he came back with his captain and woke up Danny for a second time. Danny looked at the lance corporal and then the captain, who was also looking furious.

The captain said to Danny, "Did you tell my lance corporal to fuck off?"

Danny replied, "Yes, sir."

"Are you refusing to stand to?"

"Yes, sir, I am refusing. We are visitors, leaving tomorrow morning. We don't have assigned 'stand to' positions. We don't know your call or reply passwords, so if we go outside, we could get shot by one of your trigger-happy paras... sir."

The captain looked annoyed, but Danny was making sense. He retorted angrily, "Corporal, you and your team can stay where you are for now, but make sure you come to see me in my office before you leave in the morning."

Danny replied, "Yes, sir," and rolled over, going straight back to sleep as the captain and lance corporal left the Nissen hut.

The 'stand to' only lasted a couple of hours, not that Danny knew that at the time. He was fast asleep, as were Mark and Kevin. When he woke up the next morning, Danny realised he might be in a bit of bother. He walked down to Holdfast HQ with its Union Jack proudly flying outside. The captain was waiting in his office.

Danny knocked, and the captain said, "Come in."

Danny walked in. "Sir, you wanted to see me," he said, standing to attention.

The captain looked at Danny and said, "Who the fuck do you think you are telling my lance corporal to fuck off?"

Danny stayed standing to attention. "Sorry, sir, it had been a long journey, followed by work, followed by a few beers, and I was fast asleep, but I shouldn't have told him to fuck off."

The captain looked at Danny with disdain, "Don't let it happen again, Corporal!"

Danny said, "I won't, sir," thinking that the army captain probably wouldn't want to deal with any formal type of disciplinary action with a RAF corporal. It was just too much paperwork, and they were leaving anyway.

The captain muttered, "Okay, Corporal, get on with whatever you are meant to be doing."

Danny replied, "Thank you, sir," saluted, turned, and left his office.

Danny went outside and climbed into the Land Rover. Mark and Kevin looked at him inquisitively. "Just a slap on the wrist from the grunt, now let's get the fuck out of here!" Danny said, and they all laughed.

* * *

Sisasi and the children were getting closer to the border and still unharmed, but they now had to get through the final few miles across dense marshy jungle. After that, Sisasi and the children had a stretch of open farmland to cross before finally escaping from the dangers of Guatemala into the relative safety of Belize. Sisasi had not heard or seen any soldiers, and the children were very tired, so she decided to stop for a rest. She was unaware that the soldiers following their trail had already reached Uaxactun and were now closing in on them.

CHAPTER 9. THE HUNT IS ON

Fabio and his revolutionary comrades gleaned as much information as possible from the three soldiers, then tied them to the same trees that Father Michael and Magda had been tied to. Two of Fabio's younger comrades were tending to Father Michael and Magda, who were now rehydrating and had started talking more. Magda's mouth and tongue were both still too swollen and sore to allow her to eat anything. They were both feeling very traumatised and still very weak, probably too weak to leave Colina. At least they had recovered some of their strength. Fabio asked two of his comrades to stay behind and continue looking after them until Father Michael had recovered sufficiently to enable him to look after himself and Magda.

Fabio said to them, "Once Father Michael is on his feet, follow the rest of us to Uaxactun." Fabio explained that they were heading along the old eastern road. They had all travelled that route before, so knew their way. Fabio looked at his other comrades and said, "We must find the army platoon before they catch up with the villagers they're tracking! You know what will happen if we don't get there in time!"

Fabio then spoke to Father Michael and explained, "Father, the soldiers from this platoon have not only burnt down the houses in Colina but in many other villages too. They have killed many of our people without mercy. The villagers who have managed to escape are still in mortal danger, so I'll have to leave you and Magda with two of my most trusted comrades until you are well enough to travel."

Father Michael said in a hoarse whisper, "Thank you, Fabio, for saving our lives. Go, son, go with God, and save anyone you can. Your sister Sisasi may be with them. Although the schoolhouse has been burnt to the ground, there were no bodies, and no children, so I can only think that Sisasi and all the children must have escaped."

Fabio had already realised that his sister may be with the group of villagers mentioned on the platoon's two-way radio, which stated they were heading towards Uaxactun. He put his hand on Father Michael's shoulder and replied, "Yes, Father, I'm assuming that Sisasi may be with the group too. We must remain hopeful, and head east immediately if we are to catch up with the army platoon and have any chance of saving them."

* * *

Garcia, as ordered by his lieutenant, Carlos Cruz, had been moving south quickly with his half of the platoon, and they were only a few hours away from the turn onto the old path to Uaxactun.

Fabio and his comrades had already reached the turn to Uaxactun. They were travelling light, and carrying fewer provisions than the platoon soldiers, so they were able to maintain a faster pace for much longer. This meant Fabio and his comrades were able to keep closing the gap between themselves and the forward half of the platoon with Carlos while increasing the gap between them and Garcia's half of the platoon, who were still hours behind them. They were determined to keep up their pace and catch up with the forward half of the platoon, hopefully before the soldiers caught up with Sisasi and the children.

Carlos had just arrived in Uaxactun, it was dusk, and getting dark. He and his soldiers were tired and hungry, so he gave orders to stop and rest, break out the rations, and get then get some sleep. They would be leaving at first light. The soldiers sat and relaxed on the edge of the Uaxactun village. The village was known to the army; it provided cheap labour for the local farmer, who owned a large farm nearby. The older, frailer villagers that could no longer work at the farm had spotted the soldiers and were watching them suspiciously. They stayed in their houses and called in all the children.

It was eerily quiet as the soldiers wandered down to the water pump and filled their canteens. Mosquitoes and flies buzzed around the pump. It was that time of the day when all the biting insects became much more active and persistent. The soldiers filled their canteens quickly while constantly swatting them away. As they were still filling their canteens, an open truck filled with men and women from the village came up the road towards them. The weary farm workers were on their way home after a long hard day working on the land.

Carlos walked over to the driver as he pulled up near the water pump. The villagers got down from the vehicle and whispered to each other, wondering why the soldiers were there.

The driver looked down from his cab, nodded deferentially towards Carlos, "Can I help you, sir?"

"Yes, can you tell me where the nearest bar or restaurant is?" Carlos said.

"There's a bar that does food and drink just outside the farm, a couple of miles down the road. You will find some very friendly women there too," the driver said, raising his eyebrows and winking knowingly. It seemed like a place that he knew quite well.

Carlos took the driver's 'knowing look' as a good sign and decided it was time for his men to eat some decent food and have a few drinks. "Can you give us a lift there?" he said to the driver.

The driver agreed, "Sure, get aboard."

"Two minutes," Carlos said.

He went to his men and told them of his plan to take them for a proper meal and a few drinks. They were all excited to be having a break from chasing the reds, and all got into the back of the pick-up, chattering and laughing excitedly. They headed down the road to the local restaurant and bar. It was only a five-minute drive along the bumpy dirt and gravel road, but it was much nicer than walking there. The restaurant was just

a large wooden shack with a thatched roof, situated on the intersection between the road from Uaxactun and the track to the farm. A large hand-painted sign swung gently in the breeze above the main entrance. It read, 'El Cuerno Grande', and had a picture of bull's head painted on it.

When they arrived, it was quite busy, mainly filled with younger male farmworkers who had decided to let off steam after a hard day's work. Some were sitting outside on the veranda, some drinking beer and smoking cigarettes, while others had a bottle of white rum with a large ice bucket filled with bottles of Coca-Cola. A couple of tables were set up for poker, the players holding their cards close to their chests and focussing on their game. Other patrons were enjoying flirting with the waitresses. The waitresses knew all these men intimately; some they liked, and some they didn't. They gave special attention to the men that they liked, especially those who paid the best tips. The waitresses outside looked at the soldiers arriving with interest; drunken soldiers always parted with their cash quite easily and paid good tips. They were already starting to lose interest in the local men.

Carlos walked past them and went inside. As he walked past the locals, they looked at him suspiciously. To the left was a wooden bar, with an old man standing there handing out trays of drinks to the waitresses. As Carlos walked into the bar, the normal levels of noise and laughter had become subdued. Some of the regulars whispered to each other, wondering why the soldiers were there.

Carlos walked over to the bar and said to the old man, "Can I bring 18 thirsty, hungry soldiers in here?"

The old man leaned forward and put a sawn-off shotgun on the table, "As long as they give me no reason to use this!"

Carlos looked at the wrinkly old barman and smiled, "Don't worry, old man, my men will not cause any trouble. We are just tired, hungry and thirsty."

The old man smiled and pointed to the waitresses. "And horny." He smiled, rubbing his thumb and index finger together, indicating that for a little extra cash, the waitresses were available for other more personalised services in the rooms they had at the back of the bar. Carlos looked around and liked the look of some of the girls.

The bar belonged to the farm owner, and the bar manager sent a driver with a message for him. After 20 minutes, the owner turned up and separated one half of the bar into a private area for the soldiers. Carlos liked this treatment; a man that respected his authority, and obviously a wealthy man because he was giving them free bottles of rum and the four prettiest waitresses.

All the staff knew the drill. They needed the army on their side, and they treated them all like VIP customers. The farm owner was generous to the soldiers and showered them with compliments. Carlos liked the middle-aged man. He was very overweight with leathery looking sun-tanned skin that reminded him of his own father, also a fat farm owner. The farmer called over a particularly well-endowed waitress and tapped on his lap. She sat down obediently, and he pulled down lightly on her white elasticated top to reveal her voluptuous breasts; she was his favourite. She put her hand on the back of his head, cheekily pulling his face into her ample cleavage, and shimmied her shoulders – a well-rehearsed move that had happened many times before. The farmer loved it and laughed out loud. The soldiers laughed too as they looked on with envy. This well-practised marketing ploy did the trick, and every few minutes, one or two of the soldiers would disappear out the back with one of the waitresses and return about 15 minutes later with a smile on their face and their wallet feeling a little bit lighter.

Carlos had told his men that there would be a midnight curfew as they all needed to be up early to carry on with the search for the escaping reds, but by midnight, Carlos had managed to drink half a bottle of rum and was enjoying the joint attention from two of the prettiest waitresses. *Now is not the time to go back to our camp in Uaxactun, fuck it, I'm going to cancel the midnight curfew,* he thought.

He shouted, "Men, your attention please!" They all expected him to say that they must drink up and looked quite disappointed. Carlos laughed out loud at the look on their faces and yelled, "Curfew is cancelled tonight!" much to the delight of his men and the farmer – whose takings were on a roll. There was a big roar of approval. They carried on getting more drunk and enjoying the frivolities until two in the morning when Carlos eventually called time. The soldiers groaned and moaned about leaving, so eventually the farm owner got one of his drivers to round them up and take them all back to their makeshift camp near the well in Uaxactun.

They were all in high spirits, drunk and happy, and by time they settled down, it was gone 3am. They were meant to be up at dawn, around 5am, but actually slept through until 6.30am, when the noise of villagers milling around, and the sound of the farm's transport vehicle, woke them up.

Carlos woke up first upon hearing the sound of the pick-up's loud and leaky exhaust pipe and the smell of the smoke from its old diesel engine. His head ached, but he remembered the night before. *It was worth it*, he thought to himself as he rubbed his tired red eyes. He walked around shouting at the soldiers to get up, and kicking a few of the soldiers that didn't respond to his shouting. His head hurt, and he still felt drunk. By the time they got going, it was 7.30am. Many of his men were suffering with hangovers, just as Carlos was, but they were all happy. They laughed and joked as they drunkenly remembered and reminded each other about some of the events of the previous night.

* * *

Magda looked across at Father Michael sleeping on the bed, on the other side of the room. She was weak but her anger gave her extra strength. She stood up very slowly, initially feeling a little dizzy. She placed one hand against the wall to steady herself and waited a few seconds for the dizziness to subside. She walked slowly over to the doorway and looked outside into the sunshine, where the other houses had once stood. The devastation that surrounded her broke her heart. She remembered the deaths of her husband and grandson at the hands of these soldiers. Tears welled up in her eyes, but the sadness gave way to anger and hatred.

The two revolutionaries that had stayed behind to look after her and Father Michael were surprised to see Magda on her feet, standing in the doorway.

Walking over to her, the first rebel said, "Magda, you must rest and recuperate," and offered his hand for support, but she brushed it aside.

Her tongue and lips were still sore and swollen, so speaking was difficult, but she whispered, "Leave me alone, I'm fine. I just need some fresh air."

Magda was feeling incensed, which gave her enough physical strength and resolve to walk slowly towards the well to get a drink of water. She glanced over towards the trees where the soldiers were tied up, and could see that one of them was the soldier that had shot her husband dead. The soldiers were bewildered to see her standing there and surprised that she was still alive. They looked at her in absolute astonishment, it was only yesterday morning that she had looked like a dead corpse covered in flies.

She was a strong resilient woman, who had spent her whole life farming and doing housework. She was much tougher and stronger than anyone had realised. She changed direction, now walking slowly and deliberately towards the soldiers. When she got there, she reached down and picked up a rock about the size of a large orange and walked over to the first soldier; the one she had witnessed shooting her husband. Holding the rock in both hands, she lifted it above her head, summoning all her energy, and swung the rock hard into the face of the soldier.

He tried to move his head out of the way, "Please, no! no!" he pleaded with her.

The first blow hit him just above the bridge of his nose, between the eyes. He screamed in pain and fear as the rock shattered both of his eye sockets. He turned his head from side to side, trying to avoid more blows, but she struck him over and over again until he stopped moving and was completely unconscious. Magda had never killed anyone in her life. She was a gentle woman, but was so overcome with anger and grief that it was as if she were in a dream. She saw red, and did not truly understand the real extent of what she had done until one of the rebels ran across and took the rock out of her hands. She looked at the mangled face of the soldier, now completely unrecognisable, and was horrified. As the red mist lifted, her strength seemed to suddenly drain away, and she moved away slowly and sat down on the edge of the wall, next to the village well. She looked back at the soldier, allowing herself to take in the extent of his injuries, but she felt nothing for him. The anger had gone, the sadness was gone, there was just nothing at all. She sat there, absolutely still, feeling emotionally numb. Magda was in complete shock, covered in splatters of blood and bone, but feeling no regret as she sat motionless on the wall.

During the commotion, Father Michael had woken up. Looking across to the trees, he could see the old lady smashing the rock into the young soldier's face. He was horrified, the soldier was tied to a tree, so he could not avoid her blows, all he could do was roll his head from side to side, but the blows had kept coming. An eyeball was hanging out of its socket, but still she kept smashing the rock into the young man's head, which was now drooping forward and still.

Father Michael could see two of Fabio's comrades moving quickly towards Magda, they had both been surprised at her strength, but got there too late to stop her. The young soldier was already unconscious and dying. The first rebel to get to Magda carefully took the blood-covered rock out of her hands and threw it on the ground; it landed close to the feet of another soldier. The rebel looked at the other soldier and said, "You're next." The other three soldiers looked down at the rock with terror in their eyes, it was covered in their friend's blood. They wondered if they would really suffer the same fate.

They could no longer look at their friend tied to the other tree; the sight of him was just too awful to look at. Father Michael walked over and said the last rites to the unconscious and dying soldier, after which he went to Magda. She was still sitting on the wall, in complete shock and exhausted.

"Please give me some water," he said to one of the rebels. They gave him a canteen filled with water from the well. Father Michael used it to wash Magda's hands and then his own. The two rebels watched in silence as Father Michael said to Magda, "We need to leave this place as soon as possible." Magda looked at him wretchedly and nodded in agreement.

Father Michael asked the two rebels to leave them, "I can look after Magda. As soon as she is able, I'll take Magda with me on my motorbike to the missionary halls of residence," which was where Father Michael resided.

The other three soldiers were still tied up, and the two rebels spoke quietly to each other, too quiet for Father Michael to hear their words. One helped Father Michael to get Magda back into the house, where they sat her on the side of bed and gave her some water.

There were three loud shots outside. Father Michael looked out of the doorway and was horrified. "Was that really necessary? Such young men..." he said to the rebel.

The rebel replied, "Yes, Father, it's the only way to keep you and Magda safe. If they managed to escape, they would implicate you, Magda, all of us in the death of the other soldier, but especially Magda."

Father Michael walked over to the other soldiers and blessed them. All of them were slumped forward. They had all been shot between the eyes. He knelt down and prayed quietly for their souls.

CHAPTER 10. BACK ON THE ROAD

Sisasi was pleased that the villagers living in the thatched wooden houses near the lakeside turned out to be very hospitable and accommodating. As was their way, they shared their food and their homes with Sisasi and the children. They had seen other physically and emotionally exhausted people passing through this way. Some of them were carrying injuries and also escaping a merciless enemy, and just like Sisasi, they hoped to find a safer and better life across the border. At least they were able to offer a little respite to these school children and their teacher. They listened to Sisasi's horrific story as she recanted the destruction of the village and their escape from the soldiers in Colina.

Her hosts were saddened but not surprised by her story. They had witnessed this many times as people passed by their village, heading for the border, telling tales of violence and death. They hoped and prayed the violence would not come to their remote homes. The villagers told themselves that it would be unlikely for them to be attacked because they paid the government's licence fee to the farm on this land. They believed that the licence they held to live and farm here should give them protection from the soldiers, but they still felt uneasy with the situation.

Sisasi sat chatting with the adults while also keeping an eye on the children. The children seemed to have found a resurgence of energy since they had eaten. Some were playing hide and seek with the local children at the lakeside, others were jumping into the water from the small wooden jetty, laughing loudly. Sisasi enjoyed this small break from reality, it was uplifting to see the children playing and smiling, as the last few days had been tough going for them. It felt good to be with these people and have some normality, but she knew that by being there, it might be putting these very kind and hospitable lakeside people at risk. She mulled it over, *We'll have to move on to the border in the morning, but for now, we must rest and try to recover our energy.* She explained her plans to the village elders, who agreed that she could not stay too long, but they could find them all a place to sleep for the night.

She woke the children at first light, the same time the villagers were also getting up, and prepared themselves for their day. Some of the villagers on the lake shore wished Sisasi and the children a safe journey. They had been very kind to them the previous evening, sharing their food, and this morning, giving them even more to take with them on their journey. They waved goodbye, and then one of the older boys from the village joined them for the start of the journey as a guide. He knew his way around the area, and much of the land around here was swampy and dangerous. He guided them, using a safe shortcut through the swamp to the other side of the wetland, where the land was much firmer underfoot as it rose up and away from the swamp. He said goodbye to Sisasi and the children and wished them a safe journey to the border. Sisasi, Polo, and the children waved goodbye to the boy and then continued heading east.

* * *

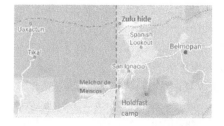

Danny and the team left Holdfast Camp and then headed north in the Land Rover and trailer, driving past San Ignacio and Spanish Lookout. After a couple of hours, they arrived at a crook in the road, where they turned left and headed into the jungle for about a quarter of a mile. The journey so far had been typically bumpy, dusty and noisy – a mixture of tarmac, rock, potholes, dusty dry roads, and slippery, muddy roads.

Danny was driving, keeping a watchful eye on the trailer in the rear-view mirrors. A mile before they arrived at the hide, there was a narrow ravine with two large wooden beams across it. This was the final 'bridge' they  needed to cross to get them to the jungle clearing where 'Zulu hide' was located. Danny stopped just before the narrow ravine, switched the engine off, and got out to check the bridge. There was a five-yard drop to the river below, and the ravine, carved by the river through the bedrock, was around six yards across. The wooden bridge, constructed by the Royal Engineers from two large reinforced wooden beams crossing the ravine, was exactly the right width for the Land Rover. Danny and his team checked the concrete plinths at either end and the steel bolts that held the two wooden beams in place.

Danny said, "Looks good to me, guys." Kevin and Mark agreed. Kevin unclipped the winch hook on the front of the Land Rover and released the clutch lever on the winch, pulling the steel rope out as he walked across the bridge to the other side of the ravine. He wrapped the steel winch cable around a large tree, clipping the winch hook back onto the winch cable. When he got back to the Land Rover's winch, he re-engaged the gear and pressed the button to take up the slack in the cable. Mark's job was to steady the trailer, he held a short rope attached to the rear of the trailer and took up the slack to stop the trailer from sliding to the left or right.

Danny put the Land Rover into low ratio, four-wheel drive and slowly drove onto the start of the bridge, where he stopped to allow Kevin to take up the slack on the winch. They carefully and very slowly took the Land Rover and trailer across the bridge. Danny looked out of the driver's window, and just downstream, he could see a small group of women who were washing clothes on the rocks in the ravine. They were watching with interest, not only at the exercise of moving the vehicle across the bridge but also at the vehicle itself. They were fascinated by how difficult it seemed to be. One of the women mused with the others, "Surely a donkey would have been better?" After a few minutes they were on the other side and relieved to be over the bridge and back on firm ground.

When they arrived at Zulu hide, a jungle clearing to the north of Spanish Lookout, they set up their camp first. Mark and Kevin dropped the tailgate on the trailer and took out a large trunk. The trunk, labelled 'Rations', contained all their food, a polystyrene icebox with bottles of water, and a case of beer. Mark and Kevin opened the large metal trunk and then opened a can of Belikin each before starting work on servicing and refuelling the generators. The radio operator, Mark, reported back to Holdfast Camp and Airport Camp to let them know they had arrived safely at the hide. Everything was going as expected, with the most exhilarating thing being the crossing of the ravine.

They had only been in Belize for a few weeks, but they were already acclimatised to the heat and the humidity. They enjoyed having the freedom to set their own schedule of work, travel around the different hides, work at their own pace, and see different places; it felt a little surreal, but it was exciting to be there. As long as all the landing sites were operational, they could chill out, it was a relaxed pace of life, but they still needed to be on their guard. Zulu hide was less than a mile from the Guatemalan border. It wasn't unusual to hear gunfire and the occasional explosion in the distance. Danny, Kevin and Mark had become accustomed to this occasional background noise. They always listened out carefully for small arms fire – today, the gunfire seemed closer, short bursts, and occasionally the noise of a deeper, more rumbling explosion, maybe from grenades or mortar rounds.

* * *

Sisasi and the children had moved away from the swamp onto the safer and higher ground, so it was now becoming much easier underfoot. The jungle was still dense here, but they were moving at a reasonable pace. Sisasi said to Polo and the rest of the children, "Not far to the border now, children. Once we are across the border, we'll be safe, the soldiers can't follow us there, and then we can find some good people to help us."

She hoped that she would find help across the border. *So far, so good*, she thought.

The people they had met so far along their escape route had all been kind and considerate to them. Polo could see Sisasi was deep in thought, and looked at her with immense pride; she was so beautiful, clever and strong. He was completely infatuated with her, but he knew it was a hopeless situation. He could take solace in the fact that she always asked him for help first, so he felt like he was the closest to her. He thought proudly, *I'm her favourite*, and was happy to be near her, staying right by her side, ready to do whatever she wanted.

They were now a long way from Colina and Sisasi was playing mind games with herself. *Am I doing the right thing? What if I turned back? Maybe the soldiers will have gone away?* Then her thoughts were interrupted by the distant sound of automatic weapons, and she realised that she must get the children across the border to safety. Once in Belize, she could send a letter to Father Michael to let him know where she and the children were. *Yes, that's the best plan. When Father Michael gets the letter, he will be able to tell everyone that we are all alive and safe, and when he writes back, I'll know what to do*, she decided.

Polo looked at her and said, "Miss Sasi, are we going to be okay?"

"Yes, of course we are, Polo." She smiled. "We're not too far from the border now. Once we get into Belize, I'll ask a local church there for help, and we can then decide what to do next. We all just need to stay strong, don't we, Polo?"

Polo responded, "Yes, Miss Sasi, we must all be strong," as he raised his arms, flexing his skinny biceps and puffing out his chest, "like a good soldier," he said, with a cheeky smile on his face, and his chin jutting up proudly.

Sisasi smiled at him and said, "Yes, Polo, like a good soldier!"

The other children also started raising their arms in a muscleman pose, mocking and teasing Polo with his own words, "Like a soldier, like a soldier…" He shook his fist at them and gave them all an angry glare.

Sisasi intervened, "That's enough, children, we need to move on now, follow me," and she started walking away. They all quickly stopped their teasing of Polo and followed her east towards the border.

* * *

Carlos and his men were hungover after the previous night's escapades, but feeling happier and relieved to find that the trail had not gone cold. They had tracked and followed Sisasi all the way to Uaxactun and felt they were closing in. Carlos called his platoon towards him – he picked up a stick and drew a line representing the border and a rudimentary map in the dust, showing where they were and where he assumed the reds might be. He said, "We are still tracking these reds, and we are not far behind them, a few hours only. If we don't catch them today, it will probably be too late because they will cross over the border here," pointing the stick at the map he had drawn. His men grunted in agreement and Carlos said to the corporal, "Go and ask the locals if they have seen anyone or know anything; my gut says we're closing on them."

They knocked on a few doors and came back with the news, "No one knows anything or has seen anything, sir!" the corporal reported to Carlos.

He wasn't surprised in the least, he looked at his map and pointed to a location on it. "We need to get to here!" he said, pointing at the high ground on the far side of a large lake, "Let's get going."

The corporal shouted his order, "Move out!"

They eventually arrived at the small lakeside village. The village was very quiet, the people here did not trust soldiers with guns. When the soldiers appeared on the treeline, an alarm was raised and most of the villagers took their boats out from the jetty or went out into their crops. Carlos could see the villagers moving around and took no notice. He discussed the village with his corporal, "Any reports of rebel activity here, Corporal?"

"No, sir, no reports. This is reported as a licensed fishing and farming village, selling some of their fish and other produce to the local market and other traders. Should be quiet."

They carried on towards the village, carefully surveying the surrounding area for any signs of ambush, but everything stayed calm. When they got to the village, a few older people had stayed around.

His corporal asked them some questions, "Have you seen any strangers here?" It was clearly obvious that the reds from Colina had passed through this way as their tracks were easy to see and follow.

If they lie, they're obviously reds too, or at least supporting the reds, and will soon be dead reds! Carlos thought to himself.

One of the village elders replied truthfully, saying, "Yes, a woman and some children passed through here. There were no soldiers that we could see." The elder knew that there was no point in lying, he had heard stories and believed he and his fellow villagers could end up dead if he didn't tell them what they wanted.

"When did they come through here?" the corporal asked.

"They came through just after first light," the old man said, pointing towards the east, "they went that way."

Carlos had come close to the point of ordering his platoon back to barracks, but now he knew he was so close, he felt motivated to continue with the hunt. His corporal said, "Looking at the tracks, I think the old man is telling the truth, they definitely came through this way. We could probably catch up with them before they reach the border, sir."

Carlos agreed with his assessment and shouted, "Okay, let's move out immediately. We'll continue east towards the border." Raising his arm towards the sky, Carlos indicated to the platoon that they would keep going. He shouted again, "Move out!"

The elders of the lakeside village felt relieved as they watched the soldiers fade into the distance.

The platoon moved quickly. After this long chase through the jungle, they were even more determined to catch up with the reds.

* * *

Fabio and his men had also been moving quickly, and they were nearing Uaxactun. Fabio bent down, carefully inspecting the trodden ground and said, "These are fresh tracks, soldiers boots here," pointing at footprints on the path, "they're only a few hours old, we are catching up with them." "There are other tracks here too, children," he said in a concerned voice, again pointing down at the path. Fabio thought about the fate of his sister Sisasi. He knew what would happen to her if she got caught. "We can't relax the pace, comrades, let's keep going as quickly as we can!" They all felt the urgency in Fabio's voice and moved out at a jog. The ground was easy going, the soldiers, Sisasi, and the children that had already walked this way had cleared the path for them and left easy tracks to follow.

They were able to maintain a good pace until they reached Uaxactun, where they stopped to pick up water. Fabio spoke to an old lady in the village. She could see he wasn't a soldier but still didn't trust him. He spoke to her in a quiet and gentle voice, explaining that the soldiers were chasing his sister Sisasi, and a group of children from his village.

She recognised the name, "Sisasi, you say?"

"Yes, she is my sister; a teacher from Colina. She's trying to escape from soldiers that destroyed our village," Fabio explained.

She knew that this was the schoolteacher who had asked her for directions to the Belize border. She looked into Fabio's eyes and believed his story. There was truth in his eyes and concern written all over his face. She relaxed and said to him quietly, "You are a few hours, maybe half a day, behind the soldiers. They're searching for your sister, who they claim is a communist rebel, and also the children that are with her. You will need to move like the wind to have any hope of finding them before the soldiers do." She gave Fabio directions to the route that Sisasi had taken. He quickly thanked her, and after filling their water flasks, Fabio and his comrades went off at pace, jogging on the eastern path towards the border.

CHAPTER 11. AN ENGAGEMENT
ON THE WAY

The Guatemalan government had a long-held claim that Belize had been taken from them illegally by the British, which the British government refuted. The British forces had been ordered to stay out of the civil war to avoid any further friction. They couldn't afford another territorial conflict. Margaret Thatcher, and her government, complained to the US Reagan administration about them secretly arming and training the Guatemalan army, but she also didn't want to see Guatemala becoming a communist country either. The British government therefore 'turned a blind eye'.

Fabio and his comrades were closing in on Carlos and the front half of the platoon. They had been given some useful intelligence by the lakeside villagers and already knew from the radio interceptions that the platoon was only at half strength. Having spent six months training in Cuba, his team of highly trained and motivated rebels versus half of a Guatemalan platoon didn't seem like bad odds to them. Fabio felt like they had a fighting chance if they could catch them.

They pushed on, moving quickly through the jungle, where the path before them was well-trodden and clear to see. Fabio was up front, worrying that he may already be too late. They had been jogging for hours, but this is what they had all been trained for, and his sister and the children from Colina needed rescuing. Fabio was lost in his thoughts when he looked up and saw the rear of the platoon moving through the trees in the distance. He put his arm out, palm to the ground, and dropped to one knee. His comrades all followed suit.

Fabio said, "The soldiers are only a few hundred yards ahead of us, cock your weapons now... quietly, be ready, be careful. I'll get as close as possible before opening fire. Once I start, we will take defensive positions and open fire. Let's kill as many of these murdering bastards as possible; and then, on my signal, head south five hundred yards and try to outflank them."

They all drew back the cocking levers on their weapons quietly and allowed the first round to slip into the chambers of their automatic weapons. The adrenalin kicked in, and they followed Fabio as he jogged down the path, his weapon held up and ready to fire. They were not more than one hundred yards behind the rear of the platoon. The noise of the jungle was enough to mask the sound of them approaching. Fabio's heart was racing as he silently clicked off his safety catch at 50 yards, he increased his speed to a sprint, 40 yards, 30 yards. Carlos and his half of the platoon were not prepared for the ambush, their weapons were not even cocked, and they were only thinking about the hunt, never realising they themselves were being hunted.

At 20 yards, the soldier at the rear heard a quiet 'crack' as Fabio stepped on a twig, he could hear someone was approaching quickly from behind him but wasn't quick enough. As he grabbed for the cocking lever on his weapon, it was already too late for him; Fabio opened fire and kept firing before stepping to the edge of the path, and dropping down onto one knee and allowing his comrades to have a line of sight. Almost instantaneously, his comrades clicked off their safety catches, the men at the front dropping down low and moving to either side of the path, allowing those at the rear to have a clearer shot as they opened fire. A hail of bullets came flying forward, ripping through the backs and legs of the four soldiers at the rear of the platoon. It was pandemonium, soldiers shouting, "Take cover!" and the machine-gun fire at the same time made the rest of the platoon dive into the undergrowth and then start returning fire.

Carlos was 20 yards away, near the front of the line, when he heard the sound of the machine-gun fire. He dived onto the ground, multiple shouts of "Take cover!" echoed through the trees, followed by Carlos shouting, "Fire at will!" He didn't know, but four of his soldiers were already dead on the path, and another two had been injured but had managed to get off the path and take cover.

One of the injured soldiers was screaming for help. Two rounds had hit him in the right shoulder, shattering his collar bone, blood spurted out of a severed artery, and his arm hung limply. His trigger finger was still inside the trigger guard. He looked down at his useless arm in shock, it was completely disabled. He fumbled with his left hand for a field dressing to try to stem the bleeding, not realising one of the rebels was stealthily moving through the undergrowth, creeping towards him. Suddenly, the injured soldier felt the thump of a razor-sharp machete in the side of his neck, the blade almost decapitating him. The soldier's last thoughts were for his wife and baby son. As his life drained away, he was swallowed up by an awful sadness. He wished that he could be home, just one last time, then everything faded into darkness and he was at peace.

The rebels had already stopped firing and were moving south through the undergrowth. The platoon,

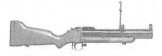 caught off guard, were firing wildly into the jungle. Carlos ordered one of his soldiers, who was carrying a grenade launcher, to fire grenades towards the area where the rebels had been firing from. They exploded loudly, sending shrapnel ripping through the branches, but they only had a kill radius of five to ten yards. Fabio and his comrades had already started moving towards their new flanking route, south of the soldier's current position. It was a hit and run tactic they had used many times before. This was how they had been taught to operate at their training camp in Cuba; ambush the enemy, quickly kill as many as possible, then escape; don't waste ammunition or lives in a long, drawn-out fight. They carried a limited amount of ammunition each, as did the soldiers they had just attacked, but there were many more soldiers, so they had more ammunition overall. Fabio and his comrades switched their weapons to single-shot mode to conserve their ammunition. Fabio knew he had stopped them in their tracks, but he also knew Garcia's reinforcements were on their way. He and his comrades needed to get out of there quickly and find Sisasi.

Carlos got on the two-way radio, not realising that Fabio had acquired one of his two-way radios from the soldiers he had left guarding the prisoners in Colina. Fabio listened attentively as Carlos spoke to Sergeant

Garcia, who was closing in on their position with the rest of the platoon.

Carlos said, "Garcia, we are under attack. What is your position?"

"We've just come through Uaxactun, sir, making good progress," Garcia replied.

Carlos thought for a moment, "Okay, you are probably two hours behind us, come as quickly as you can, but keep an eye open for the reds, we've just lost five good men and have one injured."

Garcia replied, "Yes, sir, we'll get there as quickly as we can, out."

Fabio was listening in on the stolen two-way radio, and said quietly to his comrades, "Their reinforcements are coming down the path from the west; we need to move quickly. We'll save this fight for another day. Let's go."

The soldiers were only two hundred yards away, but in the thick undergrowth, they were impossible to see. He knew it was too dangerous to use the path, so they would have to move carefully through the jungle, circumventing the soldiers. Fabio decided it would be better to keep moving south and then try to get ahead of the platoon. He led his comrades through the jungle south then southeast, for about a mile, until he felt they were in a position to stop and discuss their next move.

Fabio said, "We can't go back to the path, there are more soldiers on their way from the west. Our best bet is to continue travelling east through the jungle until we reach the border, try to find Sisasi and the others, and make sure we get them safely across the border. The soldiers won't follow us into Belize. I think we still have a good chance of manoeuvring around the platoon in time to find my sister and the children."

His comrades couldn't see any reason for not following Fabio's plan, he was a good man, and they trusted him completely. They set off immediately, skirting around the soldiers, in a race to reach Sisasi first.

Carlos beckoned to his corporal; the corporal crawled through the undergrowth towards his lieutenant. Carlos whispered, "Corporal, wait here with half the men, and hold this path until Sergeant Garcia arrives; it may only be a couple of hours. I am going to take the rest with me to catch up with those fucking reds we've been chasing since leaving Colina."

The corporal nodded, "Yes, sir," he said in a quiet but slightly concerned voice.

Carlos pulled together his team and told them that the plan was to continue going after the reds to stop them from reaching the border.

They stayed off the path initially, to be safe, proceeding east through the undergrowth for half a mile. It was slow going, and Carlos was getting frustrated, so he decided to risk going back onto the path. He thought it would be safer now and worth taking the risk so they could move more quickly.

* * *

Danny and Kevin had just refuelled and started up the Houchin diesel generator at Zulu hide. It was the first time it had been started up in two weeks, and the thirty-year-old engine needed some encouragement. As Danny pressed the starter button, he shouted, "Now, Kev!" It coughed and spluttered, with grey smoke rising out of the exhaust. Kevin immediately sprayed ether into the air filter, which got drawn into the combustion chamber of the engine, strengthening the fuel mixture to hopefully get the old engine going, which then pleasingly burst into life. It was a tried and tested method they had used many times before on these old generators. The smoke rose high above the canopy and then subsided after a couple of minutes as the engine warmed up.

When Fabio and his comrades had opened fire on Carlos's platoon, unbeknown to them, Sisasi and the children were less than a mile away. Sisasi and the children could hear the commotion, sudden bursts of machine guns, mixed with the distant sounds of men screaming in pain and the shouting of orders in the distance. Sisasi and the children went from being fairly calm to feeling terrified. Adrenalin was coursing through Sisasi's veins, and she said to the terrified children, "Run, children, run!" Picking up the smallest child, she and all the children started running down the path through the jungle as quickly as they could. After a few minutes, the shooting stopped, so they slowed down to a walk. They were all exhausted and sweating profusely, with their legs badly scratched from running through all the undergrowth. Some of the children were crying, and she tried to reassure them that everything would be alright, while knowing it might not be.

Polo was a great help to her. *My little soldier*, she thought. He followed her lead, asking the other children to calm down, and holding the hands of two of the youngest children. Sisasi didn't have a map, but she knew she must be close to the border. They gathered themselves and she kept reassuring all the children; with Polo's help, they all calmed down and carried on walking towards the border. They didn't know it yet, but Sisasi and the children were only 10 minutes' walk from the treeline of the border when she heard the rumble of an engine in the distance. The sound of it misfiring could be heard clearly as it coughed and spluttered into life, then a cloud of grey smoke billowed high over the treetops. She looked at the smoke in the sky and wondered if they might be close to the border. She knew that she needed to be extremely careful until she and the children had crossed over to the safety of Belize.

* * *

After a few minutes, even over the rumbling sound of the diesel engine, Danny and his team could hear the bursts of small arms fire and the sound of grenades exploding, coming from the east. Danny went over to the generator and switched it off, the engine falling silent. It wasn't the first time they had heard distant gunfire and even explosions, but this time it felt different.

The sound was much less muffled by the jungle, much clearer, and therefore much closer than they had experienced before. They all looked at each other with raised eyebrows.

Kevin said, "That sounds a lot closer than usual, Danny. What do you think?"

Danny listened intently and said, "Yeah, I agree, Kev, it definitely sounds closer."

Mark looked at them with a concerned expression, nodding in agreement and said, "Absolutely, guys, it sounds too close for comfort!"

The normal hubbub of background noise in the jungle had been temporarily suspended by the small arms fire, becoming subdued to a mere murmur. It was as if the jungle's menagerie were so concerned that even they, the animals in the jungle, paused from their normal activities to stop and listen. Some of the birds decided to take flight and move to a quieter, less volatile location. It all felt slightly surreal.

Kevin and Mark looked at Danny, waiting for his assessment. Danny thought about it for a moment.

Should they wrap up and leave? Or finish their work there? He said, "Mark, get your whip aerial up and find out if any of our lot are carrying out military exercises around here. Also, ask HQ if there are any Belizean Defence Forces training in this area too."

Danny continued, "Kev, let's go and get our weapons out of the Land Rover, just as a precaution, and we'd better get the ammo boxes unlocked too." Danny could see a look of concern on Mark's face; his eyebrows were raised with a questioning look. "Just as a precaution, Mark."

Mark replied, "Let's bloody hope so, Danny."

Danny pulled his Sterling submachine gun from the metal gun mounting clips situated behind the driver's headrest in the Land Rover. The clips snapped closed with a metallic clunk. He unlocked the hinges of his submachine gun's shoulder butt and folded it under the weapon's muzzle cooler. He then loaded a full magazine and dropped another loaded magazine into the left pocket of his jungle fatigues jacket.

Danny threw the shoulder strap over his head and held the gun in his left hand, close to his body.

He positioned the weapon at around waist height, checking that the length of the strap was 'just right' for grabbing the gun quickly if needed. He felt his pulse racing a little as the adrenalin started to kick in.

Kevin pulled the two SLR assault rifles from under the bench seat and four loaded magazines. All their weapons were specific to them. Danny was left-handed, so his sights were set up for the way he held and fired the weapon. It was the same for Kevin and Mark, their weapons were set up for them. Kevin handed Mark his rifle and

two of the loaded magazines, and then, just to check, he pressed down on the top cartridge of each magazine. There was a little give, but he could feel from the weight and the spring tension that the magazine was full, and he clipped it into the rifle with a slight feeling of trepidation. Mark did the same, pressing down on the top cartridge, then clipping the magazine in, gripping it and giving it a little push back and forth to make sure it was properly loaded. They dropped their spare magazine into their pockets and carried on with their preparations.

Mark walked over to the Land Rover, where his radio was located, and got the whip aerial out of the back. Mark assembled it and dropped the aerial into the slot on the Land Rover before connecting it to his radio. Danny glanced over, and even though he had seen it many times before, it always impressed him how high the aerial was, like an extremely long fishing rod. Mark switched on the two-way radio and contacted HQ to notify them of their location at Zulu hide and to check on any patrols or exercises in the area. When he got off the radio, he walked over to Danny and Kevin and said, "Guys, there are no reports from HQ of any British or BDF military exercises in this area, and from the direction of the sound, it must be coming from the Guatemalan side of the border, across no man's land. It could be the Guatemalan army on exercise, you know how they sometimes like to fuck around, just to irritate and test our patrols, or maybe they're engaging with rebels near the border?"

Danny looked down at their map of the area. He could see that the start of 'no man's land' was not that far from the hide, maybe a ten-minute walk through the jungle. No man's land was a cleared strip of land between the Belize side of the disputed border and the Guatemalan side, approximately six hundred yards wide, that went in a straight line down the border; from the Mexican border in the north to the neck of the Mopan River a few miles to the south.

The team had been well briefed before leaving the UK, and they knew that the sovereignty of all this land was disputed by the Guatemalan government, who claimed that it belonged to them. In fact, they considered the whole of Belize as part of Guatemala, saying it had been stolen by the British in the eighteenth century, so the British and Belizean armed forces now worked together to keep an uneasy peace by patrolling the border regularly.

The Guatemalan government had major issues of their own, with their own civil war going on, so the British forces had assessed it was highly unlikely they would start any territorial battles with the British forces that were patrolling the border. There had been a few minor exchanges over the past 10 years, with both Guatemalan soldiers and rebels crossing over from the Guatemalan side, but they had been easily dealt with.

Mark was still waiting for a response from Danny and said again, "Danny, Ops are saying no exercises. What do you want to do?"

"Yes, I heard you the first time, Mark. I'm thinking, just a moment please." He paced back and forth, weighing up the options in his mind, and decided to investigate, "Okay, by my reckoning, the sound of the gunfire is coming from the west, across the border, which we know is not that uncommon, so it's probably nothing to be too worried about, but let's take a quick walk to the edge of the treeline and have a look across no man's land. If we think it's too dangerous to complete our work here, we'll wrap up and head back to Airport Camp, but if we leave, we'll only have to come back in a few days. Then we'll have to do that shitty drive again, so, if at all possible, I would prefer us to crack on and get it done before we leave."

Danny and his team knew that they weren't too far from the Holdfast British army camp and hoped that there were some British army patrols nearby if anything kicked off.

CHAPTER 12. NO MAN'S LAND

It took 10 minutes for Danny, Mark and Kevin to walk from the hide through the jungle to the treeline on the Belize side of the border. They stood there, hidden in the shadows of the trees at the edge of no man's land, looking out across the fields of maize. The firing had stopped and it had become eerily quiet. Danny took out his binoculars and looked across no man's land to the opposite treeline, only six hundred yards away. He adjusted the focus and zoomed into the shadows on the Guatemalan side of the border. He couldn't see anything unusual. Kevin and Mark were standing next to him, also looking at the opposite treeline. Their weapons were slung over their shoulders, and they felt slightly nervous but also excited. This was the closest they had ever been to no man's land. This was a departure from their normal duties of servicing and refuelling the ground support equipment at the various aircraft hides and British forces camps along the border. Danny handed over the binoculars to Kevin, saying, "Do you want a look? I can't see anything unusual."

Mark and Kevin both took turns with the binoculars, scanning the opposite side, but also didn't see anything out of the ordinary. No man's land was full of waist-high maize being grown by the locals. They had taken the opportunity to grow crops here when the border had been cleared of trees by the British decades before. They planted their crops and tended to the land, and these farming activities kept a very clearly defined border. The British forces turned a blind eye to the farmers using this strip of land; it made it easier for them to patrol the border and also improved their relations with the locals.

* * *

After leaving his corporal with half of the men to guard the path where the rebels had ambushed them, Carlos and the rest of his men had moved east towards the Belize border as quickly as possible.

They were now making good time, finding it easy to follow the tracks left by Sisasi and the children. Carlos was a few paces behind the lead soldier when the soldier pointed ahead and then raised his arm up straight and opened his fist twice, splaying his fingers wide to indicate to the rest of the platoon that he could see approximately 10 targets ahead. Carlos gave his order, "Cock your weapons!" the soldiers cocked their weapons and then waited for his order to open fire.

Sisasi had reached the treeline on the Guatemalan side of the border first. She looked east, across the fields of maize, and could see the opposite treeline on the Belize side of the border, not very far away. She looked left and right along the border to check it was safe to cross, and could see that the jungle had been cleared of trees for as far as the eye could see to the north and south. "Polo, children, we must move quickly to the other side, we'll be safe over there. Polo, please can you stay at the back, and I'll stay at the front?"

Yes, Miss Sasi." Polo replied.

Sisasi then proceeded to lead them into the maize crop, picking out a route through to the other side.

Danny and his team were just about to turn around and head back, when Kevin, still holding the binoculars to his eyes, said, "Danny, there are some people over there, a woman with a group of children; I would say there are about 10 or 11 of them. They've just come out of the shadows of the treeline on the other side."

Danny reached out and took the binoculars from Kevin. He focussed in on the group coming towards them and wondered what they were doing there? "You had better report this back to base, Mark. Radio it in to HQ and see if they have anything to say about what we should do with regard to this group crossing no man's land." Mark started to radio in their report.

Sisasi started guiding the children across no man's land, completely unaware she was being watched from the other side.

Carlos and his men soon reached the outskirts of the treeline on no man's land. Sisasi and the children were already crossing through the field of maize. *We have finally caught up with the reds!* Carlos thought.

One of the soldiers reported, "Sir, they're already in no man's land; what should we do?"

Carlos felt pissed off, he knew he wasn't allowed to open fire into no man's land or even enter no man's land, but he was angry. *We've lost good men today, and who would know or care, anyway, if we opened fire here, we are in the middle of nowhere? After all, they're just reds, better dead than alive,* Carlos thought. He gave the order to open fire, "Go after them, kill them all before they get to the other side and bring back their bodies! Open fire at will!"

Danny lifted the binoculars to his eyes and adjusted the focus, he could see the woman clearly. Her jet-black hair was whipping around as she seemed to be giving instructions to the children, especially to an older boy near the back of the group, who was holding the hands of two younger children. They started moving as quickly as they could through the maize, and were heading straight towards Danny and his team. Her machete was sweeping back and forth through the maize, making the path easier for the children following behind. He could hear worried shouts coming from some of the younger children, who weren't much taller than the three feet high maize, and probably afraid of being left behind.

Danny could see the older boy more clearly as they got closer; he looked to be around 12 or 13 years old. The woman looked like she was in her early twenties and was carrying a young girl on her left hip. She continued forward, expertly wielding the machete in her right hand to cut a path through the maize. He watched them as they approached, then something else caught his eye; he re-focussed his binoculars onto the opposite treeline and could see some armed soldiers coming out of the shadows. Then he was appalled to see them start opening fire on the woman and children coming in his direction. Loud cracks of gunfire ripped through the quiet serenity of the maize field as the soldiers opened fire. Danny's heart sank at the thought of what might happen to the defenceless children and the woman leading them.

On Carlos's orders, his soldiers cocked their weapons and opened fire on Sisasi and the children. They were still two hundred yards away from the Belize side of no man's land. Danny could see the soldiers running into the field of maize with the obvious intention of killing these civilians.

Luckily for Sisasi, the accuracy of the soldier's weapons at that distance and while running was not very good. As soon as she heard the first shots, Sisasi and the children had time to instinctively drop to the ground, vanishing into the field of maize.

Danny shouted, "Take cover!" and stepped back behind a tree, dropping onto one knee. He couldn't believe what he was witnessing, there were loud thuds as some of the rounds impacted with the trees around them, it sounded like hammers hitting nails, and splinters of wood flew out from each impact. Danny, Mark and Kevin stayed down, trying to avoid the stray bullets heading towards them.

Sisasi and the children were halfway across no man's land, they could hear bursts of gunfire, and the children started screaming in terror. Sisasi reassured them, saying, "Stay down, try to keep quiet and follow me, everything is going to be alright. Keep crawling forward, but if I say 'run', we must get up and just keep running as fast as we can." The urgency of their situation was clear in her voice as they continued to crawl through the crop of maize towards the safety of the Belize side.

Danny could still see the soldiers moving forwards through the maize and firing their weapons into the maize in short bursts. The woman and children had temporarily vanished after coming the first few hundred yards, but he thought, *The soldiers must be closing in on them*. The children could still be heard screaming in terror as the bullets continued ripping through the maize around them. The woman was clearly trying to get them across no man's land to safety, but the soldiers on the other side were closing in on her position. Danny had no idea whether any of them were injured, but he knew it was his duty to try to help them.

It all seemed surreal, like it was happening in slow motion. Danny felt outraged at the sight of these soldiers opening fire on an unarmed woman with a group of children. The soldiers were out in the open, moving through the field of maize and getting closer to their targets.

Danny couldn't spend any more time thinking about it, "Mark, radio this in, a group of what appear to be Guatemalan soldiers are firing on an unarmed woman with a group of children," Danny said in an urgent voice.

"Kevin, we can't just stand by and watch them being massacred."

Kevin was momentarily stunned. He looked very concerned. "So what are we going to do, Danny?"

Danny looked back at the developing situation; the soldiers were closing on the last position where the woman and children had dipped below the height of the crop. They walked through the crop and fired sporadic bursts of gunfire, like beaters trying to flush out hunted animals.

"We are going to help. Open fire on the soldiers. Aim high, we don't want to hit the woman or any of the children," Danny said.

Without any further hesitation, Danny stood up, raised his machine gun, and started firing short volleys towards the soldiers coming towards them.

Mark was still on the radio when Danny opened fire, "...Yes, sir, civilians under fire. West of Zulu hide. Our NCO is engaging with them now. Over and out."

The signals officer relayed the message straight to Brigadier Davies.

"Sir, we have a situation being reported in from Zulu hide. Three of our men have become involved in a firefight with Guatemalan soldiers attacking unarmed civilians, a woman with approximately 10 children, currently crossing no man's land from the Guatemalan side. I can clearly hear gunfire in the background. Our men have opened fire on the Guatemalan soldiers in an attempt to save the civilians, and they're requesting immediate backup."

Brigadier Davies instantly gave orders for the Harrier pilots to be scrambled. Within a few minutes, four fully armed Harrier Jump Jets were accelerating down the runway, their Rolls Royce Pegasus jet engines roared  deafeningly as they were taking off. They headed due west towards Zulu hide at 700mph; the journey time was only seven minutes. One of the Puma helicopters happened to be at Holdfast

Camp delivering supplies. The order went out to the Two-Para commander at Holdfast Camp to use the Puma helicopter to deploy 20 armed soldiers to Zulu hide.

The signals officer radioed Mark, "Twenty soldiers from Two-Para are on their way from Holdfast Camp as reinforcements, their ETA is 15 minutes. Four Harriers are also in the air, ETA is seven minutes; over."

Mark responded, "Understood; over and out."

Carlos and his men were initially confused that they were being fired upon and fell to their knees, the crop immediately hiding them from view.

Danny couldn't see them, and they couldn't see Sisasi and the children. The gunfire stopped, and there was a lull in the action. Sisasi seized the moment and shouted, "Now, children, run!" they all sprang up and started running towards Danny's position.

"Use the fucking grenade launcher!" Carlos shouted his order. One of the soldiers in no man's land stood up, aimed towards the last known position of the reds, and pulled the trigger. The grenade was launched.

Suddenly, a grenade exploded 30 yards behind Sisasi and the children. Danny looked through his binoculars and could see the soldier in no man's land reloading his grenade launcher. He was intent on firing again and was running towards them through the maize. Some of the other soldiers jumped up and started firing again too. Sisasi and the children kept running towards the treeline on the Belize side of the border, hoping to find safety in amongst the trees. Danny pointed at the soldier with the grenade launcher and said, "Look to one o'clock, the soldier with the grenade launcher, we need take him out."

He handed over the binoculars to Kevin, and they focussed their fire on the soldier with the grenade launcher, but the grenades kept coming, exploding about two hundred yards from their position, probably at its maximum range. Currently, they were missing their target, landing short of the woman and children but getting closer to them with each attempt.

Danny felt the anger rising up inside him and, without warning, said, "Cover me. I'm going to get them." He ran forward into no man's land, emptying his magazine in the direction of the Guatemalan soldiers that had been coming towards them.

Carlos couldn't believe what he was seeing. He and his men all dropped to the ground as the volley of machine-gun bullets and rifle bullets from Mark and Kevin ripped through the air around them.

Mark and Kevin couldn't believe what they were seeing either. Danny was running out into no man's land. They kept firing their weapons at the enemy soldiers, but their ammunition had almost run out. Danny had no rounds left in his magazine and needed to reload; he also knew that with every yard that he got closer to the soldiers on the other side, the better their aim would get. He could hear the whistle of bullets flying past him as he approached Sisasi.

As he closed in on her position, a bullet struck, he felt a sharp tug on his front right-hand side, just above the waistband of his trousers. Danny fell, spinning to the ground and vanishing into the maize. He lay on his back momentarily and pulled his jacket up to look at the wound, it was bleeding but not too painful. *For fuck's sake!* he thought, then he let his jacket drop back into place, clicked the empty magazine off, and loaded the full magazine and tentatively got back up on one knee. He felt terrified, but there was no turning back now.

When Danny disappeared into the maize, Kevin and Mark thought he might have been hit and momentarily stopped firing.

"Now what should we do?" Kevin said to Mark.

"Keep fucking firing; help is on its way!" Mark replied.

* * *

Fabio and his men were still making their way through the jungle when they heard machine-gun fire coming from the northeast towards no man's land. They pushed hard and, moments later, came running out of the jungle, half expecting to find Sisasi and the children being executed by the soldiers. They were a few hundred yards to the south of Carlos's position. Fabio looked through his binoculars, he could clearly see that it definitely was Sisasi and the children, and she was already crossing no man's land. A British soldier was running towards Sisasi while shooting at the Guatemalan soldiers in the maize fields. Fabio was pleased and relieved to see that Sisasi was still alive but also immediately realised that she and the children were in grave danger.

He said in an urgent voice, "Comrades, we must take out the soldiers on our side if we are to save my sister and the children."

They could see Carlos and his men, but they were still three hundred yards away, so Fabio and his rebels started running north along the treeline to get closer before using their limited ammunition. As they closed in, they could see Carlos and his men running through the maize crop towards Sisasi and the British soldier. The soldiers were sporadically opening fire with their automatic weapons, and one of the soldiers was firing grenades. The soldiers were completely focussing their attention on Sisasi and didn't see the danger closing in on them from Fabio and his men.

Sisasi and the children had, by now, realised that the soldiers on the Belize side of the border were trying to help them and shooting at their aggressors, not them. When Sisasi saw Danny running towards them, she knew instinctively that this was their chance to save themselves and to get to the far side.

Danny had loaded the second full magazine into the breech of his machine gun. He then reappeared, kneeling, and started firing his machine gun at the soldiers again. He looked at Sisasi and flicked his head towards the Belize treeline, and said, "Run! Go now!"

Sisasi understood and shouted to all the children to run, "Now, Polo! Now, children! Now, run, run!"

The moment Polo stood up to run, he felt like someone had hit him very hard with a club just below his shoulder blade. The high-velocity round had hit him so hard that it sent him spinning forward like a ragdoll. The bullet had hit him in the back, puncturing his right lung and then exiting. There was a large hole in the front of his chest, where the bullet and wound debris had ripped through the chest wall.

Polo realised immediately that he had been shot, and he tried to say to the two younger children that were with him "Run!" but his throat was full of blood. Instead of words, he coughed up a bright red plume, it was spurting like a macabre fountain from his mouth. Strangely, he felt no pain, as if the pain was being masked by the memories that were flashing through his mind, like a vivid slide show. Hundreds of colourful images from his past, his mother, his father, the village, school friends, and Sisasi. He realised how sad they would be when they found out he was dead. He wanted to say "goodbye" to all of them. He could see his mother crying. "Don't cry," he wanted to say to her.

He felt sad about all the people he was leaving behind and was absolutely certain that he was going to die here and right now. *I don't want to die yet,* he thought despairingly, as tears ran gently down his cheeks. He remembered happier times, it seemed as if time itself was now slowing down, and as he faded into unconsciousness, the light faded from his eyes, and he felt himself being picked up and taken away.

CHAPTER 13. TIME TO LEAVE

As Sisasi ran past Danny, leading the children to the Belizean side of the border, he was focussed on firing his machine gun at the attacking soldiers on the other side. Sisasi briefly glanced at him, with a look on her face of both relief and exhaustion. Danny was watching the soldier with the grenade launcher coming towards them, he could see the puff of smoke and hear the sound of the next grenade being fired. With each grenade, the soldier was finding his aim, and this one was coming in a long arc, straight towards them.

Danny shouted, "Get down!"

Sisasi had her back to the grenade and didn't see it coming, it landed just 15 yards away. She had heard Danny shout just as the grenade exploded but couldn't get down in time. Around the explosion, the grenade had turned into metal confetti ripping through the maize but due to the nature of the explosion, the fragments travelled in a V-shape upwards and outwards, narrowly missing the children. Some of the children screamed as they were hit by the blast-wave. Sisasi's ears were ringing, and at the same time, a sharp fragment of shrapnel sliced through the top of her head, tearing through her hair and leaving a gaping wound in her scalp. She was thrown forward by the blast and felt momentarily concussed. Libi, the four-year-old child she had been carrying, was thrown out of her arms as if the little girl had been shot from a catapult. Another child that had been holding Sisasi's hand was also thrown forward into the maize by the shockwave.

As Sisasi lay there, temporarily confused and waiting for her senses to return, she felt a strange warmness running from her hair, down her forehead and into her eyes, she couldn't see properly. She wiped both her hands across her face as if to wipe it away and cleared the blood from her eyes with the tips of her fingers. Blood was smeared over the whole of her face, making her features almost unrecognisable, as if she was wearing a strange red mask. The blood was still pouring from the wound in her scalp. She held her hand on her scalp to stop the bleeding, and as her senses came back to her, she got back up and shouted to the children again, "We must run! Follow me." With every step, they came closer to the safety of the Belize treeline.

Garcia and the rest of the platoon had pushed hard and could hear weapons being fired in the distance. They finally arrived to join the rest of the platoon and pushed their way forward into the maize to rendezvous with them. Carlos looked back to see Garcia bounding through the maize towards him, "Garcia! Great to see you and the rest of the platoon. There's a small group of British soldiers on the far treeline, and one of them is about three hundred yards away, where we are focussing our fire. Keep your weapons trained on the opposite treeline. We'll advance through the crop and take out the reds that are hiding there." Garcia ordered his men to keep firing short bursts into the opposite treeline. Kevin and Mark returned fire, but their ammunition had nearly run out. Carlos, with Sergeant Garcia and the rest of their platoon, started advancing through the crop, feeling like victory was almost at hand.

Danny had thrown himself to the ground when the grenade exploded but almost immediately got back up and opened fire again, still focussing his aim on the soldier with the grenade launcher. Out of 30 of the rounds in his magazine, only two hit their target, but that was enough to make the grenades stop. *Time to leave!* Danny thought. He had run out of ammo and was two hundred yards from Kevin and Mark's position.

Danny's left trouser leg was torn near the top of his thigh, where a piece of shrapnel from the grenade had struck him when it had exploded. He could see that he had been wounded again, but there was too much happening to concentrate on his own injuries right now. It didn't feel very painful, but when he looked down, he could see a lot of blood was soaking through the camouflaged material of his left trouser leg; the material felt wet and claggy against his skin, and the reddish stain ran down to his knee. It stuck to his leg as he moved quickly through the maize, and his leg was throbbing painfully, but he just knew he must keep running back to the treeline if he had any chance of staying alive.

As he sprinted back, he spotted the older boy lying in the maize, with two other children kneeling next to him, calling his name, "Polo! Polo!" He was lying on his back, blood pumping out of a hole in his chest that was the size of a man's fist. Danny stopped immediately and dropped down onto one knee, looking down at the boy. He could see Polo was alive because a rhythmical spurt of blood was squirting from a torn blood vessel in the hole in the boy's chest, and he was still breathing enough to be choking on his own blood. *I have to stop the bleeding, but I can't do it here*, Danny thought. He picked him up quickly and draped Polo over his shoulder in a fireman's lift. The two other children with him were crying and frozen with fear. Danny picked the smallest one up with his free arm and gestured to the other one to follow him, saying, "Come with me!" He started running towards the treeline, hoping they would get there without any more injuries.

Fabio had also seen the soldier with the grenade launcher, three grenades had already been fired, and his accuracy was improving with each shot. Fabio saw the next grenade land very close to its target, arcing three hundred yards over no man's land and exploding very near to Sisasi, the British soldier, and the children. He could see his sister and the others were thrown forward by the blast, and he realised that he and his comrades may have arrived too late. A surge of anger erupted inside him, he just wanted to kill these soldiers that were attacking his people, but by now, they were very outnumbered and getting low on ammunition. He exploded into action, cocking his weapon, clicking off the safety lever, and opening fire as he ran towards the platoon.

Carlos and his platoon now found themselves under fire from a different enemy. This surprise ambush from the southern flank could thwart their mission. Sergeant Garcia shouted, "Take cover, take cover!" The platoon dropped to the ground and were again hidden by the crop.

Fabio had his weapon trained on the area where he had seen the soldiers go to ground. He just wanted to make sure Sisasi and the children had enough time to escape. He needed to keep them pinned down.

Carlos shouted, "Garcia, take out those fucking rebels!"

Garcia replied, "Yes, sir!" and ordered the men around him, "On me, fire at will!" he stood up and started to charge towards Fabio and his men.

Fabio pulled his trigger first, while shouting, "Open fire!" The clatter of his weapon was deafening as it sent a spray of bullets straight towards Garcia. Three rounds hit Sergeant Garcia in the chest, and as he fell, the final round ripped through his neck. The soldiers following him dropped back to the ground at the sight of their sergeant being mortally wounded. One of his men crawled over and tried to stop the bleeding from his neck. The bullet had severed a major artery and he was bleeding out. The soldier could see he had stopped breathing; there was nothing he could do. He shook his head at a colleague who had come over to help, indicating there was no hope. Sergeant Garcia was dead.

Sisasi and seven of the children were ahead of Danny, running towards the safety of the Belize treeline. They could hear more terrifying gunfire behind them, not realising that some of the gunfire was coming from the rebels, led by her brother, trying to protect them. Sisasi, and the children that were still with her, got to the trees very quickly, running the last stretch in less than a minute, though it actually felt so much longer.

Kevin and Mark looked at Sisasi's face, it was covered in blood, and her features were difficult to make out. Mark looked directly at Sisasi and patted the ground, palm down, saying, "Get down, get down!" Sisasi immediately understood and obeyed his signal, dropping to the ground behind him and Mark with the children. Mark could see that the skin on the top of her head was torn wide open, and blood was pumping into her hair, which by now was wet and matted. He pulled a field dressing from his left trouser pocket, ripped it open, and threw it over to her, patting his head to indicate what to do with it.

Sisasi was very grateful, and nodded saying, "Thanks," and then pressed the dressing against the wound to stem the bleeding. She looked around at her group, counting the children, and suddenly realised that Polo and two of the younger children were missing. Sisasi immediately looked back towards no man's land, Danny was running towards them through the maize, and she could see Polo was draped lifelessly over his shoulder. The smallest child was under Danny's arm, and the third child was following behind him. On the other side of no man's land, she could hear more shots being fired, it felt like mayhem. She could see a new group of men in the distance just to the south of the soldiers, who were firing their weapons at the soldiers. She placed her hands on the ground and said quietly, "Thank you, God, for bringing us help, thank you." She didn't realise that it was her own brother, Fabio, leading the group that was now attacking Carlos's soldiers.

Kevin looked through the binoculars, he could see Danny running towards them. *Thank God!* he thought briefly before turning his attention back to the soldiers, who were now being fired upon. He zoomed in, "Rebels,

I think. There are rebels attacking the soldiers from the south! We need to get the fuck out of here, and quickly!" Incredibly, Danny managed to reach the treeline less than a minute after Sisasi. He quickly put Polo down, grabbed a field dressing, pressing it into the large wound in his chest to stem the bleeding.

Sisasi's eyes focussed on Polo, she immediately realised that his situation was dreadful. She moved over to Danny and could see that he was helping Polo. Danny said to her, "Do you speak any English?"

Sisasi replied, "Yes, a little."

Danny could see she had sustained a head injury, but she was more concerned about Polo, and so was he. He took her hand and said, "What's your name?"

She replied, "Sisasi."

Danny said calmly, "Sisasi, can you hold this bandage in place for this boy?" pointing at the already blood-soaked field dressing on Polo's chest.

Sisasi said, "Yes, I can." Sisasi looked at Polo and cried, tears streaming slowly down her face, washing away her own drying blood and leaving clean lines on her cheeks, giving a macabre look to her expression. She whispered into Polo's ear, "Polo, Polo! My little soldier, fight, don't give up now, fight!"

Polo was unconscious, in critical condition, and in need of urgent medical attention.

* * *

Brigadier Davies commanded the British forces in Central America and had met the commander of the Guatemalan armed forces on a couple of occasions, and didn't much like him, but was under orders from his superiors to keep a respectful peace. There had already been a territorial war in the Falklands that year, and Margaret Thatcher didn't want and couldn't afford another war. Neither he nor the commander of the Guatemalan armed forces wanted an international incident, but the brigadier was incensed by the intelligence he had received from his signals officer, and he was not going to stand for it.

Brigadier Davies called the commander of the Guatemalan army. After a momentary pause, the brigadier could hear the voice of the commander, "Hello, Brigadier, what can I do for you?"

Brigadier Davies responded with a stern tone in his voice, "Hello, Commander, we have an intrusion by your forces into no man's land on the border, approximately 10 miles north of San Ignacio. They're apparently trying to kill a woman and a group of children. This goes against the Geneva Convention, and our troops have legally engaged with your troops to save these civilians. I thought you should know that we already have four Harrier fighter jets armed and already in the air, and additional reinforcements on their way from our Holdfast Base near San Ignacio. They will be there within minutes and will be instructed to open fire if you do not confirm that you have stood your men down and started moving them away from the border. I'll order our air support to empty their munitions into your side of the treeline if they do not retreat at least one mile. I would advise not trying to send in any air support of your own. If you do, we'll assume it to be a further act of aggression and we'll shoot them down. Do I make myself clear, Commander?"

The commander responded, "I have no idea what you are talking about or what has happened there, but I'll look into this immediately and get back to you, Brigadier."

Brigadier Davies responded, "You have less than five minutes left before my fighter jets arrive, Commander. I will not wait a minute more than that; I must know that your soldiers are retreating away from the border."

**

After Fabio and his comrades had attacked, Carlos and his men had retreated back to the treeline. The radio was buzzing, the radio operator handed over the two-way radio to Carlos, saying, "Sir, it's the boss, he needs to speak to you urgently."

Carlos spoke to the company major on the radio, who said angrily, "Our commander has issued urgent orders to move all troops away from the border,

Lieutenant, what the hell are you doing in no man's land? Are you trying to start a fucking war?!"

Carlos responded humbly, "No, sir. I was following a group of reds here; some of them have now escaped across the border, but only with the help of the British troops, who are still firing on our position, and we are now also under fire from rebels to our south."

The major could hear the roar of the Harriers arriving in the background and shouted at Carlos in an angry voice, "Lieutenant Cruz, I order you to immediately stand down and get out of no man's land. Report back to base immediately. Is that understood?"

Carlos replied, "Yes, sir. Understood. Out."

Danny had decided they should get back to Zulu hide. As they headed back, Danny said, "Mark, what's happening? Are we getting reinforcements?"

"On their way, Danny. Two-Para should be here any minute, coming in a Puma from Holdfast Camp. Also, four fully armed Harriers are on their way from Airport Camp," Mark replied.

As Mark finished speaking, they could hear the roar of the Harriers' engines coming overhead. As they flew over Zulu hide, they were so low, they could see the pilots in their cockpits. The trees shook as they passed overhead, gradually slowing down to a hover over the fields of maize, while the pilots looked around for targets, with the blast from their engines flattening the crops.

The Harriers hovered ominously, seemingly pointing their whole arsenal at the enemy. It was quite a sight. Danny, Mark and Kevin roared with approval and suddenly felt much safer. They looked across and could see the soldiers and the rebels vanishing into the shadows. Mark was giving a 'sitrep' update to the signals officer at Airport Camp.

Everything looked calmer, they could no longer see the soldiers or rebels. When the jets had arrived, the soldiers and the rebels had all momentarily stopped to look up in awe at the powerful and destructive fighter jets bearing down on them and then retreated.

Fabio signalled to his comrades to leave and said, "I think it is time to go; lets live to fight another day." His comrades looked up at the sky and agreed. Fabio didn't like leaving his sister, but he also knew that the British soldiers would protect her.

Sisasi and the children were now on the Belize side of the border, and Fabio decided that it was too dangerous to try to follow them. They knew the border was patrolled and heavily defended by the British forces, and they could see from the safety of the shadows that a large helicopter was arriving from the south, doors open and full of armed soldiers.

Danny felt much safer now the Harriers were still hovering over no man's land. They had no order to open fire yet, so they just hung there in the sky like four fearsome dragons waiting for the order to breathe their fire.

Danny still had a piece of shrapnel embedded in his thigh. He dropped his trousers to inspect the wound. There was a piece of flesh partly torn away. It looked a lot worse than he had imagined. *I wish I'd left my bloody trousers done up!*

Mark sounded concerned, "For God's sake, Danny! Let me help you." He took out a roll of medical tape from the first aid kit, pushed the flap of flesh back into position, and placed the field dressing over the wound. Mark used the tape to make sure the dressing was held securely and then said reassuringly, "That should do for now, Danny; you'll be fine."

The Guatemalan commander called the brigadier back, "Our soldiers have been ordered to stand down and return to base."

Disappointingly for the brigadier, he then had to order the Harriers to stand down too. The Harrier pilots received their orders to return back to Airport Camp without a shot being fired.

A couple of minutes later, the Puma landed at Zulu hide, dropping off the Two-Para contingency. The parachute regiment created a cordon, taking up defensive positions around Zulu hide while the Puma loadmaster boarded the passengers and casualties. Sisasi, the children, and Danny were going to be flown back to the medical centre at Airport Camp. The medic checked Polo's vital signs, his blood pressure was very low, but he was still alive. He spoke to Danny, "It's not looking good, Corporal, his pulse is very weak. I'll put him on a drip and give him some adrenalin; that will help."

Danny nodded in acknowledgement and said, "Okay, let's hope that's enough."

Mark and Kevin watched the Puma helicopter take off and then packed everything away under the protective cordon provided by the parachute regiment.

"What a fucking nightmare today!" Mark said as they drove off towards Airport Camp.

Kevin agreed, "Yeah, I can't believe what Danny did. Crazy fucker! I hope he'll be alright."

"He didn't look too bad when he left, fingers crossed he will be fine in a few days. We will have to look in on him when we get back."

It took them a couple of hours to drive back to Airport Camp, and as they drove back, they mulled over the events of the day. When they finally arrived back, they dropped off their weapons at the armoury before heading to the medical centre to see how Danny and the rest of the casualties were doing.

Chapter 14. Repercussions

The Airport Camp medical centre was a small but fully functional medical facility, with two in-patient wards and one operating theatre. The senior officer in charge of the facility was Wing Commander Edmunds, a trauma surgeon. Like many of those serving in the medical branch of the armed forces, he had a relaxed, easy way about him. He had already seen active service in the Falklands, where he had tended to many serious injuries that had been inflicted on the battlefield. This posting was meant to be a six-month 'jolly' for him; sun, sea, and relaxation. When the message came in that there had been a firefight on the border, the thought of having casualties came as a bit of a shock.

In the 30 minutes it took the Puma helicopter to make its way to Airport Camp, they had prepared the operating theatre, making it ready for the more serious

injuries, and a walking wounded triage area had been set up for those with less serious injuries. The helicopter touched down on the playing fields opposite the medical centre and lowered the steps. The medic was holding up a drip for the young boy, Polo. "This one first, sir," he said to Wing Commander Edmunds, who switched into triage mode, examined the boy's wound, and quickly realised he didn't have much time if he was going to save his life.

He turned to the stretcher-bearers and said, "Take this one straight to the operating theatre, I'll be there in a minute." He looked at Danny's blood-soaked jacket and trousers, "How are you doing, Corporal?"

"Bullet wound in my right side, shrapnel embedded in my left thigh, sir, but I feel okay, and the field dressings have stemmed the bleeding. Please sort out the boy first. He has a very serious chest wound," Danny replied.

"Okay, Corporal, I'll leave you in the capable hands of my team and see you afterwards."

He headed to the operating theatre, leaving the junior doctor and medics to deal with the other casualties. People had started coming out of their offices and accommodation blocks to watch the medical team dealing with the wounded and were all wondering what had happened.

The medical team got Danny, Sisasi, and all the children over to the medical centre, where the medics quickly triaged the injuries. Danny was taken to one cubicle, Sisasi to another, and the rest of the children were quickly checked over. Thankfully, none of them seemed to be in a serious condition, only Polo had sustained a life-threatening injury. The flight lieutenant was a general practitioner, not a surgeon, but he was happy to see that all Danny's vital signs were stable; there was some blood loss, but his blood pressure was normal. He said to Danny, "We'll need to get you into theatre to look at that bullet wound, the leg wound I can clean and deal with now." He injected some local anaesthetic around the wound on Danny's left thigh and cleaned up the wound, removing a fragment of shrapnel before carefully stitching up the flap of skin. He looked up, holding the curved needle between his index finger and thumb, and smiled at Danny saying, "All done, Corporal; a good job, even if I do say so myself. We'll get you into theatre next to look at that bullet wound properly. It is not bleeding, and your blood pressure is stable, so we'll just monitor you for now until the theatre becomes available." He left Danny to be monitored by one of the nurses while he did the rounds, checking up on the rest of the casualties.

Polo came out of the theatre. He was sedated, and an intubation tube had been inserted through his mouth into his throat to help him breathe; a transport ventilator hissed rhythmically as it pumped oxygen-enriched air into his lungs via the tube, doing the breathing for him.

The junior doctor, Flight Lieutenant Dobson, said to Wing Commander Edmunds, "I've got another one for you, sir. Corporal Sinclaire has a gunshot wound through his waist on the right side. I've cleaned the entry and exit wounds."

They cleaned down the operating area, then put Danny on the operating table. The surgeon, Edmunds, inspected the wound. *In at the front, out at the back*, he thought.

He looked at Danny and said, "We are going to give you some gas to put you to sleep, Corporal, then I can sort out your wound."

The nurse looked down, and holding Danny's hand, said, "Count to 10, Corporal."

Danny started counting aloud, "One, two, three, four..." It felt a little uncomfortable breathing in the gas, but the anaesthetic did its job, and he was unconscious before he could finish.

Edmunds said to his team, "Turn him on his side so I can see both the entry and exit wounds," and they carefully turned Danny, as requested. He looked at the wounds and said, "Scalpel, please," to the theatre nurse who was assisting. She handed over the scalpel, and he carefully used it to cut the skin from the rear hole to the front hole, gently pulling the skin apart to look for any internal damage.

Edmunds looked at the team around the table. "He was incredibly lucky, no internal organs damaged, the bullet has just travelled under the skin before exiting." He cleaned the wound and stitched him up. "Okay, all done. Take him back to the ward. He should make a good recovery."

Flight Lieutenant Dobson smiled at Sisasi sympathetically and said, "Hello, young woman, my name is Ben. I am a doctor; do you speak any English?"

"I speak a little English, Doctor, but not very good," Sisasi replied.

He responded, "Well, it sounds very good to me. I need to get your wound cleaned up so I can take a closer look, is that okay? And can you tell me your name?""

Sisasi responded, "Yes, Doctor, that's fine. My name is Sisasi."

The doctor called a nurse over to where Sisasi sat on a treatment couch and said, "Please can you clean up Sisasi's wound? Cut back the hair around it, just enough for me to be able to examine the wound before I stitch it up. Please call me when you're done."

It was quite a long wound, the shrapnel had torn through the skin, but there was no damage to the top of her skull. The nurse washed the blood off Sisasi's face, her skin glistened again, and the nurse said with a smile, "There, I can see your face properly now, that's better," and she then thought, *what a beautiful young woman*.

She cleaned Sisasi's scalp, carefully cutting away the blood-matted hair around the wound with a pair of right-angled scissors, and when she had finished, called

Doctor Dobson back, who said, "Thank you, Nurse, that's perfect."

He smiled at Sisasi and took out a suture to close the wound. After very carefully examining the wound, he said positively, "Well, Sisasi, you will be pleased to know that there's no damage to your skull, it could have been much worse. I can now stitch up your scalp, and you will be feeling much better within a few days." He then used the suture to stitch the wound closed and eventually said, "All done, Sisasi," smiling at her.

"Thank you, Doctor," she replied with a look of relief on her face.

The commander in Guatemala complained bitterly to their Foreign Minister about the British troops engaging with his soldiers.

"My men were only trying to stop the communist rebels from escaping across the border!" he complained.

The impact of the British forces engaging with the Guatemalan forces went right to the top. The US administration had been working secretly with the Guatemalan President, General Ríos Montt, to eradicate the communist threat, and were providing military training and weapons. Reagan's office was informed about the British troops opening fire on the Guatemalan soldiers.

Ronald Reagan wasn't happy with the situation and called Margaret Thatcher. "Hi, Margaret, are you well?"

"Hello, Ron, I am, thanks for asking. How are you?"

"I am fine, Margaret, thanks. We have a situation in Guatemala. Did you know your troops attacked Guatemalan forces while they were in the process of trying to stop communist rebels from escaping across the border into Belize?"

Margaret replied in a suitably sarcastic tone, "I've been briefed that there was a skirmish on the border, where our troops opened fire to protect an unarmed woman with 10 children trying to flee across no man's land. What does this have to do with the US? I read in the newspapers that you were staying out of Guatemalan politics?"

Ronald sounded irritated. "Margaret, my intelligence briefing states that these were commies carrying weapons and shooting back, not just women and children. Six Guatemalan soldiers are dead, two of them were apparently killed by your guys, and the others by Cuban-backed commies. You are a politician like me, the USA can't stay out of the Guatemalan civil war, in the same way as we couldn't stay out of the Falklands War, because we must help our friends. You know it is in both American and British interests to stop these commies taking over Central America. We just can't have your trigger-happy men allowing them to escape across the border into Belize."

Ronald went on in a more patronising voice, "You do understand the importance of dealing with this commie issue, Margaret? We just need you to support us by defending the border. If you can't do that, at least leave us to help Montt to get the job done."

Margaret thought about it for a moment. "I understand, Ron, you are right, I wouldn't want commies in my back yard either. Leave it with me. I'll speak to my people."

The next day, Brigadier Davies received a secret communication from defence intelligence stating that, according to US intelligence, the Guatemalan forces had been engaging with communist rebels when the British forces had opened fire. By firing on the Guatemalan soldiers, the British had allowed the communist rebels to escape, and they had also contributed to the deaths of six Guatemalan soldiers, who were US allies in the fight against communism in Central America. Brigadier Davies had orders from the top to fully investigate whether the British troops had assisted the communist rebels to escape and also to investigate their role in the killings of the Guatemalan troops.

Brigadier Davies was a straightforward soldier with 20 years of experience. He leant back in his chair, scratching his head, and looked annoyed by the intelligence report in his hand. *What a crock of shit!* he thought. To him, it was so obviously biased and wrong, but he had been ordered to carry out a full investigation by defence intelligence, so he had no other option.

Brigadier Davies's secretary called Captain Crawley of the military police at Airport Camp, "Hello, Captain Crawley, Brigadier Davies is on the line. Are you available to speak to him?"

Captain Crawley replied, "Of course, put me through."

The brigadier's voice came on the line, he seemed agitated, "Captain Crawley, I have a secret communication from defence intelligence. I need you to come to my office to discuss it as soon as you can."

Captain Crawley replied, "Yes, sir, I'm on my way now."

Captain Crawley walked into the brigadier's office and stood to attention in front of his desk, giving the customary salute. "Morning, sir."

Brigadier Davies responded, "Morning, Crawley, please have a seat."

The brigadier pointed to the chair in front of his desk. He pushed a file over to Captain Crawley, and said, "You need to read this. Apparently, the yanks are saying we've aided commies to escape from Guatemala into Belize, apparently putting the whole region in jeopardy of being taken over by communist rebels. It goes on to request a detailed and full investigation into what exactly happened during the firefight at Zulu hide. It implies we broke international laws on both the rules of engagement and assisting communist rebels to avoid justice. They're requesting we return all our Guatemalan casualties to go through their own legal processes."

Captain Crawley took a look at the report and said, "It looks like feathers have been ruffled at the top by US intelligence, sir. I'll look into it immediately and report back to you once I've examined the preliminary witness statements."

Captain Crawley headed over to the medical centre and knocked on the door of Wing Commander Edmunds. "Come in."

Captain Crawley went in, closing the door behind him, stood to attention, and saluted, saying, "Morning, sir."

Edmunds looked up over the rim of his glasses, "Morning. Have a seat, Captain. What can I do for you?"

"Sir, Brigadier Davies has ordered me to carry out a thorough investigation of what happened yesterday at Zulu hide. I'll need to interview everyone involved, including all the casualties brought in yesterday, but especially Corporal Sinclaire."

"I understand, Captain, but one of the casualties is a thirteen-year-old boy with a serious gunshot wound. He is currently sedated and ventilated, so you can't see him, but you can speak to the rest. You will need a translator for the children. None of them speak English, but their teacher does."

"Thank you, sir. I'll start with our own troops first and find out what their versions of events are," Captain Crawley replied.

"Follow me; I'll take you to the ward." The wing commander stood up and beckoned the captain to leave his office.

They walked to Danny's bedside first, where the wing commander asked, "Corporal Sinclaire, are you ready to answer a few questions about what happened at Zulu hide?"

Danny replied, "Yes, sir, that's fine."

Sitting on the chair next to Danny's bed, the military police captain introduced himself, "Hello, Corporal, my name is Captain Crawley. I have been assigned to carry out a full investigation of what happened on the border near Zulu hide yesterday."

Danny went on to explain the whole incident in his own words while Captain Crawley made some notes.

Captain Crawley asked, "Did you request permission to open fire, Corporal?"

"No, sir, there wasn't time to do that," Danny replied.

"Did you know you were engaging with Guatemalan soldiers?"

"Yes, I assumed that was the case, sir."

Captain Crawley went on, "Did you issue any warning before opening fire?"

Danny started feeling irritated by the captain's questions and frowned, saying, "No, sir, they were six hundred yards away. What's the point of all these questions?"

The captain responded in a business-like manner, "I am just trying to get to the facts, Corporal. I need you to write a full statement of what happened in your own words, then I can give a detailed report to the brigadier."

"I understand, sir. I'll get my statement written up as soon as possible."

Captain Crawley replied, "Today please, Corporal. I need it completed quickly."

"Yes, sir, will get started straight away," Danny replied.

Captain Crawley called in an interpreter and spoke to all the children, their stories all checked out. He could see from the evidence that the claims of escaping 'communist rebels' appeared to be completely untrue. He finished off by speaking to Sisasi, the only adult in the group that had been rescued. Captain Crawley listened to her story of how the soldiers had attacked her village and they were forced to flee, or they would have surely died. Captain Crawley believed that she was giving a truthful account of their escape from Colina and that she had no idea who the other group were that got involved in the battle and had opened fire from the south.

According to the secret communication the brigadier had received, the Guatemalan army had claimed Sisasi was part of that same rebel group. The rebels in the report had attacked and killed two soldiers, but none of the children were capable of launching any sort of offensive, and their teacher was only interested in escaping and keeping the children safe. It just didn't make any sense to the captain.

Captain Crawley went back to his office and spoke to the police sergeant on duty, "I need you to get statements from the corporal's two subordinates, the pilots and crews that were involved in the incident at Zulu hide."

The sergeant nodded and said, "Yes, sir. I'll get onto it straight away."

"Thanks, Sergeant. Also, one more thing, find out if the cameras were running on the Harriers and the Puma. If there are any videotapes or reconnaissance photos, I want to see them all."

The sergeant replied, "Will do, sir," saluted and left the captain's office.

The sergeant called his team together, briefed them all, and sent them away to gather as much evidence as possible.

Danny's wounds were sore and itched constantly under their dressings. He wanted to scratch them all the time but knew he shouldn't. He also couldn't wear any trousers because they would have rubbed against the injury on his thigh, so the nurse had given him a long baggy theatre gown to wear. It was not the most flattering look, but at least he was recovering well and able to walk around. He hoped that he would be able to leave the medical centre within the next few days.

Danny had become quite a celebrity on Airport Camp and had lots of inquisitive visitors wanting his first-hand account about what had actually happened at Zulu hide. It was the only subject being discussed in the NAAFI bar.

Chapter 15. The preliminary investigation

There was a fridge full of Coke and Fanta bottles in the patients' lounge area. Danny longed for an ice-cold bottle of Belikin beer, but he would have to make do with a Coke for now. A radio in the corner played pop music from the British forces BFBS radio station, and there were a few magazines and newspapers scattered around. Danny wandered over to the lounge and was surprised to see Sisasi sitting there in hospital pyjamas, reading a newspaper. She looked up at Danny but didn't recognise him immediately in his long blue gown. Danny looked across at her and smiled, saying, "Hello, very nice to see you. Able to escape the ward, I see?"

Sisasi put down the paper she has been reading and looked up, "Ah, it's you," she looked genuinely happy to see him. "You are the man that saved us. Thank you so much!"

Danny said, "Yes, that was me and my colleagues, Kevin and Mark. My name is Danny, what's yours?"

"My name is Sisasi," she replied, relieved that he did not look badly injured. She looked at him and realised that his green eyes reminded her brother, Fabio. She momentarily wondered, *Where is he now?*

They sat and chatted about the days leading up to her rescue, and it just confirmed Danny's feeling that he had done the right thing.

Sisasi said, "They won't let me see Polo, but I have seen all the other children."

Danny said in a questioning tone, "Polo is the boy with the chest wound?"

"Yes, that is Polo," Sisasi replied.

"He is still in a critical condition, Sisasi. That's why they won't let anyone see him yet," Danny said. He sat down next to her and said reassuringly, "We have the best doctors and nurses here, he is in the right place." He looked at the shaved strip on her head, with the long row of black stitches, neatly holding her scalp together. "It looks sore," he said sympathetically, running his finger across the top of his own scalp and pointing at her injury.

"Yes, they've made an awful mess of my hair and stitched in a zipper!" She looked at Danny, screwed up her cheeks, and lifted her palms upwards.

Danny laughed out loud, "Yes, not the best hairstyle, or a great place for a zip, and they have put you in pyjama trousers and a jacket, and me in a long blue dress!" He mimicked her, raising his palms towards the ceiling and screwing up his own cheeks.

She also laughed out loud and realised it was the first time that she had laughed for a very long time. It felt good to laugh again and to feel safe. She liked Danny and appreciated his company and his friendly smiles.

Sisasi held out a letter addressed to Father Michael at the Petén Missionary Hall in Guatemala. "Can you get this letter posted for me, Danny?"

"Of course I can. I'll ask Kevin or Mark to post it first thing tomorrow."

Danny took the letter from her.

"I've written a letter to our local priest to let him know where we are and that we are all safe. He can then pass on my message to the villagers, including my own parents, who were working away on the local farm when Colina was attacked."

They continued talking for hours. Danny was surprised that English was her third language because she spoke it so well. He soon realised that she was a strong, resilient, and intelligent woman who had managed to protect the lives of all the children in her care. He had been there at the border, but it was her strength and perseverance that enabled them to get that far and be here now, safe and sound.

Mark and Kevin were regular visitors, coming to the medical centre every day to see how things were going. They were pleased to see Danny's rapid recovery and were enjoying getting to know Sisasi. Danny gave Kevin the letter Sisasi had written to Father Michael, and he posted it the same day.

After a few days, the military police had collected all the witness statements, with the exception of Polo's. He was still on a ventilator and unconscious, but although he was still in a critical condition, his vital signs remained stable. The findings of the preliminary investigation were now well underway, and Captain Crawley was ready to give an interim report on his investigation to the brigadier. He called the brigadier's office to arrange a time to give him the interim report and was asked to come over immediately. Captain Crawley was ushered into the brigadier's office and asked to sit down after completing the usual salutations. Brigadier Davies had been feeling the pressure from high command. This incident had caused repercussions all the way to the top, and he wanted to 'nip it in the bud' as quickly as possible.

"Captain, give me the shortened version of your report," he said, expecting it to be a set of relatively 'cut and dried' findings.

"Sir, we now have sufficient evidence to understand why Corporal Sinclaire opened fire on the Guatemalan troops, which, according to the corporal's evidence statement, was to save the lives of unarmed civilians. Although I understand his reasons, I still believe that there are charges to answer."

Brigadier Davies looked bemused and said, "Really, Captain Crawley?"

Captain Crawley replied, "Unfortunately, yes, there are, sir. Look at these photos."

He proceeded to pull out a series of black and white still photographs and place them, one by one, onto the brigadier's desk. "These are some of the aerial photos from our Harriers. If you look here, just to the south of the Guatemalan soldiers' position." Captain Crawley handed the brigadier a magnifying glass and pointed to a location on the aerial photo. "There were armed rebels there, who were also firing upon the Guatemalan soldiers. We also have video footage from the Harriers showing them firing, then eventually running into the shadows when they see our fighter jets bearing down on them."

He carried on, "There are accusations coming from the Guatemalan Embassy in London that our forces opened fire on their soldiers during an ongoing battle with communist rebels. According to their version of events, they were trying to capture the communist rebels before they crossed the border. They claim that they were only trying to apprehend fleeing communist rebels at the border."

Brigadier Davies felt very annoyed because he had been to visit Danny and had heard his first-hand account of what had actually happened. "These were not 'soldiers', but just a bunch of trigger-happy thugs!" he said to Captain Crawley, pointing at the soldiers. "Sounds like complete bollocks to me, Crawley!"

Captain Crawley responded, "Although I understand your thinking, sir, the facts before me are that our men were at Zulu hide to do a specific job. They should never have left Zulu hide to go out to see what was happening on no man's land. Corporal Sinclaire put himself and his team in unnecessary danger and has also caused an international political incident because of his actions. According to the reports I am receiving from the UK, this incident has gone right to the top, to the prime minister herself. She is communicating directly with the White House, who are questioning why we are damaging counterinsurgency operations that are intended to stop the spread of communism." Crawley paused, the brigadier looked absolutely furious, but he said nothing, so the captain continued, "As you know, sir, we should not be involving ourselves in another country's affairs."

Brigadier Davies then stood up and responded in an angry voice, "The corporal and his men saved an innocent woman and 10 children. Are you trying to say we should press charges against him?"

Captain Crawley responded, "I'm saying that we have no choice, sir. It is out of our hands. Military law states that we should not engage with soldiers of another nation without authority. Corporal Sinclaire did not seek any authority. Military law clearly states that you cannot aid enemy insurgents. The Guatemalan Embassy in London is accusing us of doing exactly that. When

Corporal Sinclaire is well enough to leave his sick bay, we must arrest him and charge him. We must go through the due legal processes. The other two men that were with him were following his orders and did not go into no man's land; therefore they have no case to answer."

Brigadier Davies looked pensive. "I understand what you are saying from a legal perspective, but do you have any actual evidence that this woman, who our men rescued, is part of the communist insurgent group? This seems absolutely mad!"

Captain Crawley replied, "No, sir. We don't have any evidence to prove the woman or the children were part of any communist group or were involved with the rebels that opened fire on the soldiers. All the statements that we've taken so far confirm that they were the victims, and our men's action potentially saved their lives. That seems to be the truth when you look at the current evidence and the way the firefight played out. The fact that there were armed rebels firing on Guatemalan troops may just be a coincidence, but we don't know that for certain. I'm in touch with defence intelligence who are keeping a close eye on this incident. All our aerial images have been sent for further analysis, and we included photos of the woman, Sisasi, and the children, just to make sure that there isn't any intelligence being held on any of them."

Brigadier Davies deliberated, "So, if I understand correctly, you are saying that according to military law, we must follow the due legal processes and press charges against Sinclaire?"

The captain could see the brigadier was unhappy. "Yes, sir. That is the only course of action. I've collated all the witness statements, and unfortunately, it appears that there has been a breach of British and international military laws. Corporal Sinclaire does have a case to answer. If we do not charge him, there may well be accusations of a cover-up. We need to present all the evidence and have his actions assessed against the witness statements."

The brigadier said, "Captain, I think we need to wait and see what the top brass comes back with after reviewing the witness statements, photos, and documentary evidence before we take any further actions. In the meantime, Corporal Sinclaire is not to be charged."

Captain Crawley reluctantly agreed, "Okay, sir. I'll not press charges yet, and let you know as soon as I've received any responses back."

"Thank you, Crawley, that'll be all for now," the brigadier responded.

The captain got up and left the office.

The children were all in a dormitory ward together. At the entrance to the ward, there were two self-contained single rooms, with Danny occupying one room and Sisasi the other. The nurses would come around every few hours to check up on everyone, provide meals, and ensure that they had everything they needed to fully recuperate, including toys for the children.

Danny and Sisasi played with the children in the hospital garden, it had been a week since the incident, and the speed of recovery in all of them, with the exception of Polo, was remarkable. They were all oblivious to what was happening in the background with regard to the ongoing investigation.

Sisasi enjoyed improving her English with Danny and enjoyed his company too. He was kind, funny, and obviously enjoying spending time with her. Danny thought Sisasi was incredible; he listened to her stories about being brought up in the jungle and how she worked in the village school with Father Michael to become his teaching assistant. He was dazzled by her wonderful smile, her inner strength, and her bravery. Danny enjoyed listening to her speak and the swishing movement of her long black hair as she waved her arms about when telling her stories.

She would mimic some of the animals and birds that she described, crouching like a panther, or flapping like a bird, making Danny laugh out loud at her antics. The more they laughed, the more the incident on the border faded away into the background.

Flight Lieutenant Dobson, Wing Commander Edmunds and the nurses carried out regular checks with all their patients, and they were very happy with their progress, with the exception of Polo. He would be on a much longer road to recovery, but his vital signs were steady and his wound was healing, so they were hoping to wean him off the ventilator soon.

Edmunds had spoken to the brigadier about the children, there was no need for most of them to be in the medical centre anymore. He had visited the local convent school on the outskirts of Belize City that had an attached orphanage. The nuns were willing to take in the children once they were suitably recovered. There were already other refugee children living there, and it would be better for them to be there with other children and learning in the school, rather than living in a medical centre on an armed forces base.

The wing commander came into the common room where Sisasi and Danny were sitting. "Corporal, do you mind if I have a few minutes with Sisasi in private?"

Danny stood up and said, "Of course not, sir," and left the room.

The wing commander smiled and sat down in one of the armchairs. "Hello, Sisasi, you and all the nine children in the general ward are now well enough to leave. In light of this, I've spoken to the local convent school, who operates an attached charitable orphanage, and they have agreed to accommodate all nine children. Unfortunately, they cannot stay here indefinitely in the medical centre, and neither can you. Also, when I spoke to them, they said that, due to the increase in the number of refugee children, they may be able offer you a temporary teaching post, subject to an interview. This would include a salary and accommodation, if that would be of interest to you?"

Sisasi was very happy with the suggestion and said, "Could I possibly meet with them and have a look around?"

"Absolutely, I'll arrange for a driver to take you there, probably tomorrow now. Thank you, Sisasi, it has been a pleasure looking after you." He said goodbye and headed back towards his office.

As soon as the wing commander left, Sisasi went off to find Danny. He was outside, playing football in the garden with the children, helping them to recover from the horrors of the battle, and enjoy being children once more.

She watched him for a moment, he made her smile. "Danny," she called and waved at him.

Danny stopped and looked over. "Hello, Sisasi, what's up?" he called back, leaving the children playing, and went to sit on the bench with her. He was getting closer to her every day, and she also felt closer to him. He deliberately sat right next to her, he was being cheeky, and she liked it.

"Well? What did the wing commander say?" Danny asked.

Sisasi smiled broadly and said, "I may have a temporary teaching job with accommodation at a convent school on the outskirts of Belize City. There's an attached orphanage at the convent, where the children can be moved to. I think it will be good for them, at least until I hear back from Father Michael. Wing Commander Edmunds is organising a visit for me tomorrow. Can you come too?"

Danny said, "Wow, that sounds amazing. I'll check, but I can't see any reason why I couldn't come along with you."

Sisasi felt relieved, she was getting used to having Danny around; he made her feel safe. She hugged him impulsively and said, "Thank you, Danny, it will be easier for me if you are there."

The next few days were a whirlwind of activity. Sisasi and Danny went to visit the convent school, which had around four hundred pupils, split into 12 classes. The orphanage building was an annexe attached to the boarder's accommodation and represented almost a fifth of the pupils there. The fees taken for the boarders and the day pupils covered most of the costs of running the orphanage and allowed them to offer some free tuition to the less fortunate local pupils.

The mother superior was a plump elderly woman, dressed in a long black tunic, with a white coif head covering that framed her kindly wrinkled face. She showed Sisasi, Danny and the children around the school and then took them to the dormitory, where each of the children was given a bed and a wardrobe, and then taken to the stores to pick up their black school uniforms and some spare clothing.

Sisasi got on well with the mother superior and accepted the temporary teaching position at the school. The post, teaching Spanish to the younger pupils came with a small salary and tied accommodation – a small one-bedroom wooden house, furnished, and perfect for her needs. It was only a ten-minute walk to the school, so she could easily have regular contact with the children from Colina.

Danny helped Sisasi to move into her new home and give it a good tidy up. He looked around at the wooden slatted walls and corrugated tin roof. *More of a shack than a house, but at least it is a roof over Sisasi's head*, he thought. They went shopping together, and Danny treated her to new bedding, pillows, and clothes. Danny was happy to pay for everything, but Sisasi insisted that she would pay him back when she got her salary. The next few days were all about getting Sisasi set up in her house and in her job. They had nearly forgotten about the awful time they had endured at the border, and were now focussed on sorting out the old ramshackle wooden house and making it into a comfortable home. Danny went around the outside of the house doing a few repairs to the wooden boards and oiling the squeaky hinges while Sisasi continued sorting out and cleaning up inside. They both worked hard all day, and the house was finally spruced up, comfortable and clean. The two of them decided to celebrate by going to a popular restaurant in the city, where they ate a lovely meal, washed down with a few glasses of white wine. They were both feeling a little bit tipsy as the taxi stopped outside Sisasi's house. She hadn't been this happy in quite a while; things seemed to be on the 'up and up'.

Danny smiled and gave Sisasi a big hug, saying, "Thank you, Sisasi, I've had such a lovely day, topped off by a wonderful evening." He reluctantly stopped hugging her and stepped back a little, and thought about how lucky he was to be able to spend so much time with her.

"Yes, Danny, I had a lovely evening too, and thank you for all your help today."

She looked back at him, and he held her gaze momentarily before pulling her gently back towards him until their bodies touched, and then he kissed her, "Goodnight, Sisasi."

She stood there waving from her front door as the taxi took him back to Airport Camp and thought, *I wish he had stayed*. Danny was thinking the same thing as the taxi drove away.

The next day, Danny called the convent school and left a message for Sisasi. Polo had come off the ventilator and was making good progress; breathing for himself and conscious, but still weak. He was missing Sisasi and all his school friends and feeling very confused. Sisasi was still in the classroom teaching, but the secretary said she would pass on his message.

Danny was also recovering very well. He had now moved out of the medical centre and been temporarily allocated a single-man room, normally reserved for more senior ranks, to aid his recovery. He looked around his new room. *Much nicer than living in that eighteen-man Nissen hut!* he thought. He picked up some extra clothes and his wash kit from the Nissen hut and invited Mark and Kevin over to see his room.

"So now I know why you got yourself shot!" Kevin joked, sweeping his arm around as if presenting the room. "Not too shabby, eh?"

They all laughed. "I agree, Kevin, definitely not too shabby," Danny said, nodding good-humouredly.

Sisasi arrived at Airport Camp later that day. The taxi pulled up at the gate, and Danny was standing there with a big smile on his face, obviously very happy to see her. He signed her in at the guardroom, and they walked towards the medical centre. Sisasi was chatting away excitedly about her day and waving her arms around expressively. Danny was delighted to see her so happy and animated; he was hooked on her every word.

When they arrived at the medical centre, Polo was propped up in his bed and was very happy to see Sisasi, his eyes lighting up brightly. When he spoke, it was still painful, and he could only speak in a hoarse whisper. His throat was still dry and sore from being intubated and on the ventilator for so many days.

Sisasi touched his shoulder and spoke softly to him, "I'm so happy to see you are awake and improving, Polo, my strong little soldier." Her voice was very soothing, and he felt comforted. She explained where she and the rest of the children were and that there would be a place for him once he was well enough to leave the medical centre. Danny watched her as she talked and was filled with admiration. They stayed there with Polo until he fell asleep and then walked back to the gate to get a taxi.

A row of taxis waited for fares outside the Airport Camp gate. Danny and Sisasi opened the rear doors of the front taxi. "Belize City, please," Danny said.

"Yes, sir," the driver replied, leaning forward and switching his meter on.

Danny lifted his left arm up and rested it across Sisasi's shoulders, gently pulling her towards him. She enjoyed being close to him and leaned in closer, resting her head on his chest, feeling absolutely safe and at ease. Danny felt very pleased that Sisasi wanted to spend more time with him.

As they neared the city, Danny gave the driver directions to Sisasi's house. When they arrived, they paid the driver and went into her house, which was looking cleaner, and feeling more like a home. They sat on the old two-seater sofa, playing card games on the small wooden side table, sipping rum and talking until the early hours. The time he spent with her was never enough, they had become more than just good friends, and he loved being close to her. He found the smell of her hair intoxicating, and the way she smiled could lift a room full of people. Sisasi was always flamboyant, her arms had a life of their own when she was telling a story, and he realised how special she was becoming to him. Just being in the same room with her made him feel contented.

"I'd better get a taxi back to base," Danny said unenthusiastically.

Sisasi leaned towards him and asked flirtatiously, "Why don't you just sleep here tonight?"

Danny was thrilled, "I suppose I could get a taxi back in the morning..." he replied ecstatically and then kissed her passionately. Her lips were soft, warm and inviting, and he tenderly pulled her up off the sofa and towards the bedroom.

CHAPTER 16. THE CHARGES

Captain Crawley of the military police presented the evidence and potential charges to Brigadier Davies. There was pressure coming from the top brass in London to set an example by pressing charges against Corporal Sinclaire.

"Sir, I've shared the evidence with the RAF prosecuting authority, who have deemed that there are potentially four breaches of military law, and therefore we should proceed with the court martial of Corporal Sinclaire."

Brigadier Davies felt exasperated that it was going to be taken so far, "Are you serious? If we court martial Corporal Sinclaire, we could have a bloody mutiny on our hands. For God's sake, Crawley! Everyone agrees that he's a hero for saving that woman and those children!"

Captain Crawley looked perplexed. "Not everyone agrees, sir. The actions taken by Sinclaire have triggered accusations of interference by British forces in Guatemala's internal affairs. This is coming from both the Guatemalan foreign ministry and the US Embassy in London. As you know, the US are providing weapons and training to their army to enable them to eradicate the Cuban-backed communist rebels in their country. The prosecuting authority are stating that we do have sufficient evidence to court martial Sinclaire for four offences."

Brigadier Davies sat forward in his chair. "That's bloody ridiculous, Crawley! What are these 'so-called' four offences then?"

The captain went on, "The first charge is that he assisted an enemy attack on Guatemalan soldiers by supporting the communist rebels. The second charge is misconduct on operations – unnecessarily abandoning Zulu hide without a reasonable excuse, thereby leaving the landing site undefended. The third charge is that with intent or recklessness, he failed to carry out the planned operations assigned to him, put the lives of his own team at risk, and caused the death of at least two Guatemalan soldiers. The fourth charge is that he contravened standing orders. It clearly states in our orders that British forces are not allowed to enter no man's land. These four charges carry a maximum punishment of life imprisonment, sir."

Brigadier Davies looked aggravated. "Unbelievable! It's an absolute travesty!" he muttered angrily.

Captain Crawley could see that the brigadier was angry. "Sir, I'm not saying this is at all fair to Corporal

Sinclaire, but the order to carry out this court martial is coming right from the top. I've just collected and presented the evidence, as required by the law."

Brigadier Davies realised that Crawley was looking stressed. "Okay, Captain Crawley, I understand that we are all in a difficult position, tell me what you have to do. What's going to happen next?"

"We must first charge him, and explain the charges to him. At this point, he is still considered innocent until the court martial takes place and determines whether he is innocent or guilty of any of the charges. The trial will require a presiding officer to be brought over from the UK, or potentially, you could be the presiding officer, but only if you can get the major general's approval. We will also have to bring over a military prosecutor and a defence lawyer from the UK. These will be commissioned officers, who are qualified lawyers, and familiar with military law. Once charged, I recommend that Sinclaire is confined to Airport Camp until the court martial is completed."

The brigadier thought for a moment. "Don't charge him yet, not until we've identified the prosecution and the defence lawyers. There's no point in confining him to camp until the court martial is able to proceed," he responded.

"Understood, sir. I'll get back to you as soon as I have more information," Captain Crawley agreed.

Danny's wounds were healing nicely, and the stitches had been removed. He sat on the wooden steps of Sisasi's house, watching the land crabs running around in the gutter. He was in a world of his own when Sisasi touched him on the shoulder and handed him a mug of tea.

"Ah, thanks, darling," Danny said with a smile on his face. "I was thinking about us possibly going away for a weekend, maybe to Caye Caulker. What do you think?"

Sisasi sat down on the step next to Danny and contemplated the idea of getting away from the city. "That sounds like a lovely idea, Danny; how will we get there? Where will we stay?"

"Leave all that to me. I'll sort out all the details, just pack enough clothes for the weekend," he said.

The next day, Danny went to the local travel agent and booked a double room at the Waterfront Hotel in Caye Caulker, which included a private speedboat transfer. On Friday afternoon, they got into a taxi and headed to their transfer jetty in Belize harbour. The boat was waiting for them, and within a few minutes, they were skipping across the waves towards Caye Caulker. Every now and again, sea spray would blow into the boat, and they both howled with laughter. It was a very exciting, hour-long thrill ride. The speedboat driver had been at full power for most of the journey, but as they got closer to the island, he throttled right back, slowing the boat down, before finally coming alongside the wooden jetty outside their hotel and tying the boat up.

They both climbed up and out of the speedboat onto the hotel's private pier and were helped by a member of the hotel staff. He welcomed them to their beautiful island and escorted them to the check-in desk while one of the hotel porters carried their bags.

The young receptionist was very welcoming, "Hello, sir, madam. I would like to welcome you both to Caye Caulker with a complimentary cocktail. Would you both like a pina colada while we sort out the paperwork?"

Danny smiled and agreed, "Yes please, two Pina Coladas sounds great."

The young receptionist continued, "And the names you are booked under please?"

"We have one room booked under my name – Danny Sinclaire," he replied.

"We've given you a sea view room, as you requested, sir, overlooking the jetty. You will be able to watch the boats coming and going. If you are interested, we have a barbecue on the beach later?"

"That sounds nice; how much?" Danny said.

"Ten dollars each, including a free cocktail," she replied.

Danny agreed, handing over the 20 dollars in cash.

"Seven o'clock next to the pier, you can't miss it," she said.

They took the key to their room and walked upstairs and along the corridor. Danny put the key in the lock and opened the door. Sisasi had never been in a hotel room and walked around like an excited child discovering everything for the first time. "There's a bathroom," she exclaimed. "Oh wow, we have a balcony!" She threw herself onto the bed and laughed excitedly. "The bed is so soft, Danny."

Danny was laughing too and lay next to her on the bed. They were both delighted to be there and rolled towards each other, wrapping themselves in a happy holiday embrace. Danny undressed her and marvelled at her smooth, silky skin; he thought she was like a living work of art. They made love all afternoon, and it felt like they were the only people on the island. It was paradise.

Eventually they got up and showered together, then headed downstairs to the bar.

The receptionist was now the barmaid. "Hello again, what can I get you two lovebirds?"

Danny thought *lovebirds?* and wondered how soundproof the wooden walls were. He smiled at the barmaid. "Two rum and cokes, please," he said, expanding his smile, hoping to get generous measures of rum. He was not disappointed, she was very liberal with the rum, and even before the barbecue had started, they were already starting to feel the effects of it.

They spent the evening marvelling over the barbecued food, drinking more rum, and enjoying the company of the hotel staff and the other guests. Eventually they found out, while stood around the blazing fire on the beach, that the receptionist who had booked them in was also the owner.

At the end of the evening, Sisasi said to her in a slightly slurred voice, "You are a lovely lady, and we've had a wonderful evening, thank you very much," and gave her a big hug.

"Time for bed, I think," Danny said, smiling at the hotel owner.

The next day, they both awoke with a slight hangover, got dressed and made their way downstairs. The breakfast waitress showed them to a table and pointed out the coffee area; a large stainless-steel urn was filled to the brim with very strong, very hot, black coffee. Danny pulled on the tap, filling the two mugs, and heard a voice from behind him saying, "That'll help with your hangover!" He turned to look, it was the hotel owner, she laughed and gave Danny a wave. Danny laughed and waved back at her. Sisasi looked annoyed and jealous; she didn't like Danny waving at the other woman. She moved closer towards him and put her arm around his waist as if to say, *He's mine!*

Danny could see the jealous expression on Sisasi's face and whispered into her ear, "Don't worry, not my type, I only have eyes for you." He smiled and pulled her even closer.

Danny hired some snorkelling gear from the hotel, and they walked out onto the beach where he showed Sisasi how to use the mask and snorkel. He then took his T-shirt off, revealing his lean, muscular physique and the recent battle scars that were still very red and angry looking. He could see other people on the beach staring and felt a little self-conscious until Sisasi, very gently, ran her fingertips over them. "Don't worry, Danny, you are beautiful." She pulled on his arm, and they walked into the warm shallow water to try out the snorkelling gear. The whole weekend was perfect, and in the speedboat on the way back to Belize City, they looked back at the island, wishing they were still there.

The following day, Danny smiled and waved goodbye from his taxi as he headed back to Airport Camp, and Sisasi waved back just before walking into work at the school. She had never been as happy as she was at this very moment. She felt completely elated, realising that she was completely smitten with Danny.

He arrived at Airport Camp and went for his check-up with Wing Commander Edmunds at the camp medical centre. Edmunds examined him and said, "Your wounds are healing very nicely, Danny. You can go back to work this week but only doing light duties." He gave him a medical chit, assigning him one month of light duties. Danny spent the next day helping out in the office. He found that doing paperwork was tedious and that administration was definitely not a strength of his.

He kept looking at the clock, waiting impatiently for five o'clock to come around, so he could get a taxi back to Sisasi's house.

At four thirty that afternoon, Captain Crawley phoned the engineering office. The flight sergeant called over to Danny, "Pick up the extension, Danny; it's for you."

"Hello, Corporal Sinclaire. It's Captain Crawley here, military police. I need you to come to my office tomorrow morning at 9am."

"Yes, sir. Can I ask what it is about?" Danny sounded confused.

"I'll explain when I see you in the morning, Corporal."

"Okay, sir, I'll be there at nine."

Danny wondered what was going on. *Shit, I've probably been seen leaving Airport Camp alone.* In Airport Camp's standing orders, it stated that *'no one can leave camp alone, groups of two as a minimum'*. He was sure that this must be the issue, but there was also a midnight curfew which he had been ignoring recently. *It wasn't doing any harm staying at Sisasi's*, he thought to himself. He had now got used to staying overnight with her. He enjoyed having her fall asleep in his arms and was concerned that it might have to stop.

He still got the taxi outside the camp gates that evening. *In for a penny, in for a pound*! he decided.

He arrived at Sisasi's house and could smell seafood cooking on the stove. He walked in. "Hello, gorgeous, where's my kiss?"

She was happy to see him and came running over, wrapping her arms around him, and repeating his words back to him, "Hello, gorgeous, here's your kiss."

She kissed him firmly on the lips and then said, "I'm making us some food, a crayfish salad with some boiled potatoes."

"Excellent, sounds very tasty," Danny replied.

"I think you should know that I may have a slight problem at work. I have to go to see the military police captain tomorrow morning. I think I may be in a bit of trouble for leaving camp alone, but I don't know for sure if that is the reason, the captain wouldn't say over the phone. It may be just another follow up about the battle at Zulu hide, I'm not sure."

Sisasi looked concerned. "What if they won't let you come here on your own again? I like you coming here on your own."

"So do I, darling. I love being here with you, just the two of us. I'm sure we can sort it all out somehow," Danny replied.

The next morning Danny walked into the military police office and booked in at the desk. He was then taken through the whitewashed police building, to Captain Crawley's office, by the corporal that had booked him in.

A fan was whirring slowly on the ceiling, Danny stood to attention and saluted the captain.

Captain Crawley pointed at the seat in front of his desk and said, "Corporal Sinclaire, please have a seat." Danny sat down and noticed a sergeant from the military police had joined them and had sat down on a seat against the wall holding a notepad and pen. The captain went on, "The sergeant is here to make notes and also act as a witness to our discussion."

"Okay, sir," Danny replied, now feeling even more concerned.

"As you know, Corporal Sinclaire, we have been conducting a thorough investigation into the incident that happened at Zulu hide. You may not realise this, but what you and your team did there has resulted in international repercussions, with complaints from both the Guatemalan foreign ministry and US foreign ministry that you have interfered with the legitimate pursuit of communist rebels and that, by your actions, you aided their subsequent escape."

Danny interjected, "But, Captain Crawley, I only acted in the interest of saving a group of unarmed civilians. My understanding of the Geneva Convention is that it is illegal for military personnel to attack unarmed civilians. Surely, that needs to be taken into consideration?"

"That may be the case, Corporal, but we have shared all our witness statements and photographic evidence with the RAF prosecuting authority in the UK, who have deemed that there is sufficient evidence to prosecute you for four breaches of military law."

"Sir, really? Four! What breaches?" Danny sounded completely shocked.

"Firstly, that you assisted an enemy, namely the communist rebels, to escape. Secondly, misconduct on operations by abandoning Zulu hide without having orders to do so. Leaving your post, and therefore leaving the site undefended. Thirdly, with intent or recklessness, you failed to carry out the planned operations and put the lives of you and your team at risk and also caused the death of at least two Guatemalan soldiers. Fourthly, and last, you contravened standing orders. It clearly states within our standing orders, *'not to enter no man's land'*. I also need to tell you that if you are found guilty by the board, these charges can carry a maximum punishment of life imprisonment."

Danny couldn't quite believe what he was hearing. *How can this be happening after everything I did?* he thought.

Captain Crawley went on, "I need to ask you how you intend to plead to each of the four charges?"

"This is ridiculous, sir! I'm not guilty of any of these charges!" Danny responded angrily.

"Sergeant, please note that the defendant pleads not guilty to all four counts," Captain Crawley said.

The police sergeant replied, "All done, sir."

Captain Crawley addressed Danny again, "Corporal Sinclaire, you are suspended from work and confined to camp until your court martial, which is scheduled to start two weeks from today. The major general has given approval for Brigadier Davies to act as the presiding officer, and we have assigned a board of four commissioned officers and three senior non-commissioned officers. The court martial board members' role will be to act as the jury. Their decision will be made by a simple majority. If they acquit you, you will be free to leave and carry on with your work and life as normal. If they find you guilty, you will be sentenced in accordance with military laws and procedures and returned to the UK to serve your sentence. Our commanding officer, Brigadier Davies, will act as judge and will have powers of punishment. This has been approved by the major general. We have arranged for a lawyer to defend you; she will be arriving tomorrow. Do you have any questions?"

"Yes, sir, although I'm confined to camp, am I allowed any visitors?"

"You are allowed visitors, Corporal, but make sure they're booked in at the guardroom and leave before the midnight curfew."

"What about the other two guys in my team, Mark and Kevin. Have they been charged too?"

"No charges are being pressed against them. They were just following your orders, so these four charges are only against you."

"I didn't do anything wrong either, sir. I'm not guilty," Danny protested.

Captain Crawley replied, "That is for the board to decide, Corporal. You can leave now and I'll be in touch."

Danny left Captain Crawley's office in disbelief, it was still only 11 in the morning; he needed to get someone to speak to Sisasi.

He called the office where Mark and Kevin were working in the engineering flight. When he relayed the conversation to them, they were both shocked and angry but also a little relieved about not having to go through this themselves. "Guys, I need someone to collect Sisasi and bring her here tonight so I can explain what's happening," Danny said.

Kevin and Mark agreed to collect Sisasi, and after finishing work, they both jumped into a taxi and headed over to Sisasi's house. Sisasi was excited to see the taxi pulling up, thinking Danny had arrived, but instead of Danny getting out, it was Mark and Kevin.

She recognised them both and immediately felt stressed, and thought, *What has happened to Danny?*

Mark and Kevin briefly explained to Sisasi why Danny had been confined to camp. They were here to take her back to Airport Camp to see Danny if she was able to go.

"Of course I'm coming!" she said without hesitation and got into the taxi with Mark and Kevin.

CHAPTER 17. THE BRIEF ARRIVES

Danny was waiting at the guardroom as the taxi pulled up. Mark, Kevin and Sisasi all got out, and Danny waved at them from the other side of the gate. They waved back, with Sisasi touching her lips and blowing him a kiss. "Thanks, guys; let me buy you both a beer." They both turned down Danny's polite offer, knowing that he really wanted to update Sisasi about what was going on.

"I think I'll have that beer, but another time, Danny," Kevin said, with a slightly raised eyebrow.

Mark agreed, "I'll do the same. Maybe we'll see you in the bar later," and winked at Danny.

Danny and Sisasi called in at the medical centre to visit Polo. There were a few Spanish children's books sitting on his bedside table. Polo was still recovering from his injury, his chest was completely wrapped in bandages, but he was now able to be propped up and able to read a book. When he saw them both walk in, a beaming smile appeared across his face. He still felt a lot of pain with every single breath, but he said in a quiet voice, "Hello, Miss Sasi."

"Hello, my little soldier." She touched him sympathetically on the shoulder. He looked very gaunt and was still weak. Danny and Sisasi stayed with Polo, chatting about how all the other children were doing at the school and then their weekend trip to Caye Caulker. After about an hour, Polo started drifting off to sleep, so they said their goodbyes and left him to rest.

They walked down the road to the Palms restaurant. It was just after seven in the evening, and the restaurant was quiet. They got a table in the corner, and Danny explained that the military police had charged him with four offences and that the defence and prosecution lawyers had been appointed for his court martial.

Sisasi could not believe that Danny was being treated this way and asked indignantly, "Could they actually find you guilty of a crime? You saved my life and the lives of 10 children. How is that a crime? You are a hero, everyone knows that, and so are Mark and Kevin!"

"I know it sounds unfair, but the police are insisting that I broke international military laws by intervening," Danny replied.

"What laws?" Sisasi asked angrily.

"They're accusing me of assisting the communist rebels to escape, abandoning my post, recklessly putting the lives of my team at risk, killing two Guatemalan soldiers, and also contravening standing orders by entering no man's land on the border. These are very serious charges, Sisasi," Danny replied.

They talked all evening about the possible consequences, the unfairness, and what they could say to counter the charges until Danny eventually had to walk Sisasi back to the gate just before midnight and watch her leave in a taxi.

The next day, Danny met his defence lawyer, Squadron Leader Ruth Lockwood, in her temporary office at the headquarters building. Danny had been feeling very worried about the court martial; he knew that if he was found guilty, he could go to jail for a very long time. He walked down the corridor and knocked on the open office door. The squadron leader was sat at her desk with a pile of evidence folders.

She looked up and smiled, "Come in, Corporal Sinclaire, close the door behind you."

He entered the room, stood to attention and saluted, saying, "Ma'am."

She said, "Thank you, Corporal, please have a seat."

Danny sat down, and Squadron Leader Lockwood continued, "We are going to spend a lot of time together, so, if you don't mind, while we are on our own, you can call me Ruth, and I'll call you Danny. Is that okay with you?"

"Yes, ma'am, I mean Ruth, that is fine."

Ruth wanted to put Danny at ease. She had spent the last two weeks going through the evidence and believed that the case was not cut and dried, but a *'not guilty'* plea could be argued based on the witness statements she had read.

"So, Danny, let's work through all the charges against you one by one. If I am going to get an acquittal on each of the four charges against you, we need to put enough doubts into the minds of the seven members of the board, effectively the jury, for them to agree that you are innocent. I'll describe the charges against you and then explain a summary of my legal arguments against those charges. If you have any questions or suggestions, we can work through them over the next few days.

"Charge number one, you assisted an enemy, namely the communist rebels. According to all the transcripts, you were already leaving no man's land when the communist rebels arrived. We have reliable witnesses, Mark, Kevin, and Sisasi, that will positively testify that you were already exiting no man's land when the rebels opened fire on the Guatemalan army and therefore could not be assisting them."

"I didn't know they were there at all, let alone that they were communist rebels," Danny defended himself.

"I know, Danny, I've read all the witness statements. Let me explain the charges, and then we can develop our defence arguments afterwards."

"Charge number two, misconduct on operations by abandoning Zulu hide without any orders to do so, thereby leaving your post and the site undefended. I will argue that this site is often undefended, most of the time in fact, as it is an unmanned and infrequently used hide. The fact that you had no orders to leave is a red herring, as you never have orders to leave those hides. You are the person in charge, and whichever hide you are at, you make all the decisions and set the work schedule on behalf of your team, including when to arrive and when to leave.

"Charge number three, it says, with intent or recklessness, you failed to carry out the planned operations, and put the lives of you and your team at risk, and caused the death of at least two Guatemalan soldiers. I will argue that you did put your own life at risk, and the lives of your colleagues, but not in an illegal way, according to international military laws. You were the non-commissioned officer in charge, and as such, made decisions that were not reckless, but in fact necessary to save civilian lives. All your decisions were legal, in accordance with the humanitarian laws of the Geneva Convention. You were presented with a situation which left you with no choice but to help these civilians evade an illegal attack from another country's armed forces.

"Charge number four, you contravened standing orders. It clearly states within standing orders that

British forces are not allowed to enter no man's land. I will argue that you took proportionate action to save the lives of civilians, and the only way to do this was to enter no man's land. You were seeking to protect people who were not communist rebels and were not taking part in the rebel hostilities, and in fact, were also unarmed.

"As you know, Danny, if the board finds you guilty, these charges can carry a maximum punishment of life imprisonment. I believe we have a strong case for acquittal, and I will argue that all these charges are completely unjustified."

Danny had been listening very carefully. When she stopped explaining the charges and the counter-arguments, he said, "Thank you, Ruth, that makes me feel like we have a chance of winning, and there may be light at the end of the tunnel."

* * *

Fabio had made his way across the border alone, leaving his comrades to return to their rebel camp. He wanted to find his sister, to listen to her version of what had happened in Colina and understand what the British troops were going to do with her and the children. So many unanswered questions.

There was a hotel in Belize City called the Victoria Hotel. It was owned by a slightly unscrupulous Mexican man called Rodrigues. He sympathised with the Cuban-backed rebels in Guatemala and was receiving Cuban funding to help hide escaping rebels until they could find a way back for them. The Victoria Hotel was used as a refuge for guests who did not ask questions of each other and did not want to answer questions; they all kept themselves to themselves. That area of Belize City where the hotel was located was known for being laissez-faire. Drugs, gambling, and prostitution were rife, and the illicit goings-on were ignored by the local police, who were paid handsomely for turning a blind eye. After 10 days of travel, Fabio finally arrived in Belize City and made his way to the Victoria Hotel, a large wooden and slightly dilapidated building on King George's Street; the most dangerous street of Belize City.

There was a community of Guatemalan refugees living near King George's Street, most of them living along the side roads, in simple wooden houses with corrugated tin roofs. It was a place of poverty and depredation, which was known as 'Mugger's Alley' by the locals and by the British forces. It was the most dangerous place in the city, where drug dealing, fencing of stolen goods, and other illegal activities were carried out with impunity in the open street. There were regular fights, muggings, and even killings taking place. King George's Street was a complete no-go area for both the police and the British forces, so a perfect place for criminals, or a communist rebel, to hide out. The local thugs had learnt, over time, not to target anyone staying at the Victoria Hotel. When it had happened in the past, the culprit had usually been found face down in the local river.

The Victoria Hotel had a fearsome reputation to uphold, a highly notorious place, whose guests were rarely seen and best avoided. When they did come out, they tended to do so in the evening and move in the shadows. A couple of surly-looking men were guarding the entrance door, with large machetes hanging by their sides.

Fabio walked towards the entrance door, "Can we help you, sir?" they said to him.

He replied, "I'm a friend of Rodrigues," and then repeated it in Spanish.

The two men stepped apart and opened the doors for him to enter the hotel.

Fabio walked past them into the hotel lobby. The reception desk was empty, and although it was still light outside, all the window shutters were closed. Upon first entering the building, it looked completely dark, but as his eyes adjusted to the dim light inside, he could see shadowy figures at the tables, some drinking beer, some eating, and others playing cards. They stopped to look at him, "Hey, you! come over here!" a voice called out from the centre of the saloon area. "Over here."

The man who had called to him was sitting with two other suspicious-looking men. All three of them carried large machetes attached to their belts with leather scabbards.

The man asked, "Who are you, and why have you come knocking on my door?"

Fabio walked up to the table and introduced himself. "Hello, sir, my name is Fabio. I've come from Guatemala, and I was assured I could find assistance from a man called Rodrigues at this hotel, and it would be somewhere safe for me to stay."

"Hello, Fabio, I am Rodrigues and the owner of this hotel. What assistance do you need?"

Fabio was tired from his journey; he pulled a chair out and sat down, saying, "I'm here searching for survivors from my village, Colina, in Guatemala. My sister and a group of children were recently picked up by a British Puma helicopter while we were trying to rescue them near the Belize border, just north of San Ignacio."

Rodrigues said, "Ah, so she's your sister. Yes, we've heard about the rescue. The British forces have been very animated when talking about it in the bars around the city. Please tell me more, but first, would you like a beer, food, or anything else?"

Fabio replied, "Thanks, a beer please, that'll do for now," then carried on with, "I was there, on the border, just before the helicopter arrived. We opened fire on the soldiers that were trying to kill my sister."

Fabio went on to explain how his village, and other villages, had been burned to the ground, and how most of the people had simply vanished, and how he had tracked the soldiers and his sister to the border.

As he spoke, the other men listened intently, they could hear the raw emotion in his voice. Rodrigues agreed to help and quickly found out that Sisasi was now working as a teacher for the local convent school. He gave Fabio her address, and that evening, Fabio left the Victoria Hotel and got a taxi to Sisasi's house.

As he climbed out of the taxi, he could see an oil lamp was glowing brightly through an open window. It was attracting moths and other insects that were crashing into the fly screen on the window. He knocked on the door and waited. Sisasi wasn't expecting anyone and was getting ready to take a taxi to Airport Camp. Danny was expecting to see her this evening.

She walked to the door, opened it, and initially didn't recognise Fabio. He had grown a thick black beard, which covered up a lot of his features, and he looked taller and broader, "Hello, Sisasi, it's me, Fabio," he said. As soon as he spoke, she knew it was him.

Sisasi instantly flung her arms around him, hugging him and crying with joy and relief. She had not seen her brother for over two years and had thought she may never see him again.

"Fabio, is it really you?" she exclaimed as she leaned back to look at his face. "What are you doing here? How did you find me? Come in, come in!"

He walked through the door, and Sisasi was not able to take her eyes off him. "Where have you been for the last two and a half years, and how did you find me here? And what are those awful clothes you are wearing?" she said excitedly. He was wearing a short-sleeved black vest, with black trousers and black army boots.

"You look like you are going to a funeral dressed all in black," she commented.

Fabio laughed and said, "Better for hiding in the shadows, sister. I'll tell you everything, but no one can know what I'm about to tell you. You must promise to keep it a secret."

"I promise," Sisasi said.

"Coffee, Fabio?" She pointed at the coffee pot on the stove.

"Yes, please, two sugars with milk." Sisasi poured two coffees and then sat down.

Fabio went on to explain that he had joined the rebel forces two years earlier. He had been recruited while working at the local farm to the south of Colina and was then taken to the rebel training camp in Cuba. That was where they trained him to be a soldier, learning how to use weapons, navigate, and lead an armed ambush.

Sisasi was very concerned for her brother, the conversation had become very serious and scared her. "Fabio, you must not go back, they will kill you. Stay here with me."

He replied, "I've come here to find you, and to take you home, Sisasi. We have a well-defended rebel camp in the north, near the Mexican border, where you will be safe. You and all the children can come back with me. We'll all be safer there."

Sisasi said, unenthusiastically, "Fabio, I'm already safe here. The children from Colina are also safe in the orphanage at the convent. We all need me to stay here for now, at least until the troubles settle down at home. Also, Polo is still recovering at the British medical centre, and he needs me to stay here. I've also met a very special man called Danny. He is kind, funny, and he saved our lives when we crossed the border."

Fabio didn't like his sister being with a man from the British forces and said, "You cannot trust him! The British are part of the oppressive western regime killing our people. I order you to stop seeing him immediately!"

Sisasi was very annoyed by her older brother and said, "Order me! How dare you! I'm an educated, grown-up woman, and I'll do whatever I want to! You can't order me to do anything!"

Fabio knew that his sister could be very forthright when she wanted to be and replied, "You don't understand, Sisasi. You were wrong about it being the British that saved you. You didn't know it, but my comrades and I actually saved all of your lives. We attacked the soldiers coming after you, slowing them down, then moved around them to the south and stopped the soldiers from firing at you. We were attacking them from the south, and drawing their fire towards us, just as you escaped across the border. If it wasn't for my comrades and I, you, your British soldier friend, and all the children would probably be dead!"

Sisasi's mouth dropped open in shock. She was astonished to hear that he had been there at the border, although she did remember that some men had opened fire from the south. Fabio and Sisasi went over each other's movements, and it became clear to Sisasi that both her brother and Danny had helped to save her life and the lives of the children. Nevertheless, she could not go back to Guatemala, not yet, it was still far too dangerous.

CHAPTER 18. AN UNEXPECTED GUEST

Danny had gone down to the front gate to meet Sisasi at seven, just as they had agreed, and he had waited from seven until eight, but she didn't turn up. Danny was getting worried; he had to know if she was safe, and needed to find a way to get in contact with her. His only option was to see if Mark and Kevin would take a taxi to her house again and try to find out why she hadn't turned up. Danny walked over to their Nissen hut. They weren't in, so he went over to the bar, and thankfully, they were there.

Danny walked up to them, "Hi guys, I know this is a bit cheeky of me, but Sisasi was supposed to meet me at seven, and she hasn't turned up. If I pick up the tab, would you two mind getting a taxi to her house to see if she is okay and try to find out why she hasn't turned up tonight? I'd go myself, but I can't risk getting into any more trouble."

Kevin said in a tongue-in-cheek, sarcastic voice, "You are a pain in the arse, Danny, take, take, take! Only joking, of course we will. Come on, Mark."

"No probs, Danny, we'll find her for you, your personal cupid service!" Mark replied.

Danny replied with a smile on his face, "Yeah, Mark! Now get going."

They both went down to the front gate, signed out, and then jumped into a taxi. After 20 minutes, the taxi pulled up outside Sisasi's house. Fabio looked out of the window and asked, "Are you expecting visitors tonight?"

"No, Fabio, but I was supposed to be getting a taxi this evening and meeting Danny at Airport Camp around seven."

She walked over to the window and looked out. Two men were getting out, she recognised them immediately and said to Fabio, "It's Mark and Kevin; they're friends of Danny's."

"They can't know I'm here; get rid of them," Fabio said.

She replied, "Go into the bedroom, I'll call you when they have gone."

Mark had already spotted a man through the window when they were pulling up outside.

Kevin said to the taxi driver, "We won't be long, please can you wait here a few minutes?"

The driver nodded and said, "Yes, sir, that's fine."

Kevin and Mark walked up to the door, and Sisasi was already standing there, "Hello, you two, nice to see you. What are you doing here?"

"Danny asked us to come and make sure you were okay," Mark responded.

He looked through the doorway and could see two coffee cups on the table in front of the sofa. "Are you okay, Sisasi? Is someone else here? Danny was expecting to meet you at the gate at seven."

Sisasi looked at her watch and said, "Oh my God, I must have fallen asleep after work and didn't realise what the time was! No, there's no one else here. Please can you tell Danny I am fine, and I'm sorry. It's too late to come over now, so I'll see him at seven tomorrow night instead. Please can you say sorry for me."

"Are you sure? You're welcome to come back with us and share our taxi, I don't think Danny will think it is too late." Mark said.

Sisasi replied, "Not tonight, Mark, I also have a headache, so I think it's better that I have a rest this evening."

Mark and Kevin said goodbye and got back into the taxi, "Back to camp, please, driver," Kevin said. Mark looked at Kevin and said under his breath, "I think there was someone else in there, Kev. When we pulled up, I'm sure I saw a man looking through the fly screen out of the lounge window; difficult to see properly because of the fly screen, but I'm sure that she had a man in the house with her."

Kevin nodded in agreement, as Mark continued whispering, "There were two cups on the table near the sofa too, and I thought she was acting suspiciously, didn't you?"

"Yeah, I saw the coffee cups too, and she was acting strangely. It is not like her to forget to visit Danny, I thought they were both very loved up. I hope she's not seeing another man. Danny has enough going on, the last thing he needs is Sisasi messing with his head. He will be gutted!" Kevin frowned and folded his arms.

They arrived back at camp and went straight to the NAAFI bar, where Danny was waiting patiently. He stood up as they walked in and said anxiously, "Did you find her?"

They both responded, "Yes," and then Mark went on, "she said she fell asleep and didn't realise what the time was. We asked her if she wanted to come back with us in the taxi, but she said she had a headache and to tell you that she will see you tomorrow, at the usual time, seven o'clock at the gate."

Danny could tell that something was not quite right, "Really, that seems very odd, was that all?"

Mark and Kevin looked at each other, and then Mark said, "You've got a lot on your plate already, Danny, and I'm not one hundred per cent sure, but I thought I saw a man at the window when we arrived. We didn't go into the house and couldn't see anyone from the door, but there were two cups on the table in the lounge. He could have been hiding somewhere;

sorry, mate, I'm not trying to cast aspersions on Sisasi, but I'm just telling you what we saw."

Danny looked confused and upset. "A man, what man?"

"Like we said, by the time we got to the door, he had disappeared, and Sisasi told us that she was on her own. Maybe I was mistaken." Mark said.

"Okay, guys. Well, at least I know she is safe at home, but I don't like the idea that she may have another man in her house," Danny said dejectedly.

The next morning, Danny was meeting Squadron Leader Lockwood, his defence lawyer. He walked into her office, closed the door, and sat down in front of her desk, "Morning, Danny," she said.

"Morning, Ruth," he said miserably.

"Are you alright?" she sounded concerned.

"Yes, I'm fine, thanks," Danny said despondently.

Ruth assumed he was worrying about the court martial. "You must remain positive, Danny, you don't know what the outcome will be, but we definitely have a strong case to refute all four charges."

Danny pulled himself together. "Yes, that's because they're trumped-up charges!"

They carried on discussing the court martial, but Danny's mind kept wandering back to Sisasi and whether or not she had been with another man the night before. He felt let down, jealous, and angry, but had no real evidence; other than what Mark and Kevin had said about seeing a man in the window. Sisasi knew what he was going through, and yet said she fell asleep; none of it made any sense to him.

That evening, Danny got to the gate at ten to seven and waited impatiently. He felt agitated as he watched the taxis come and go and felt slightly less sure that she would turn up, but at seven o'clock, Sisasi climbed out of a taxi, smiling and waving. Danny smiled and waved back, but it felt forced, he wasn't feeling the same way about her; something had changed. She signed in at the gate, and they hugged, kissed as usual, and then walked towards the Palms restaurant, stopping on the way to visit Polo again. He was getting stronger every day. When they got into the restaurant, they both knew there was tension between them, something was wrong, and Danny said, "Sisasi, I was upset you never came to see me last night, and I still feel upset. Why didn't you come?"

Fabio had made it clear to Sisasi that he was not to be discussed, so she stuck to her headache story. "I had a headache and fell asleep, and I only woke up just before Mark and Kevin arrived. I had no idea what the time was." She didn't like lying to Danny, but she needed to keep her promise to her brother. Danny snapped immediately back at her, "So there was no other man there then? Mark said he thought he had seen a man in the window!"

She didn't realise that Fabio had been spotted in the window, and she certainly didn't want Danny thinking there might be someone else, "I'm sorry, Danny. I'll tell you the truth, but I made a promise not to tell anyone, so if I tell you, you must promise not to tell anyone else. Do you promise?"

"I don't know what you are going to say, but I promise not to tell anyone, Sisasi, just put me out of my misery. Is there another man?"

Sisasi felt relieved to not have to lie to Danny anymore and returned to her normal self, telling Danny, "My brother Fabio turned up last night; he has been searching for me. I haven't seen him for over two years, that's why I couldn't come last night. Fabio made me promise not to tell anyone he is here, staying at a hotel somewhere in the city. The manager of the hotel found out where I was living and gave him my address." She communicated her conversation with Fabio from the previous evening, which left Danny wishing that he had never asked. He now had hold of important intelligence about a communist rebel leader staying in the city, and he was Sisasi's brother. It was a complete nightmare scenario.

The way Sisasi spoke about Fabio made Danny question; who were the bad guys, and who were the good guys? All the briefings he had attended in the UK and at Airport Camp were about how Cuban-backed communist rebels were waging an illegal war. They were ambushing and murdering Guatemalan soldiers and dealing in drugs. It was his duty to report this intelligence to the military police, but this man, Fabio, and his communist rebel group had helped to save their lives. It was a conundrum that Danny didn't want to contemplate at that moment in time.

At the border, Danny hadn't known it was Sisasi's brother that had opened fire from the south, but now he did, it made everything more complicated. It meant that he and his men had been helped to escape by a communist rebel cell. Danny had a set of black and white photos in his evidence pack. He walked back to his room with Sisasi and took them out, "Which one is your brother?" Danny said.

The black and white aerial photos were blown up, and although a little bit grainy, she was able to point out her brother, "That's Fabio there," Sisasi said. "He and his men risked their own lives to help us." She paused, looking at Danny. "They're good men, Danny."

Danny replied, "I agree with you that your brother and his men, through their actions, helped to save our lives. They bought us just enough time to escape on the helicopter, but they're also communist rebels, attacking the Guatemalan army, which is illegal. They're enemies of the state." Danny went on, "What does Fabio know about the soldiers that were attacking you and the children?"

Sisasi replied, "The soldiers that attacked us had already targeted and destroyed many of the local villages around Colina. We were just the next village on their list. My brother and all his comrades are from our district. They're only trying to protect us, save our villages, and our livelihoods, but there are not enough of them; the army is far too powerful."

Danny felt confused and disconcerted. It was his duty as a serving member of the British armed forces to share this sort of intelligence, but it might damage his relationship with Sisasi, and he owed his life to her brother. He felt conflicted and said, "Under international military laws, what those soldiers are doing is completely illegal, and the world needs to be told. Do you think Fabio would testify with you and me against these soldiers?" Danny asked.

"There's no point, Danny. Fabio is considered a traitor by the Guatemalan army. Our country is not like your country, they will execute him immediately," she replied.

"Sisasi, if I could guarantee your safety, and that of your brother, would you be willing to testify then?" Danny asked again.

Sisasi said, "I would, but Fabio definitely won't. He insists on remaining in the shadows."

"Perhaps you can try to persuade him to testify? He might listen to you?" Danny said.

Sisasi nodded, "I'll ask, but I'm not optimistic that he will agree."

They carried on chatting until Sisasi had to leave just before the curfew at midnight. As they parted at the gate, Sisasi said, "Danny, please say nothing about Fabio."

Danny agreed, "I won't say anything, I promise. Goodnight, Sisasi," then they hugged and she left in a taxi to go home.

The next day, Danny had another meeting with his lawyer.

"Hello, Ruth, good morning."

He seemed in a better mood today, she thought. "Good morning, Danny, please sit down. I have some news about the court martial. It takes place the day after tomorrow. You will need to be prepared for some difficult cross-questioning. Do you have any questions for me?"

"No, Ruth, I'll tell the truth and hope that the board sees it my way," Danny replied.

"Good, Danny. Keep your answers factual and succinct. Then we'll hopefully come out of this with the result we are hoping for."

The prosecuting lawyer, Squadron Leader Morgan, was in his final meeting with the military police captain, "Thank you for collecting all the witness statements and photographic evidence, Captain Crawley."

"That's fine, Squadron Leader Morgan, I think that is everything you need for the court martial. There is one other issue related to the case; we've just received a telegram from the UK foreign office, stating that the

Guatemalan foreign ministry is accusing the British forces of aiding a rebel kidnapper. Apparently, Sisasi, one of the defence lawyers' key witnesses, has been accused of kidnapping the children that were with her and bringing them over the border illegally. They're also putting pressure on our government to have her and the children repatriated back to Guatemala," Captain Crawley said.

Squadron Leader Morgan thought about it for a moment. "Seems like a ridiculous request to me, but I'm not here to deal with Sisasi and the children. She is a civilian, so not part of our military jurisdiction. I would advise you to forward that message on to the Belizean police headquarters and leave them to decide what to do with the information. It's actually a civilian police matter."

Captain Crawley thanked Squadron Leader Morgan and sent a copy of the telegram, by fax, to the Belizean police headquarters. Soon after receiving the fax, the police sent an inspector to question Sisasi at the school. The telegram stated that she had taken the children from the village in Colina without the parents' consent, and therefore this was a clear case of kidnapping. The police inspector read it and thought, *We don't get paid enough to deal with things like this*. She was in their country illegally, but there were thousands of illegal immigrant workers in Belize. It was tolerated, and the cheap labour was good for their economy. The police force had very limited resources, and there were far more serious crimes to investigate.

The detective inspector reluctantly went to question Sisasi and then spoke to the nine children in the orphanage, who verified her story. He believed the children were probably safer here than where they had come from. He was fully aware of their neighbours' ongoing civil war, so felt sympathetic towards Sisasi and all the other refugees in the city who had escaped across the border into Belize. He quickly assessed that although she did take the children, they had followed her of their own free will, and if they hadn't, they might have all been dead, so he didn't feel that there was any need to arrest her yet. He would need Sisasi to come down to the station the next morning and make a full written statement, and then there would be an investigation. It would be for a judge to decide what would happen after that.

"Look, young lady," the inspector said in a slow, lazy sounding voice, "I need you to come to the police station tomorrow morning at nine, where you must make a full written statement. You will probably be free to carry on with your life until the investigation is completed, but I can't tell you whether the judge will send you back to Guatemala or not – that is not for me to decide. Hypothetically speaking, you may want to consider what would happen if you did not turn up tomorrow? You would not give a statement, and there could be no investigation. That would help you, and it would help me too. Do you get my drift?"

Sisasi nodded and said, "I think so, but I'm a witness at a court martial tomorrow morning, so I can't be at the police station at nine anyway."

The detective inspector said, "If you do not turn up at the police station to give your statement, I'll have to issue a warrant for your arrest, but that may not happen immediately. I'm a very busy man, and it is a time-consuming process, with lots of paperwork to do. It could well be the next day by the time the arrest warrant is issued. My advice, off the record, of course, is that you should probably leave Belize City. That would help you, and it would help me, but I'll deny ever saying that. It's up to you now. I hope that I don't see you in the morning, and I'll say goodbye for now."

Sisasi replied, in a slightly confused voice, "Goodbye, Inspector," and thought, *I really need to speak to Danny about this.*

Chapter 19. The boardroom

Fabio was sat on Sisasi's sofa when she arrived home from work. He could see she was upset from the worried expression on her face, "What's wrong, Sisasi?" he said, looking very concerned for her.

She sat down next to him on the sofa and told him that the police had asked her to go to the main police station in the morning to make a statement about why she brought the children to Belize.

"I've been accused of kidnapping the children, Fabio," she said very emotionally. Tears welled up in her eyes as she explained, "The inspector said that I still have time to get out of the city, he won't start looking into this until tomorrow. He said that if I don't go to the main police station at nine in the morning to give a statement, he will have to issue an arrest warrant the following day." She started sobbing, "I don't know what to do!"

Fabio looked at her and said, "It is too risky for you to go to the police station, or stay in Belize any longer, Sisasi. I have a contact in the city who can help us to get to Chetumal in Mexico. It's only just over the northern border, about a three-hour drive from here. We must leave here as soon as I can get everything arranged. You will be safer in Mexico, and they have a policy of accepting Guatemalan refugees."

Sisasi sounded conflicted, "I can't go yet. I'm a key witness at Danny's court martial tomorrow, he needs me to testify, and what about the children and my job?"

Fabio paused to think, "I understand your predicament, Sisasi, Danny helped to save your life, and the children will feel lost without you. Get all your things packed up, and be ready to go by eight tomorrow morning. I'll get a car and take you to the British camp first so that you can testify. I'll wait outside the gate for you, and we'll leave for Mexico as soon as you have finished giving your evidence. You will be able to contact Danny to tell him where he can find you once we are in Chetumal. I'll return in a few days and go to the convent to explain everything to the children and to the nuns. I'm sure they will all understand."

That evening, Sisasi met Danny at the gate as usual, and they followed the same routine, visiting Polo first, "I'm so pleased that you are recovering, Polo, you look so much better every day." She smiled and held his hand. "You are still my strong little soldier, thank you for being with me on that very difficult journey to the border." She wanted to tell him that she was going to Mexico but knew she couldn't.

Polo thought she was being a bit odd and said quietly, "Are you okay, Miss Sasi?"

She smiled at him and said, "Yes, Polo, I'm fine," and then let go of his hand.

Danny could see that her eyes had started to well up as if she was about to cry. She looked at Danny and said, "I think it must be time to go, Danny."

As they headed over to the Palms restaurant, she told Danny about the visit from the police inspector and the accusation that she had kidnapped the children. Also, that the Guatemalan foreign office wanted her arrested and repatriated. It was just too much of a risk for her to take. She would have to leave.

Danny sounded outraged, "That's ridiculous, how can you be accused of kidnapping?"

Sisasi nodded, "I know, Danny, but I just can't risk staying here in Belize. If they do send me back, you will never see me again. My brother has a contact who owns a hotel in Chetumal. He will help us get across the border tomorrow. I can contact you once I get there, and send you the address of the hotel. It is not so far; Fabio says it is only three hours away by car."

"Are you sure about all of this, Sisasi?" Danny felt like his world was falling apart.

She could see that Danny didn't like the idea of her being three hours away and across the border in Mexico. "Danny, you know how much I want to be with you, we are so good for each other, and you make me very happy. I know we've been seeing a lot of each other, and that will not be possible if I am in Mexico, but hopefully, you will come to see me in Chetumal, and at least we can be together on the weekends. We can still make this work for us if we try."

Danny felt robbed, but understood she was in an impossible position, so he reluctantly agreed, "Of course I'll come to see you in Chetumal, but what about the court martial tomorrow? You are a key witness. I need you here to give your testimony regarding the events that led up to the fire fight."

Sisasi looked up at him and said, "Don't worry, Danny, I'll definitely be there tomorrow. I won't be leaving Belize until after I've testified."

Danny didn't like the idea of her not being nearby, "It will be awful not being able to see you as often, but I would rather see you safe in Mexico than being arrested for kidnapping in Belize."

They went back to his room and lay on his bed listening to a cassette. Danny rolled towards her and gently ran his fingers through her hair. He wanted to memorise every feature; her brown eyes, soft lips, silky hair, and intoxicating fragrance. He said, "I'm so lucky to have you here with me, darling. It's just not fair that you have to leave after everything you've been through." He wanted her to stay with him, so he could make love to her and watch her fall asleep in his arms.

Unfortunately, Sisasi, like all visitors, had to leave before the midnight curfew. Danny hugged and kissed her at the gate, "See you tomorrow morning at 10, darling."

She smiled, "Yes, tomorrow, at 10 sharp. I'll be right here." They reluctantly waved goodbye to each other as she left the gate in a taxi.

Danny's alarm clock went off at seven, but he was already awake and worrying about the court martial. He busied himself with getting ready, showering, putting on his uniform, and then walked over to the mess for breakfast at eight. He was going to review his papers, then meet Sisasi at the gate at 10. The court martial was starting at 11, so they had time to meet his defence lawyer, Squadron Leader Lockwood, just before the court martial started.

Sisasi knew that she had given a very clear account to the military police about everything that had happened to her and the children and was prepared to be cross-examined about her witness statement. She was waiting for Fabio to turn up and had packed a small suitcase with her personal belongings. She knew that the nuns would be disappointed at her leaving without giving any notice, but she also knew they would look after the children, and hopefully, one day, she would be able to see them all again.

She could hear a car pulling up outside; she looked out of the window and could see Fabio and another man getting out of the yellow taxi. The man driving the taxi was Rodrigues, the owner of the Victoria Hotel where Fabio had been staying. He walked up to the door with Fabio and said, "Hello, nice to meet you, I'm your brother's new friend, and now your driver too, my name is Rodrigues. Nice to meet you." The surly-looking man smiled at her and held his right hand out.

Sisasi shook his hand. "Hello, Rodrigues, my name is Sisasi. Nice to meet you," and then turned to Fabio and said, "I thought you were going to be on your own, Fabio?"

"Rodrigues is a friend. He owns a sister hotel in Chetumal, that is where we are going." Fabio handed over a large brown envelope to Sisasi. "Here are our papers, they will get us across the border without any questions being asked."

She got in the car as requested and Rodrigues put her suitcase in the boot. Fabio sat next to her on the rear seat and explained what they needed to do when they reached the border. As they drove towards Airport Camp, Rodrigues complimented her on her escape from Guatemala and how lucky she was to have such a wonderful brother. He didn't seem to stop talking. *I wish he would just shut up!* she thought.

When they got close to Airport Camp, Fabio said, "Sisasi, we are not stopping, it is too dangerous for us. We must go straight to the border."

Sisasi was taken by surprise and said, "What! What did you say? We must stop! I'm a key witness for Danny. Fabio, you promised you would let me give my evidence!" She shouted angrily, "Rodrigues, stop the car, stop it now!"

Rodrigues replied, "Sorry, Sisasi, but I can't do that. You must listen to your brother, he is only doing what's best for you. You should not worry yourself about that soldier in there, you need to be concerned about your own safety right now."

Sisasi, tried to open the door, but the child lock was on. Rodrigues turned right onto the Northern Highway and continued driving towards the Mexican border, ignoring her demands to stop.

* * *

Danny was waiting at the gate for Sisasi to arrive, his evidence folder tucked tightly under his arm. It was nearly 10 o'clock, and he felt happy that Sisasi would be there to testify for him. He stood there waiting for half an hour, wondering where she was, and was getting more and more worried with every passing minute. In the end, he had to leave, so went up to the guardroom and asked them to call Squadron Leader Lockwood when Sisasi arrived; he would just have to come back for her.

Danny walked into Squadron Leader Lockwood's temporary office, he was late, "Sorry I'm late, ma'am, Sisasi hasn't turned up yet. I have no idea where she is."

Ruth looked over her reading glasses, slightly perplexed, "Her testimony is important, Danny. I hope she makes it in time."

"So do I," Danny replied.

The two of them went over the opening statement and the arguments one last time. Sisasi had still not arrived and it was nearly 11 o'clock.

Ruth said, "Sorry, Danny, it doesn't look like she is coming; we need to go to the boardroom."

There were a group of people in the corridor standing outside the boardroom, waiting for Brigadier Davies to arrive. As he appeared at the end of the corridor, the station warrant officer called out, "Atten-Shun!" and everyone stood to attention as the brigadier walked past, until he said, "At ease..."

Everyone relaxed and filed into the board room after him. There were two military police corporals, acting as the ushers and security for the court martial, showing everyone to their designated positions. The boardroom had a number of chairs and tables set out in rows. The seven members of the board were seated to the right of the boardroom, the brigadier sat at the front, and the defence and prosecuting teams were sat on the left. There was a lectern being used to the left of the brigadier's table, where both the accused and the witnesses could give evidence statements, take questions, and be cross-examined by the prosecution and defence lawyers.

Brigadier Davies stood up, then immediately everyone else stood up. He said, "Please be seated," everyone except the brigadier sat down. He continued, "We are here today to carry out the court martial of Corporal Sinclaire, seated here on my right. Firstly, I will give way to the prosecution, who will give an account of the four charges, and the evidence they have gathered. Then I will defer to the defence team to present their arguments against the prosecution evidence. Corporal Sinclaire pleads innocent to all four charges against him. Squadron Leader Morgan, please proceed with the prosecution's case."

Captain Crawley, the military police investigator, was sat next to the prosecutor and nodded at him, saying, "Good luck."

Squadron Leader Morgan opened the prosecution's evidence file and then stood up as the brigadier sat down, "Thank you, Brigadier. The charges are as follows: One, Corporal Sinclaire assisted communist rebel forces to attack the Guatemalan army, resulting in the deaths of two Guatemalan soldiers.

"Two, He is accused of misconduct on operations by abandoning Zulu hide without any orders to do so, leaving his post, and leaving the site undefended.

"Three, with intent or recklessness, Corporal Sinclaire failed to carry out the planned operations, putting his own life and the lives of his team at risk.

"Four, Corporal Sinclaire contravened standing orders. It clearly states within standing orders that British forces are not allowed to enter no man's land without orders to do so.

"I put it to you, the members of the board, that these actions were illegal under military law. You must only consider the facts as to whether or not Corporal Sinclaire broke these military laws.

"On September the fifteenth this year, Corporal Sinclaire and his team left their post, Zulu hide, on his orders. I argue that by leaving their post, a chain of events was set in motion by Corporal Sinclaire that could have been stopped at any time. According to the Guatemalan foreign office statement, their platoon had been pursuing communist rebels that had attacked a northern village called Colina. The rebels ransacked the village and killed many of the people living there. They were also accused of kidnapping 10 children, which is another important reason that the soldiers were attempting to find them. The intention of the army, according to the Guatemalan foreign office statement, was to save these children from the rebels and then return them to their family members, some of whom were working away from Colina at the time of the attack and are fortunately still alive.

"They state it is well documented that communist rebels often capture children and train them to become militias, so it was important to avoid this. The soldiers tracked the rebels holding the children, and during this period, were ambushed by a contingent of those rebels, resulting in four of the soldiers in their platoon being shot dead. The platoon had just managed to catch up to the rebels again, near the border, and engaged in another battle with them to try to rescue the children.

"As they were carrying out their mission, Corporal Sinclaire and his men opened fire on the Guatemalan soldiers, eventually killing two and injuring two. After being fired upon by the communist rebels from the south, and also the British forces from the east, the Guatemalan soldiers had no option but to retreat. During this conflict, Corporal Sinclaire entered no man's land, supporting the rebel action, which ultimately helped them to escape. All the witness statements confirm that Corporal Sinclaire did enter no man's land and did illegally open fire on the Guatemalan soldiers. Those are the facts as we see them, sir, members of the board, thank you."

Squadron Leader Morgan sat down, and the brigadier said, "Squadron leader Lockwood, the defence arguments if you please."

Ruth shuffled her papers, then stood up, "Thank you, Brigadier. The defence refutes all four charges, and I will provide the evidence that refutes the prosecution argument for each of the charges. The statement from the Guatemalan foreign office is clearly fabricated to avoid military and political reputational damage. The evidence I am about to present clearly shows that an unarmed civilian group crossed no man's land, were attacked by Guatemalan soldiers, and then saved by British forces.

"Charge number one; assisting the enemy, namely the communist rebels. According to all the transcripts, Corporal Sinclaire was already leaving no man's land when the communist rebels arrived, and we have reliable witnesses to testify that was the case. The rebels opened fire on the Guatemalan army, but only after Sinclaire had turned his back on the Guatemalan soldiers, so the Guatemalan foreign office report is factually incorrect. Corporal Sinclaire had no way of knowing the rebels were there at all, not until they opened fire. By the time the rebels opened fire, Corporal Sinclaire had already been injured by a grenade, shot in the right side, and was carrying a seriously injured thirteen-year-old boy with a severe chest wound to safety.

"Charge number two, misconduct on operations by abandoning Zulu hide without any orders to do so, leaving his post, and leaving the site undefended. I argue that this site is often left undefended, in fact, it is an unmanned and infrequently used aircraft hide. The fact that he had no orders to leave is a complete red herring. Corporal Sinclaire's team is autonomous; he never has orders when to arrive or when to leave, he and his team set the route and times of arrival and departure. He is the person in charge, and whichever hide they visit, he is used to making all the decisions on behalf of his team, so Corporal Sinclaire decides when to leave their post, and in fact how to protect their post, in this case, Zulu hide. He decided to carry out reconnaissance, and he only did that to ensure the hide was kept safe. The brave actions of Corporal Sinclaire and his team's reconnaissance of the area allowed a Two-Para cordon to be called in and set up, ultimately protecting the site from any incursions, rebel or otherwise. I put it to the board that he was within his rights.

"Charge number three, with intent or recklessness, he failed to carry out the planned operations and put lives at risk. Yes, he did put his own life and the lives of his colleagues at risk, but we are in the armed forces; doesn't that come with the territory? Was he really being reckless? Not in my opinion. Did he cause the death of at least two Guatemalan soldiers? We can't definitively prove that he did. The prosecution already claims that there had been a previous ambush. I argue that it is impossible to say that Corporal Sinclaire killed any of the Guatemalan soldiers. I agree that he did put his own life at risk and the lives of his colleagues, but not in an illegal way according to military laws. He was the non-commissioned officer in charge of a specialist team operating in an area where there was known rebel activity, and as such, he made decisions that were absolutely necessary to save civilian lives. He was doing what he has been trained to do when presented with a situation which left him with no choice. It was imperative to help these civilians evade what he correctly assessed to be an illegal attack.

"Under international military law JSP 383, there can be exceptional cases, or situations in armed conflicts where, owing to the nature of the hostilities, an armed combatant can open fire. In Corporal Sinclaire's case, there is a clear argument for 'civilian immunity', where he is allowed to protect the civilian population of any nation, because under international military laws, the civilian population, as well as individual civilians, shall not be the object of attack. As you all know, attacks against the civilian population, or individual civilians, are prohibited in international law. Civilians are to be protected at all times against dangers arising from military operations. I argue that Corporal Sinclaire knew this was his duty; he knew he was not breaking any military laws but actually upholding military laws by protecting the unarmed civilians that he could clearly see were in mortal danger.

"Charge number four states that Corporal Sinclaire contravened standing orders, as it clearly states within standing orders that British forces are not allowed to enter no man's land. I argue that this order is under normal circumstances only, and this was in no way a normal circumstance. He only took proportionate action to save the lives of civilians, and the only way to do this was to enter no man's land. Corporal Sinclaire did enter no man's land, I am not arguing he didn't. I accept that he did, but only to stop the illegal actions of the soldiers on the opposite side, who were already in no man's land, shooting at a defenceless woman with 10 children. These facts must be taken into consideration by the board when deciding whether Corporal Sinclaire is innocent or guilty."

CHAPTER 20. THE WITNESS BOX

Mark and Kevin were sat in the hallway, and wondering when they would be called. They were chatting quietly. "Can you believe this shit?" Mark sounded annoyed.

"No, I think it's a bloody disgrace. Danny should be getting a fucking medal for what he did, not a court martial," Kevin replied.

Mark looked around, "I thought Sisasi was meant to be here too?"

Kevin replied, "She is meant to be here, I wonder what on earth has happened to her? Hopefully, she'll turn up soon."

Brigadier Davies thanked the prosecution and the defence lawyers for their opening statements and then asked the prosecution lawyer, Squadron Leader Morgan, if he wanted to call any witnesses.

"Yes, I would like to start by calling the witness Sisasi de Colina to the stand."

One of the military police corporals went outside into the corridor and called out, "The witness, Sisasi de Colina?" She was clearly not there.

Kevin and Mark both looked at him, bemused, and he said, "Not calling you two yet. Where is the witness Sisasi?"

They both said in unison, "No idea, Corporal."

He walked back into the boardroom and said, "Sorry, sir, the witness, Sisasi, is not here."

Squadron Leader Morgan didn't mind too much, she was more important to the defence case anyway. He said, "In that case, I call Danny Sinclaire to the stand."

Danny stood at the witness box and swore to tell the truth, holding a bible in his right hand.

Squadron Leader Morgan said, "Corporal Sinclaire, just give 'yes' or 'no' answers please. Did you make the decision to leave the hide and go to the boundary of no man's land?"

Danny replied, "Yes, sir."

Squadron Leader Morgan went on, "Did you fire your weapons at the Guatemalan soldiers on the other side of no man's land?"

"Yes, sir," Danny replied, stony-faced.

"Did you then enter no man's land, still firing your weapon?" Squadron Leader Morgan leaned forwards towards Danny.

"Yes, sir, I did."

"Does it state in standing orders that you are not allowed to enter no man's land?"

"Yes, sir." Danny looked at Squadron Leader Morgan with contempt.

Squadron Leader Morgan continued, "Were you and your team in mortal danger, Corporal?"

"Yes, sir."

"In hindsight, do you consider your actions to have been reckless?"

Danny looked him straight in the eye. "No, sir, I don't!"

"Thank you, Corporal Sinclaire. I have no more questions for you."

Brigadier Davies looked over to Squadron Leader Lockwood. "Any questions for the defence?"

"Yes, sir." Squadron Leader Lockwood stood up and asked Danny, "In the same situation, would you make the same decisions again, Corporal?"

Danny replied, "Yes, ma'am."

"Why?" she asked.

"It's about doing the right thing, ma'am. I don't regret what I did, but I would regret not having done it. I think that most British soldiers confronted with that same dilemma would have made exactly the same decision I did."

"Thank you, Corporal Sinclaire. I agree that you were doing the right thing. Please could you take out your *'pink rules of engagement card'* and tell me what it says about your right to open fire, with regard to you, your men, and civilians."

Danny took the 'pink card' out of his wallet and read out, "You may use deadly force without issuing a warning, in defence of you, your fellow soldiers, or innocent people."

"Thank you, Corporal Sinclaire. So, it is my understanding that you only opened fire to defend innocent people, and, therefore, you were operating in accordance with the rules. Correct?"

"Yes, ma'am," Danny replied.

"That's all from me, Brigadier."

Danny was surprised her questioning seemed so short.

Brigadier Davies said, "If there are no more questions? Corporal Sinclaire, you may return to your seat." Danny left the stand and sat down.

Squadron Leader Lockwood then said to the brigadier, "Sir, I would like to ask for an additional witness to speak. As our key witness, Sisasi, is not here to give her own account of the exact timings during the exchange of fire, especially when the rebels arrived, I would like to call the boy, Polo, to give evidence instead."

Brigadier Davies asked the prosecuting lawyer if he had any objections, "No objections, sir," Squadron Leader Morgan replied.

The boardroom doors opened, and Polo was pushed through in his wheelchair, looking a little bit apprehensive. A translator explained what was happening, and then Polo was asked a series of questions.

When did the shooting start on the Guatemalan side?

When did they hear the shooting from the east?

Polo was able to answer these questions and confirm the facts extracted from Sisasi's witness statement, but when asked about at exactly what point the rebels had opened fire, he had no recollection because he was already unconscious by then.

The board looked up with interest when Ruth said, "So, Polo, you were already injured, and in fact unconscious when the rebels starting firing from the south?"

Polo replied in almost a whisper, "Yes, miss, my last memory was seeing Danny shooting back at the other soldiers. Then I felt something hit me hard in the back, which I now know was a bullet. I thought I was going to die."

They spent the next two hours examining the witness statements in the boardroom, including questioning Kevin and Mark separately, who both corroborated everything that Danny had already said. After hearing all the first-hand evidence, Squadron Leader Morgan was starting to feel that he was losing ground, but there was nothing he could do about it now.

Brigadier Davies said to the board that would decide Danny's fate, "You have heard the case for the prosecution and the case for the defence. I'll now ask both lawyers to give their closing arguments, and then it is up to you, the members of the board, to deliberate based on the evidence presented. Squadron Leader Morgan, your closing statement please."

Squadron Leader Morgan stood up, "I ask you, the board, to only look at the facts. Corporal Sinclaire fired his weapon and ordered his men to fire their weapons on soldiers that are our allies in the fight against the spread of communism, and therefore allies of our western democracies. Corporal Sinclaire did leave his post, Zulu hide, and on his own admission, he did put his own life and the lives of his team at risk. He did not follow station standing orders and also admits that he did enter no man's land. These are all admissions; they are the facts. Please do your duty in accordance with military law. Thank you, members of the board." Squadron Leader Morgan sat down.

Brigadier Davies stood up and said, "Squadron Leader Lockwood, your closing arguments please."

Squadron Leader Lockwood stood up, and walked over to the table where the seven members of the board sat, and paused to look at each one of them. She then presented her closing statement.

"Members of the board, in my twenty-year-long career in the RAF, I have never been prouder to represent anyone. In my opinion, and in line with military laws, I hope you agree that Corporal Sinclaire did everything we would expect of him as a member of the British armed forces. He made sound decisions that ultimately saved the lives of 10 children and one woman. He understood his duty was not to 'lock up shop' and drive back to Airport Camp when he heard small arms fire nearby. It was his duty, and that of his men, to investigate. His actions allowed reinforcements to be called in and therefore secured his post at Zulu hide. With regard to entering no man's land, the boy, Polo, who was here giving evidence earlier, would not have been here without Corporal Sinclaire's quick thinking and bravery. It is also clear from the evidence that the order of events is not as the prosecution would have us believe. The roles played by the Guatemalan soldiers is clear as day, and the intended action of the rebels was to save the lives of their people – not take them.

"To save civilian lives... surely this is our duty? It is also enshrined in our military laws. I hope that you all believe, like me, that Corporal Sinclaire should be honourably acquitted of all four charges." She concluded with a respectful nod and said, "Thank you, members of the board."

Brigadier Davies stood up and said, "Everyone rise." They all stood up. "You have heard all the charges and all the arguments. I ask you, the officers and non-commissioned officers of the board, to consider the evidence and let me have your conclusions once you have come to your majority decision. The rest of you can go for a comfort break and get yourselves a tea or coffee. We'll reconvene when the board have concluded their judgement."

After less than an hour, the members of the board came back into the boardroom, and everyone was called back in to hear their judgement.

Brigadier Davies asked the board, "Have you come to a majority decision on all four charges put to you?"

The board spokesman said, "We have, sir," and then paused.

"Wing Commander Edmunds, what is your verdict?" asked Brigadier Davies.

The wing commander addressed the brigadier, "It is the unanimous decision of the board that Corporal Sinclaire be most honourably acquitted on all four charges, sir." He turned his head and smiled at Danny.

Brigadier Davies looked over at Danny and was noticeably pleased, "Corporal Sinclaire, I'm very happy to say that you can leave here and carry on with your well-deserved recovery. I'm sorry you have had to go through this court martial, but that is the legal military process. I am approving, with immediate effect, two weeks of rest and recuperation for you."

Danny was visibly relieved. "Thank you, Brigadier. That is very kind of you." Danny turned and looked at the members of the board and said, "And thank you to all the board members."

Brigadier Davies nodded at Danny. "You deserve some time off after everything that you have endured, Corporal Sinclaire." The brigadier continued, "I must also address everyone in this boardroom and tell you that this court martial, including all the evidence gathered and presented, is politically sensitive and is therefore classified as '*secret*'. It must not be discussed or divulged to anyone outside this boardroom. Is that understood?"

A chorus of voices said, "Yes, sir," and they nodded their heads in agreement.

Danny felt so relieved; every single person that had been on the board came over to congratulate him and wished him well. Wing Commander Edmunds said, "We are all so proud of you, Corporal Sinclaire. I was never in any doubt that you would be acquitted. Bloody farce, if you ask me. I think you should go and have a few beers now and celebrate with your mates."

He leant forward and shook Danny's hand vigorously, as did everyone else on the board. Finally, the brigadier came over and congratulated Danny, saying, "I'm so pleased for you, Corporal Sinclaire, your actions made us all very proud. Unfortunately for you, we have to be seen to be doing the right thing under military law, especially by our allies in the north. We were politically pressured into taking these actions, but I think I chose the board well." He raised his eyebrows and winked knowingly.

Danny smiled and said, "I understand, sir. I'm just relieved it is finally over."

Mark and Kevin were waiting outside nervously. When Danny walked out, he smiled at them and gave them a thumbs up. "Acquitted on all four charges, guys."

Kevin and Mark both punched the air joyously and said, "Yes!"

Kevin decided it was time to celebrate. "Right! Let's all get over to the NAAFI bar and get smashed! The beers are on Danny!"

Danny laughed and said, "I'll see you over there. I just want to thank my lawyer first."

Danny waited outside the boardroom as it slowly emptied, some of the board nodded and smiled at him as they walked by, and eventually Ruth came out, "Do you want to have a quick coffee and debrief, Danny?"

"Yes, I would like to do that, Ruth. I don't know how I can ever thank you enough."

"That's alright, Danny; the result is enough for me." She looked very happy.

They went into her office and closed the door, and sat down. Ruth looked at him with pride. "Congratulations, Danny, I'm sorry you had to go through that, a bit of a show trial for the politicians if you ask me. The government is stony broke, and shit scared of having another Falklands War, so anything that kicks off on the border here immediately causes the prime minister to have panic attacks."

Danny said, "It caused me a few panic attacks too! It has been an emotional rollercoaster. I thought we had a good case, but when Sisasi didn't turn up, I was very concerned. I have no idea why she wasn't here. I spoke to her only last night and she was adamant that she would be here this morning."

Ruth said, "Well, thankfully, it has all turned out well in the end. I think wheeling Polo in must have pulled on the heartstrings somewhat." She smiled. "We got the result we wanted in the end, Danny, and it was the right result."

"We did, Ruth. I can't thank you enough," Danny replied.

They finished their coffees and said goodbye, then Danny headed over to the NAAFI bar, where Kevin and Mark were already finishing their first pint.

He could see there was a pint on the table for him too. Danny walked over to them and said, "Look, guys, as much as I want to celebrate with you, I must try to find out what happened with Sisasi today. I want to know why she didn't turn up for the court martial. I feel like she has let me down badly!"

Mark and Kevin nodded in agreement, and Mark said, "Let's go then, we're coming with you, but get that down your neck first."

Danny drank his pint quickly and they headed to the front gate. He remembered that she said she was going to Mexico after the court martial, but maybe she hadn't left yet. He needed to check.

All three of them climbed into a taxi and left Airport Camp to go to Sisasi's house. Danny walked towards the wooden house and looked through the windows. It was empty, He could see that the wardrobe doors were open and the clothes were gone.

Danny realised that Sisasi had already left for Mexico and felt completely deserted.

He said dejectedly, "How could she do this to me?"

Kevin and Mark stood there silently at first, and then Mark said empathetically, "Sorry, mate, looks like she's packed up and left."

Danny said, "State the bloody obvious, Mark!" He felt angry with Sisasi and remembered that she said her brother was going to drive her to Chetumal.

"She wouldn't have just left like that, guys. It's got something to do with her brother!"

"Her brother?" Kevin asked in a surprised voice.

Danny replied, "Yes, she has an interfering brother, but you can't tell anyone. I didn't mean to blurt it out. I only just found out about him myself."

"What was he doing here?" Kevin asked.

Danny said, "He was looking for his sister and the children. He followed us here from the border. He was one of the men that saved our bacon, one of the men who opened fire from the south. I think they're both already in Chetumal. She said yesterday that is where they would be going after the court martial."

Mark and Kevin looked at each other, and Mark said, "For fuck's sake, Danny! You're saying her brother is a communist rebel? You need to keep your distance!"

Danny looked at them both and thought that he had probably already said too much. "Yes, Mark, that's right. I think it's best if we just leave it there for now."

* * *

Fabio, Rodrigues, and Sisasi made it across the border. Bribes had been paid to the right border guards to make sure everyone got across into Mexico safely.

When they arrived in Chetumal, Fabio thanked Rodrigues, but Sisasi remained silent and angry, ignoring them both. She had cried most of the way, her eyes were dry and red, and she imagined that Danny may now be locked up because she wasn't able to give her evidence. He probably hated her, she didn't know what to think or what to do, but it was all her brother's fault that she wasn't able to testify, not hers. She must find a way to tell Danny.

Rodrigues pulled up outside the Frente al Mar Hotel, a quaint wooden building overlooking the beach. It was in a scenic and tranquil place; it reminded her of the hotel that she had stayed at with Danny on Caye Caulker, and immediately, she felt like her heart was breaking.

They walked into the hotel together, and the woman on reception said to Rodrigues, "Hello, boss, these are the guests?"

"Yes, these are my guests. Look after them well."

She handed over two keys to Fabio and then Sisasi and said, "First floor, up the stairs, on the left." Rodrigues turned to Fabio and said, "This is my place, you and your sister can stay here as long as you need to. I'll get in touch with our Cuban friends and let them know you are safe. I'm usually here around once a week. I'll stay tonight and head back over the border tomorrow."

Fabio thanked Rodrigues and then went upstairs with Sisasi to find their rooms.

She was still upset, he knew his sister well. "Come on, sister. I am sure everything will be fine. Chin up."

Sisasi felt incensed and looked at him indignantly. "Chin up! How dare you?! Just leave me alone!" and pushed him away from her. She unlocked the door, walked into her room, and slammed the door hard behind her.

It was much nicer inside the room than she had expected, and there was a telephone on the bedside table. She picked up the receiver and dialled zero for the operator.

"Hello, operator speaking, how can I help you?"

Sisasi said, "Can I make a call to a number in Belize?"

"Yes, you can, madam, what's the number please?" the operator replied.

Sisasi pulled out a piece of paper from her pocket with the telephone number for the guardroom at Airport

Camp and read the number out for the operator. There was a ringing on the line, and a man answered on the other end.

"Hello, Airport Camp guardroom, can I help?"

The operator said, "Please hold, sir, I have a caller on the line for you. Madam, you can now go ahead."

Sisasi said, "Hello, sir, I was wondering if there was any way I could leave a message for Corporal Sinclaire?"

The voice on the other end said, "Do you mean Danny Sinclaire?"

Sisasi replied, "Yes, Danny Sinclaire."

He replied, "Yes, that's fine. What is your message, madam?"

"Please can you ask him to call me on the following telephone at the Frente al Mar Hotel in Chetumal, room 12."

She then gave the man in the guardroom the telephone number for the hotel, checked that he had written it down correctly, and said goodbye. All she could do now was wait and hope that Danny would call.

Danny, Mark, and Kevin stayed in the city for a few hours celebrating the acquittal, going to a nice steak restaurant, having a few too many beers, and going over the events of the past few weeks. Danny told them about the local police saying that the children had been kidnapped, and Mark commented sarcastically, "Well, we must be criminals too then. We aided and abetted the abduction of those children, and thank God we did, or they would probably all be dead by now!"

Kevin asked Danny, "What are you going to do about Sisasi, she let you down today. Do you think you will ever see her again?"

Danny was silent for a moment while he considered the question, "I think I want to see her again, even if it is just to tie up some loose ends. I just can't stop wondering why she didn't turn up this morning? Maybe I'm living in my own fantasy world, I thought she cared about me in the same way I care about her. Something just doesn't add up for me."

After a few hours, they arrived back at the guardroom and there was a message waiting for Danny. "What's that?" Kevin said.

Danny replied, "It's a message from Sisasi, asking me to call her at the hotel she is staying at, in Chetumal."

CHAPTER 21. THE FRENTE AL MAR HOTEL

Kevin and Mark talked to Danny about what he intended to do as they walked towards the NAAFI bar. "So, are you going to call Sisasi, Danny?" Kevin said.

"Yes, I'm going to give her a call now and ask why she wasn't here today. Thankfully, we were able to call Polo as a witness, but things might have gone against me if we hadn't been able to do that. She said she would definitely be there to give her testimony for me, I feel so let down. That's the second time she's left me standing at the gate waiting for her." Danny paused and said, "Well, at least the board all agreed with my defence lawyer. Ruth did a great job, so fortunately, it wasn't terminal for me when Sisasi didn't turn up. I'll try to get hold of her on the phone in the NAAFI foyer and see what she has to say for herself. What will be, will be," he said philosophically.

They walked through the swing doors at the entrance to the NAAFI building. In the entrance lobby, there was a shop on the left and a bar to the right. They could hear from the hustle-bustle coming from the bar that it was busy,

Kevin said to Danny, "You go and phone Sisasi. I'll get in the queue and get the beers in, Belikin okay?" "Yes, thanks, Kevin."

There were four public telephone booths just inside the entrance of the NAAFI bar, all with large clear Perspex hoods, two of them were in use, the other two were free. The plastic hoods were doing a good job of muffling the discussions going on, so Danny felt like he could have a reasonably private conversation if he managed to get through. He walked up to the closest vacant booth and put a small pile of 50 pence coins on the stainless-steel shelf inside, next to the phone, then picked up the receiver and dialled the number for the Frente al Mar Hotel. He held a 50 pence coin between his thumb and index finger in readiness to pop it into the coin slot when required. The receptionist answered at the other end, and as the phone started beeping in Danny's ear, he immediately pushed the first 50 pence coin into the slot.

The lady on the other end said in Spanish, "Hola, puedo ayudar?"

Danny said, "Sorry, do you speak English?"

"Yes, hello, can I help?" she said.

"I want to be put through to room 12 please."

The receptionist said, "Please wait, sir, I'll try the room. May I ask who is calling?"

"Yes, my name is Danny." She called through to the room; Danny could hear it ringing on the other end, then Sisasi's voice came on the line, "Hello."

The receptionist said, "Hello, madam, this is reception. I have a call for you from a man called Danny. Will you take the call?"

Sisasi responded, there was a nervousness in her voice, "I will, please put him through to me."

There was a click on the line as he was put through. "Sisasi, is that you?"

"Yes, Danny, it's me."

Danny felt a bit agitated after the day's events and said in a slightly raised and irritated voice, "I've just picked up your message from the guardroom. Where were you today? I was worried."

Sisasi started crying on the other end of the line while also trying to explain. Danny could hardly understand a word, then, annoyingly, the phone starting beeping again. Danny pushed another 50 pence coin into the slot, and he could just about hear her saying, "It was my brother's fault. Fabio told the driver not to stop at Airport Camp; they brought me straight here, they wouldn't stop. I tried to…" Her sobbing down the line was increasing in intensity.

"Sisasi, please calm down and just listen for a moment. If I heard you correctly, you said it was your brother's fault and not yours; we can talk more about that tomorrow. The important and good news is that I was acquitted on all four charges, and the brigadier has given me two weeks off for rest and recuperation. I've been completely exonerated, so I'm a free man again, Sisasi. I'll come to see you in Chetumal tomorrow. I should be there by early afternoon if I can get a bus ticket."

Sisasi felt both relieved and overjoyed. She had thought that she might never see Danny again, but now she would be seeing him tomorrow. She went from feeling absolutely miserable to feeling completely elated, her emotions were all over the place. She laughed with joy and cried with relief, saying, "You'll be here tomorrow afternoon, Danny?"

"Yes, tomorrow afternoon. I'll get the first Northern Highway bus up to the Mexican border in the morning and then get a taxi from there to your hotel. I should probably be there by early afternoon."

Sisasi's heart was racing at the thought of being reunited with Danny, and she said excitedly, "That's fantastic, Danny. I was so worried that I may never see you again, but now I'm so very happy. I can't wait to see you!"

Danny had run out of coins and finished off the call, saying, "Well, darling, you will have to wait; I can't get there any sooner." Danny knew he was taking a big risk going to see Sisasi, especially now his friends knew her brother was a communist rebel, but he felt like he had to go.

Sisasi decided not to mention that she knew the hotel owner, Rodrigues, was being subsidised by the Cubans. She didn't think it was a risk for Danny, especially with her brother being there, who seemed very friendly with Rodrigues.

The next day, Danny got the Northern Highway bus to the Mexican border. It was a bumpy ride along the pothole-ridden road, but after four hot and uncomfortable hours, the bus arrived on time. Danny went straight through customs without any delays, walked up to the front of a long row of yellow taxis, and said to the driver, "Do you know this hotel?" showing the driver the name of the hotel written on a piece of paper.

The driver said, "Yes, I know the Frente al Mar Hotel, please get in, sir."

The taxi took 20 minutes to get to Chetumal, then pulled up outside the front entrance of the hotel. Danny looked up and could see 'Frente al Mar Hotel' painted in large white letters on a wooden board above the main entrance.

He paid the driver and took his blue holdall out of the boot, adding politely, "Thank you."

The driver responded with a smile, "No problem, sir, goodbye."

Danny pushed his left arm through the handles of his blue RAF holdall and slid it up onto his shoulder, thinking to himself, *This looks lovely, just the sort of laid-back place I would have chosen to stay at,*' and smiled to himself at the thought of being there with Sisasi, away from all the worries of the past few months and just relaxing on a beach for a couple of weeks.

He had a quick look around the immediate vicinity as he walked towards the hotel entrance. The coral sand on the beach was bleached white and glimmered on the shore as the gentle waves of the Caribbean Sea washed over it, giving it a sheen. There were a few tourists lying on sun loungers, some in the water swimming and snorkelling, but the beach was not at all busy. A long wooden boardwalk stretched out a hundred yards over the beautiful pastel blue shallow waters covering the coral reef. Fishing and leisure boats were tied up alongside, and Danny could see a shaded platform at the end of the boardwalk, with wooden handrails on three sides, where the hotel guests could sit and enjoy a drink under the shade of the thatched roof while listening to the waves gently lapping up against the wooden columns of the walkway. Shoals of small fish flitted in and out of the shadows underneath the boardwalk. It looked, and felt, like an idyllic place to get away from the stress of the previous few weeks. Danny walked through the hotel entrance and up to the reception desk.

There was a young lady on the desk who looked him up and down, smiled, and asked, "Can I help you, sir?"

Danny put his bag down on the floor, smiled back, and replied, "Yes please, can I use your telephone to call room 12?"

Sisasi had been waiting in the bar with a bird's eye view of the entrance, and even before the receptionist was able to answer his question, he could hear his name being called. Sisasi was shouting in a very excited voice, "Danny! Danny! At last! you're here!" and ran towards him, her floral cotton dress lightly wrapping around her legs as she approached until she finally pounced on him. Sisasi almost knocked him over. He held her tightly as she wrapped both her arms around his neck. They were both laughing and then kissed. His worries seemed to vanish in that moment.

Soon after their embrace had subsided, the woman on reception said in a slightly mocking tongue-in-cheek tone, "Sir? Do you still need to telephone room 12?"

Danny and Sisasi let go of each other; Danny smiled and apologised, "Sorry, no, I don't."

The receptionist smiled back knowingly, with a glint in her eye, and went on, "That's fine, sir, so I assume you will both be sharing room 12?"

Sisasi and Danny laughed and replied in unison, "We will."

Sisasi gave Danny another big squeeze and then pulled on his arm, saying, "Come on, Danny, let's take your bag upstairs and I'll show you my room." They both went up to their room, Danny threw his holdall on the floor, they kissed again, and started undressing each other, laughing, and discarding their clothes haphazardly on the floor.

They lay on the bed, naked and contented. Eventually, Sisasi explained everything that had happened, with Fabio and Rodrigues, after leaving Belize City. "My brother lied to me, he said he would stop at Airport Camp so I could testify for you, but he told the driver, Rodrigues, to keep driving. I think he was just trying to protect me, Danny. I've already told him that I hate him for not stopping, but ultimately he was just trying to protect me; he wanted me to be in a safe place, so please don't be too hard on him when we see him later."

Danny said, "He is still here?"

Sisasi replied, "Yes, Danny, he is staying in the room next door. He knows you are coming here and is worried about what you may do. I said we would meet him on the platform at the end of the boardwalk later. I've booked a table for us; please promise me you won't be angry with him. He didn't mean to do you any harm."

Danny said, "Sorry, Sisasi, I'm not making any promises, but I'll reserve my judgement, so long as he doesn't do anything else to piss me off."

Danny was still furious with Fabio, but with Sisasi back in his arms, the world felt like a better place again.

His anger was fading away, like clouds dissipating after a stormy day to leave a clear blue sky.

Danny and Sisasi walked arm in arm along the boardwalk. It was difficult to remain angry when he had Sisasi on his arm, she was so beautiful, inside and out, and they were in such a beautiful place, it was like being in paradise. The anger had diminished to a mild irritation by the time they reached the end of the boardwalk. Fabio was sat at their reserved table and was gazing out to sea.

Sisasi called out to him, "Fabio!" He turned around, and she smiled proudly, arm in arm with Danny. The two men eyed each other up and down suspiciously, but neither wanted to cause upset for Sisasi, so there was a cool well-mannered greeting and a nod from one to the other.

Danny said, "Hello, Fabio," and held out his right hand.

Fabio stood up and shook Danny's hand, saying, "Hello, Danny, my English is not so good, but it is good to meet you finally. My sister seems to like you a lot."

Sisasi interrupted, "Hey, will one of my two favourite men in the world please call a waiter and order us some drinks? I think we need to celebrate that we are all here, all alive and all safe. I'll have a pina colada please."

Danny smiled at Sisasi, and Fabio noticed the warmth in his smile towards his sister. Danny turned to Fabio, "What would you like, Fabio?"

"Just a beer for me, Heineken please."

Danny called the waiter over, "Two Heinekens for us, and a pina colada for the lady please."

The waiter replied, "Thank you, sir," and walked off to get the order.

They all sat down. At first, it was clearly apparent that there was an uneasy atmosphere between Fabio and Danny. Sisasi stage-managed a polite but superficial discussion about how nice the Frente al Mar Hotel was, how beautiful the beachfront was, the lovely boardwalk, the sea, the friendly staff, but when the small talk ran out, they inevitably had to talk about the events of the past few weeks.

This more serious and honest discussion, interspersed with more drinking and eating throughout the evening, gradually gave way to a mutual respect and a much warmer mood around their table. Eventually, Fabio and Sisasi started recounting stories from their childhood, remembering happier times. That was all Fabio wanted for his sister and himself, happier times to look forward to. Fabio looked at Danny and Sisasi, the way they often touched each other, glanced at each other. *Maybe Danny will make Sisasi happy, and that will make me happy too*, he thought. Sisasi caught Fabio's knowing look and blew him a cheeky kiss across the table. She was feeling elated after all the trials and tribulations of the previous weeks and months. She was finally able to just sit back and relax, the tension gone, and in this moment, on this evening, she had never been happier or more at ease.

Sisasi smiled and thought to herself as she looked at the two men opposite her, *This is possibly the best night of my life; me, my lover, and my brother, all so different, and yet the same, all so troubled, and yet still able to find this oasis of happiness. Maybe we are not so different after all.*

She put her empty glass down on the table and said, "I've had enough for this evening, it has been a special day, and a special time, and I'm very happy, but I'm also very sleepy now. I need my bed, and by the looks of you two, so do you!" She laughed and grabbed Danny's hand, saying, "This is a good time to call it a night – don't you agree?"

"I do," Danny said, looking at her with his boozy but adoring eyes.

"Yes, me too," Fabio said, laughing at his inebriated sister.

It was the end of a special evening for Sisasi. They thanked the waiter and said goodnight, then headed back up the boardwalk to the hotel. Sisasi held tightly on to both men, one on either side; it felt so good to have them both here to hang on to. Danny and Fabio looked over her head at each other and smiled as Sisasi swayed drunkenly between them, regaling them with how happy she was and repeating herself many times as they walked back to the hotel.

Fabio looked at Sisasi and said, "I think you are a little drunk, Sisasi," and laughed out loud as she rolled her eyes at him.

She replied, in a jokingly obstreperous tone, "No I'm not; it is the boardwalk swaying, not me," and she laughed too.

Fabio was delighted to see his lovely sister so relaxed and so happy. Danny and Sisasi said goodnight to Fabio, and they went to their rooms.

Danny called room service and ordered two large Bailey's cream liqueurs with lots of ice, which they took out onto their balcony. They sat there silently outside their room, listening to the waves break over the coral reef and watching the moonlight shimmering off the surface of the sea; it felt so magical. Sisasi rested her head against Danny's chest, and he wrapped his arm around her, pulling her in closer. She felt his fingers running gently through her hair, and she had never felt more relaxed or at peace than she was in this very moment. Danny said, "Isn't this just perfect, darling?" She sighed contentedly.

* * *

At the end of the receptionist's shift, she carefully slipped a large brown envelope into her handbag, containing all the information she had gathered about today's arrivals. As she walked along the path towards her home, a man walked towards her holding an envelope in his right hand. She took the brown envelope out of her bag, looked around to make sure no one was watching, and they exchanged envelopes without stopping to speak to one another.

He had given her cash, she had given him the guest list, and some other intelligence that she had managed to gather about the guests. The American intelligence officer had been monitoring the 'comings and goings' of the Frente al Mar Hotel for many months. He strongly suspected that Rodrigues was being generously funded by the Cubans. He was especially intrigued and very surprised to read that Danny Sinclaire, a British serviceman based in Belize, was staying at this hotel, normally a sanctuary for left-wing exiles. This revelation could be a complete game-changer.

The End.

EPILOGUE

On Monday 14 May 2013, a Guatemalan court ordered the country's government to apologise to the Ixiles, a small Maya ethnic group, for the crimes of José Efraín Ríos Montt, who orchestrated the destruction of between 70% and 90% of Ixil villages, with 60% of the population in the altiplano region being forced to flee to the mountains between 1982 and 1983. The army, under the command of Ríos Montt, engaged in a campaign of genocide against the Ixiles. On 10 May 2013, the dictator, now aged 87, was sentenced to 80 years in prison for his role in the war crimes committed between 1982 and 1983, after 96 witnesses testified against him in court. Just 10 days later, on 20 May 2013, the Constitutional Court of Guatemala overturned Ríos Montt's conviction. His retrial had not been completed when Ríos Montt died in April 2018, aged 91. The trial raised few questions about Reagan's foreign policy at the time.

CPSIA information can be obtained
at www.ICGtesting.com
Printed in the USA
LVHW032212221021
701219LV00001B/1

9 781839 757938